Denali Rising

Chronicle of Ceres, Book 2

CL LaVigne

This novel is 100% human created.

For permissions, contact:

CL LaVigne

cindy@cllavigne.com

Cover Designed by MiblArt

Denali Rising

(Chronicle of Ceres, Book Two) - 2nd Edition

www.cllavigne.com

www.facebook.com/CLLaVigneAuthor

ISBN (paperback): 978-1-7322933-7-3

ISBN (eBook): 978-1-7322933-8-0

Contents

Dedication

To all my soldiers who carry on despite adversity.
Your past has not been easy.
But your dreams provide the fuel for a fabulous future.
Cheers to you, my lovelies!

Prologue

THE KEMPS HAD A plan to ensnare Stygian which was so risky that the chance everyone would survive was too small to measure. But it was their only hope to stop the evil beast and save the world from his terror and brutality. The warriors succeeded in vanquishing Stygian, but one of their comrades perished in the fight. While three magicians emerged bruised but alive, a fourth died, a martyr in the war against evil.

Fighting a battle is simple, but taking a life during warfare demands courage and control, especially if the target is your sister.

Chapter 1

Land of the Dead

April 2012

Guardian of battle, a warrior stands.
Denali rises, ancient and sacred.
The beast rips through the vortex.
The time is nigh. The battle approaches.
Gather the troops and reclaim the forgotten throne!

HILLY AWOKE IN A fog and was no longer standing on the beach shoulder-to-shoulder with her siblings, nor was she holding her broadsword high into the sky, luring Stygian into her trap. Her brothers and sister had followed her plan precisely including the moment when they had to thrust their swords through her body, creating a blast of pure energy that propelled Stygian into another dimension and killed their sister.

Drenched in blood, Hilly embarked on her journey to the Land of the Dead. She walked barefoot on a snowy glacier. The snow swirled around her head while glittering flakes clung to her eyelashes and her dark hair, wet from battle.

Denali, the great mountain, compelled her forward, a weary warrior walking toward the peace and tranquility of her final destination. She continued up the icy slope leading to the mountain peak which thrummed a welcome, *thump, thump*—a mother's heartbeat vibrating unconditional love for her returning child.

Hilly trekked upward toward The Great Mother, raised her hands to heart center, and bowed her head in reverence.

A hand seized her shoulder, stopping her in her tracks. Hilly whirled around. Prasad met her gaze and motioned for her to follow him. The freezing wind whipped at his clothes turning his brown skin chalky white.

With eyes growing vacant and dim, he whispered, "Come with me Hilly. You must return."

"No. I have no desire to go back. My home is here," Hilly replied angrily, pulling away from him and trudging further up the snowy mountain.

But Prasad had one more mission to fulfill in his lifetime and that was to return Hilly to The Nine Muses. He lunged for her and hugged her tightly. She thrashed and beat at his head, but he wouldn't let go of his friend.

"It's not your time, Hilly. You have a full life ahead of you and I'm making sure you get that chance."

"Let me go, Prasad!" Hilly screamed. "Denali beckons me!"

Prasad ignored Hilly's pleas and mouthed an ancient incantation that opened a portal that sucked them backwards, still entwined, through a long dark tunnel and into the Land of the Living.

Hilly awoke naked in a bathtub, her pain-racked body prone in a sweet-smelling purplish fluid. A searing pain ripped through her skull, and she heaved. The agony was relentless. Shattered bones prevented her from moving. She could only weep and stare at Darrius who hovered nearby chanting a Cererian healing spell while his hands fluttered across her ravaged body. She also saw Prasad, kind, benevolent Prasad. His body slumped beside the porcelain tub, and his hand gripped her shoulder. She realized what he'd done.

He had sacrificed his life. He had traveled to the Land of the Dead to bring her home so she could complete her destiny as foretold by The Cererian Prophecy.

Death is not always the final destination for a soul. Sometimes, a deal can be brokered if balance is maintained. Prasad cleverly negotiated to allow Hilly to return to the Land of the Living while he willingly succumbed to death's final embrace.

The ache in her body and the hurt in her heart were too much for her to bear, and she cried out in frustration. Hearing Hilly, Darrius opened his eyes. "He was successful; Prasad has returned you to us." Darrius wept openly for his deceased friend, a brother he had known for thousands of years.

But there wasn't time to dwell on the passing of a beloved friend or the homecoming of another, Darrius focused on completing the healing of Hilly's body. Her agony continued for hours as bones knitted and soft tissue regenerated. But Hilly would gladly endure another hundred hours of that pain over the heartbreak and mental anguish from losing Prasad. She comforted herself during the tortuous healing process by gazing into his serene face—a contented smile on his white lips and a single tear trailing from his vacant pale-green eyes.

Chapter 2

Hilly

July 2012

"A FULL MONTH?" CURTIS grumbled as he watched Hilly stuff clothes into three suitcases spread open on the bed. Hilly turned and stared at her husband who confronted her wearing only boxers. He assumed his familiar "I'm serious" stance: hands on hips, brow furrowed, and mouth in a crooked sneer.

Hilly chuckled. At forty-eight, Curtis still had an amazing body thanks to running and yoga. She smiled at the tight stomach muscles grinning above the waistband of his blue boxers. Dark ringlets bounced atop his disheveled long hair making him appear more like a pouting teenager than her husband of fifteen years. And she adored him.

"Yep, a full month," she replied as she scoured the closet looking for the proper shoes to take with her—four pairs of hiking boots and a cute pair of red heels—just because. "You knew this day would come. It's not like I haven't talked about my quest for the last three months."

Hilly was anxious to begin her journey to reconnect with the ancient tribes, and to walk the shaman's path. During that weekend at the estate when she, along with her siblings, discovered that she was a descendant of a powerful ancient family and possessed magical abilities, she obsessed about rediscovering herself and understanding more about how she would contribute to restoring peace to the world. Since her Revelation, her powers had multiplied, including telepathy, astral travel and manipulating fire. Her intuition and senses sharpened—a dramatic transformation that led her from a gray-washed world to one bursting with technicolor with enhanced scents, sights and sounds.

Despite her excitement about the trip, she worried about leaving Curtis alone.

Over the years, Curtis embraced her quirky psychic gifts. Though he didn't possess magical powers himself, he fully supported her and oftentimes described her to others as a witch with a strong intuition.

But Hilly had changed at The Nine Muses when the memories of her magical powers had been restored. She often wondered if their love would survive if she shared the truth—battling a beast with her siblings, dying on the beach, and being reborn in a tub of healing potions. Would Curtis accept that she possessed powers that could subdue a strong Cererian? Would he understand that aliens lived side-by-side with humans? Hilly knew this information would overwhelm him and might push him over the edge. There's nothing like discovering your wife died and returned from the Land of the Dead to make a fellow reconsider his choice of mates.

Although she was fully telepathic, she respected the privacy of others and never probed the minds of anyone including Curtis. There were many moments when she wanted to know what he was thinking like when she saw him for the first time after the battle. Having remained at the bed-and-breakfast while Hilly joined her siblings at the estate, Curtis had been extremely curious when she returned.

"How did it go?" he had asked.

She laughed.

Curtis frowned.

"I'm sorry, I'm a little punchy. I didn't get much sleep. They had a lot of activities for us." She stifled another chuckle as she turned away to make tea.

"Something's different," Curtis said, stepping closer and sniffing her hair.

"What are you doing?" Hilly asked, playfully batting Curtis away.

"You're different. I can't put my finger on it, but it's weird."

"Different? How?" she responded, acting nonchalant or as innocent as a person could behave when, just twelve hours earlier, she died brutally on a beach.

"You smell like gardenias and it looks like your skin has a blue tinge. And, your eyes are greener than they used to be." He leaned close and lightly kissed her cheek. "Your skin tastes like flowers. Were you guys working with herbs over the weekend?"

Hilly recognized that as an opportunity to avoid the full truth. "Why, yes, you'll be happy to hear that my siblings are very familiar with pagan rituals and beliefs." She hadn't really answered his question, but now he was completely thrown off the topic of how she had changed.

"That's fantastic! How did you find out?"

Hilly sighed. Curtis' questions might never end unless she was completely honest with him. She bit her lip, deciding whether to tell him everything or continue weaving a trail of half-truths. She'd throw one more at him and see if he persisted.

"We were doing an activity together and one thing led to another; and I mentioned I was a witch. Then everyone chimed in that they knew witches in their hometowns."

"Awesome. Sounds like you've made peace with your brothers and your sister. Perhaps we can get everyone together for a reunion." Curtis grabbed the whistling kettle and poured the hot water into the Brown Betty teapot. He then engulfed Hilly in a huge hug. "It's great having you back in my arms. I'm happy everything worked out." Suddenly, he pushed her back and grew serious. "Gee, babe, I hate to be the bearer of bad news. But Mr. Spatz ran away while you were at the estate. I searched for him every day but couldn't find him. I couldn't reach you on your phone."

Hilly's eyes widened. "Mr. Spatz ran away?" Her mind raced. What should she say? How would she explain to Curtis that they needed to forget about that cat? The imposter feline that shape-shifted into Stygian, whom she had battled on the beach. It sounded absurd in her head, and she imagined how Curtis would take it. Hilly exhaled. "I'm sorry to hear that. I wouldn't worry. Mr. Spatz found us and I'm sure he'll find another family willing to take him in." Hilly smiled reassuringly at Curtis while thinking about Stygian, knowing he was safely imprisoned in an interdimensional cell that only she could unlock.

Hilly mused about their lighthearted exchange three months earlier, and reconsidered sharing more of the details with Curtis before her trip to Alaska. After all, her past would eventually catch up to her. She watched him fold some clothes and stow them carefully into her luggage. He was a kind soul and she worried about what might happen to him while she was gone. Should she talk about Stygian? Should she explain why she has insisted on crystal-gridding the house every week? How would she describe the Cererians?

Curtis looked at her and smiled.

There was something about his grin. And, just like that, her mind was made up. *I'll have that conversation with him when I return from Alaska. For now, I'll leave him with something much more memorable.*

Hilly called out to her husband, "Come here, handsome." She narrowed her eyes and curled her finger beckoning him to come closer.

Always the clown, he sashayed to her as a devilish grin spread across his face.

Hilly giggled as she watched him strut toward her. Raising his arms over his head he flexed his muscles, popping his biceps and six-pack. Hilly stepped closer and teased his hair with her finger while sliding her other hand into his boxers. Curtis stiffened in response to her soft caresses. She took a step back and seductively unbuttoned her shirt. Curtis hung onto her hips and swayed side-to-side as her blouse fluttered open exposing two dark nipples standing rigid. She removed her shirt and flung it behind her. She suddenly grabbed Curtis' butt and pressed her hip against his, grinding slowly. They both moaned as they swayed together in an embrace.

Curtis kissed her neck, her cheek, and then pressed onto her mouth, parting her lips with his tongue.

Hilly whimpered and kissed him back, thrusting her tongue deep into his mouth. Her hands slid down his back until she cupped his buttocks, and then she squeezed.

Suddenly he lifted her, mouths locked together, and carried her to the bed. He swept the luggage aside, scattering the clothes, and tossed her down. Curtis hovered over her and began kissing her neck, then her shoulders, and then to her breasts where he lingered, as he teased and suckled her nipples. Hilly sighed, grabbed her skirt, and slowly lifted it, exposing a bright red, lace thong. She moaned as he moved down her torso teasing her bellybutton with his tongue. He stood up and gently removed her panties. Hilly quivered in anticipation, moistening with excitement.

Curtis wriggled his boxers down to the floor and flung them away with one foot. He gazed at her longingly. He gently stroked the outside of her legs before he spread them open and folded into her, licking her heat carefully. Hilly gasped and arched her back.

"God, oh god!" she squealed. He smiled knowing his tongue had found her trigger. She thrust her hips and he obliged by probing deeper. In a breathy whisper, Hilly demanded, "Now. Take me now."

Curtis grabbed her wrists with one hand and held them above her head as he gently kissed her face and her neck. His other hand guided himself into her warmth, pulsing with excitement. He rocked slowly, his eyes closed in ecstasy. Then he pressed faster as Hilly panted. Curtis kissed Hilly's cheek and grinned a wicked smile. "If I'm not going to see you for a month, then I'm going to make sure you have something to remember me by." And then thrust eagerly while Hilly moaned in ecstasy.

Chapter 3

Sweet Memories

Hilly watched Curtis sleep, which he often did after making love. She marveled at the peaceful look on his face and the hint of a smile on his lips—her handsome husband, the beautiful man who found her during a dark period of her life.

The first time they made love was at a Renaissance festival in North Carolina. It was the same day they met. The mountains seemed to pulse with a happy, positive energy as hundreds of free spirits arrived for competition, song, and merriment. Dressed in pure white from head to toe, Hilly wore thigh-high boots, cotton breeches, a lacy chemise and bodice, and a witch hunter hat adorned with feathers. A short sword dangled from a girdle slung around her hips.

Some of Hilly's friends referenced this as her "geek-out" weekend and didn't understand her fascination with old stuff, especially swords. To Hilly, the clothes and the weapons were as natural as breathing the air. This was her tribe, these were her people, even if it was only for a weekend. No one, not even her closest friends, understood the sorrow and yearning underneath her quick smile and jokes, which were trappings of an emotional mask, a persona she had created to move forward in life after the brutal announcement from her parents—that she was part of a big lie and was not whom she thought she was.

She strolled into the marketplace, a collection of tents and kiosks selling merchandise including clothing, food, potions, amulets, and weaponry. At the sword maker's tent, she spied Curtis studying a variety of broadswords hanging vertically from a large wooden rack. It was painfully obvious that he was a novice buyer by the way he touched and remarked about the swords. The peddler instantly recognized Curtis' inexperience and anticipated getting full price on his more expensive models. His eyes twinkled with excitement as he greeted Curtis.

"Hello, young man. I see you know your weaponry." Curtis looked around to see if the shopkeeper was talking to someone else. "I can tell an experienced swordsman when I see him." The salesman draped his arm around Curtis and led him to the more expensive weapons. Curtis allowed himself to be guided to the other side of the tent where bejeweled swords shone brilliantly in the sunshine. "Feast your eyes on these beauties."

Hilly watched the exchange between the two men. It wasn't her style to interfere but this young man was different somehow. Her little voices screamed at her. Her mother taught her long ago to always listen when intuition speaks because that is when an opportunity presents itself. Act on the impulse and you win, hesitate and you lose. Her intuition kicked at her heart demanding to be heard.

She strolled the perimeter of the booth pretending to inspect daggers while keeping a keen eye on the shopkeeper and his victim. The merchant droned on about the high-priced swords, claiming the one Curtis held was fashioned after Excalibur and was particularly rare. Hilly shook her head. *What a bunch of bullshit,* she thought. She couldn't take the nonsense anymore and sidled up to Curtis.

"You can always spot a cheap sword," she said while scanning the leather sheaths on the counter.

Curtis glanced at her, but his attention was snatched back by the peddler who overheard Hilly's remark. The merchant forced his smile while encouraging Curtis to lift the sword.

"Just feel the weight of this weapon and note the balance, perfect for fighting. Proof of an authentic replica."

Curtis did as the vendor instructed. The sword balanced in the middle of his hand, and he tried to appear knowledgeable as the seller rambled on about the amazing attributes of the prized weapon. Curtis nodded in agreement, hoping he didn't seem like a novice. This was his first time at a Renaissance festival, and his first time holding a sword. His best friend had convinced him the festival was a great place to meet women. Actually, his pal had said "hot chicks in revealing clothes" which had intrigued Curtis. When he arrived, he soon discovered his buddy chickened out and left him to fend for himself.

Now, Curtis was dealing with an overzealous shopkeeper who eagerly pushed him toward the register while babbling about a special deal on a leather scabbard, "Feel this leather. Quality...nothing but quality here. This would be perfect for this beauty of a sword that you've chosen."

Hilly positioned herself near the till, and, as they passed, she spoke softly, "It's always best to know the metal used in crafting a sword." She didn't look at either of them and continued rummaging through an assortment of medallions made of iron and gemstones.

"I beg your pardon?" Curtis asked as the merchant tugged on his arm, pulling him toward the register.

"Fly away you irritating insect," the peddler barked, flicking his hand toward Hilly.

Hilly twirled around and faced the men. "I was just wondering what metal was used in creating that sword, that's all." Hilly narrowed her eyes at the merchant while plucking his hand off Curtis' arm.

"Nobody asked you to butt in, missy," the salesman snarled.

"Wait a minute," Curtis said to the merchant. "You can't talk to my girlfriend that way."

"What?" Hilly sputtered. "What did you say?"

Facing her, Curtis continued, "Do you know anything about swords?"

"Do I know anything about swords?" She withdrew her weapon and presented it to Curtis. "I've only been practicing for almost twenty years."

"Wow. That is an amazing sword. Did you get it here?"

"Good grief, no!" Hilly giggled. "This is a booth of trinkets and cheap trash."

Overhearing the comment, the shopkeeper menaced Hilly. "That's it! Get out of here! I told you last time not to come back!"

"Well, if you insist on peddling cheap crap, it's my duty to warn others and advise them of better options."

The storekeeper grabbed a random sword and swung it at Hilly. "Get out of here, or I'll—"

"Or what?" Hilly cut him off. "You'll give me a bruise with your cheap knockoff?" Hilly whirled and sliced his sword in two with her weapon. Her actions were so swift that neither Curtis nor the merchant saw her touch her sword. The salesman stared dumbfounded at the broken blade dangling from the hilt.

"No worries, you can get your money back by collecting all the pieces and melting them down at the recycling plant," Hilly joked as she grabbed Curtis and walked away amid a storm of obscenities lobbed by the merchant.

"You shouldn't have done that...really, you shouldn't have," Curtis groaned, staring back at the weaponry tent.

"That guy and I always butt heads this time of year. If only he would stop buying truckloads of junk." Hilly then added, "Hey. What was with that girlfriend remark?"

"Um, yeah." Curtis stopped. "Sorry about that. I panicked when he started yelling at you. I didn't like what he said."

Hilly smiled. Curtis appeared so innocent, yet he projected the energy of an old soul. She found it alluring. Her intuition zoomed through her insides, tickling her ribs and causing the hair on the back of her neck to stand at attention. She needed to find out more about this young man.

"I'm Hilly Kemp," she said.

"I'm Curtis Dawson," he replied as he shook her hand. "Mind if I ask you a personal question?"

"I don't know. Ask me and I'll see if I want to answer." Hilly's eyes sparkled with mischief.

"Are you some kind of a sword master or something?"

"Sort of. Why don't we talk about it over a cold one?"

"Sure!" Curtis agreed.

They grabbed two pints of dark stouts, and sat at the end of a long table joining hundreds of other revelers eating and drinking. The massive beer tent bustled with activity as long lines of hungry people snaked between the tables. Amid the chaos two merry minstrels pranced throughout the tent playing a flute and a tambourine while bellowing bawdy songs. Because of the human traffic jam, the duo couldn't move and remained in one place tormenting the same hapless individuals including Curtis and Hilly.

"We need to get away from these musical mosquitoes," Curtis said as he led Hilly out of the tent and toward a grove of oak trees surrounding the edge of the festival. "I'll take you where we won't be bothered."

They were a hundred yards away from the beer tent when Curtis stopped and gazed around at the trees. A breeze rustled through the canopies and the leaves whispered to him. "Much better," he commented. "I can hear myself think." He whipped off his jacket and laid it on the ground next to their mugs of beer. Taking Hilly's hands, he gently guided her onto his jacket and then joined her.

"Why this place?" Hilly asked, gazing up at the deep green leafy covering protecting them from the outside world. Birds warbled welcoming melodies, annoyed squirrels chattered obscenities, and a soft breeze drifted through the branches rubbing them together in hushed murmurs.

"The trees talk to me," he responded. He spread his arms wide, closed his eyes, and breathed deep. "The positive energy flows like water here. Close your eyes and feel it wash over you."

Hilly did as he requested and immediately felt the positive vibrations. Near the tent and the mob of people, there was a crazed, chaotic energy, but here, in the stand of trees, it was as if she was wrapped in a blanket of serenity. Her psychic awareness engaged, triggered by the intense power surrounding her. She opened her eyes and witnessed the magic of nature: faint electrical lines crisscrossed the ground pulsing like a slow, steady heartbeat. She had never seen such beauty or felt so much peace.

Curtis smiled at her. "You see the ley lines, don't you?"

"What do you mean?"

"You can see the electromagnetic energy all around us, can't you?"

Now she understood why her intuition nagged her all day about this man. Is it possible her soulmate finally found her? Was Curtis her twin flame to the eternal fire of love? This man was just like her. He possessed a deep love of nature and genuinely cared for the elemental energies.

"Yes, I've always seen the energetic flow in our world and around people. How about you?"

"Yep. It's always been a part of me. As a young boy, I would try to catch the lines of energy that pulsed in my yard. My parents didn't understand. They couldn't see what I was pointing at, they couldn't feel the positive vibrations rippling around them. They sent me to several therapists who also didn't understand. Heck, they didn't even try to see the beauty I saw—that this great world hums with energy and we can all see it if we remove the veil from our eyes. That's why I love being out here under the trees. Their roots anchor the current extending around the globe and returning, completing a loop of positive energy. Out here it's pure and unspoiled by people's negative actions and thoughts."

Hilly's senses tingled throughout her body making her lightheaded. Every time Curtis spoke, she fell more in love with him. She knew without a doubt she would marry this boy. Curtis didn't know it yet, but he was the chosen one.

They sipped their beers while listening to the sounds of nature. Once in a while, a loud yelp floated from the festival and disturbed their quiet musings. They would glance at each other, shrug, and continue their peaceful daydreams.

"I could sit here all day," Hilly commented as she stared up into the tree canopy. I light breeze teased the hair around her face.

"Me, too," Curtis replied. He gazed at Hilly, absorbed in her quiet manner and graceful features. Unlike other women he knew, she was comfortable living in the moment and savoring the beauty that surrounded her. She had provided details about her life and he felt compelled to share more about himself.

"I have a small shop," Curtis blurted.

Hilly shifted her gaze to Curtis and cocked her head. "Oh? What kind of shop?"

"I live on a small, organic farm and grow medicinal herbs and plants. I sell these amazing healing ointments, salves, and tinctures I make at home."

"That's really cool," Hilly replied. A shaft of sunshine broke through the trees causing her to squint and shield her eyes.

"What do you do?" Curtis asked as he held his hand above her, blotting out the sun.

Hilly hesitated, not sure how much of herself she should reveal in the first meeting. She looked into his face, his beautiful brown eyes dancing with excitement, his full lips slightly parted as though he couldn't wait to hear her next word. But The Fates brought them together. Her intuition wouldn't lie. And, if this was preordained, then she should just spit it out. "I make my living crafting special potions and spells for my clients. I'm a witch."

Curtis' eyes widened and Hilly instantly regretted saying anything. She needed to follow up with something more descriptive, more meaningful.

After all, she's more than just a witch. "I'm a green practitioner. I work with nature and everything that grows in her realm. I do what you do, only I weave in a little magic with my healing poultices." Curtis and Hilly stared at each other.

Seconds ticked by and nobody spoke. Finally, Hilly reached for his hands, relieved he didn't resist. "Look at me," she prompted. He obeyed. Her hazel eyes flashed between green and brown with sparkles of gold. "I may be forward in saying this..." She stopped talking and looked down. For a moment she doubted herself and her instincts. Should she continue speaking or just shut up and drink the beer?

"What?" Curtis asked gazing into her eyes. "You don't have to speak. Just stay here with me."

She loved him more for saying that. "I think we were made for each other," she finally blurted out like a machine gun. "My intuition is in overdrive, my voices are screaming at me, *and* you're a child of nature." She still held Curtis' hands and hadn't realized how hard she was squeezing them. The color began to leech from his olive skin.

"Umm..., could you release my hands for a moment?"

"Oh my gosh...I'm so sorry, I've never done anything like this before."

Curtis stared at Hilly. She looked at him, her big hazel eyes searching his face, tugging at his soul. He remembered his buddy's comment, *C'mon, Curtis, go to the Renaissance festival with me. It's a great way to meet chicks.*

"I do tarot card readings," Curtis divulged. "And this morning the queen of pentacles appeared. So, when my friend suggested I join him at this fair, I didn't hesitate because I knew I would find my queen here."

Hilly gasped. She was familiar with tarot cards and oftentimes she was represented by the queen of pentacles—a beautiful woman surrounded by nature and abundance, a woman of high energy. She quivered. Shifting onto her knees she gestured for Curtis to join her.

He knelt beside her. "What's going on?" he asked suspiciously.

Hilly grinned and held his hands. “Curtis Dawson, will you do me the greatest honor of marrying me?”

Curtis stared at Hilly. “What? What’s going on? What?” He had never done anything spontaneous in his entire life and now this witch with a sword wanted to marry him.

“What do you say?” Hilly pressed. “Do you want to marry your queen of pentacles?”

Curtis stared at Hilly. His mouth had dropped open and beads of sweat peppered his forehead. He gazed into her pleading eyes, the windows to her soul, and blurted, “YES!” He lunged forward, hugging her close as they fell to the ground kissing. “Yes, yes, yes,” he called out as he kissed her eyes, her cheek, her neck.

He suddenly stopped and stared at her. She could tell he was aroused. He searched her face for her response. She returned his gaze with eyes, tender and inviting. He kissed her firmly on the mouth. Hilly parted her lips, and his tongue probed inside exploring the sensitive areas. His left hand deftly undid the laces crisscrossing her bodice, and it fell open revealing milky white breasts with dark firm nipples which he sucked into his mouth. She squealed and held his head to her chest as his hand found the buttons to her breeches.

“Stop,” she whispered.

Curtis stopped. He panted and looked at her with longing.

“Let me help you. Pull my boots off first.”

He quickly obliged, tossing each long boot over his shoulder. Hilly lay on her back and finished unbuttoning her pants. She guided Curtis’ hands to the waistband. He gently pulled them down and gasped upon seeing her naked body. He ripped at his clothes.

Hilly smiled at his awkwardness and boyish display. He tore his shirt open popping all the buttons into the grass and fumbled with his zipper before Hilly took control and guided it down, pushing slightly on his bulge causing him to moan with pleasure. She ran her fingers under the waistband before sliding his pants off.

"Oh my god!" Curtis gasped. He pressed into her. They rolled together, kissing and exploring each other with their lips, their tongues, and their hands before they came together as one allowing the pulsing energy to engulf them like a welcoming blanket. Electrons flicked off their bodies with each thrust until an explosion of sparks signaled the climaxes.

Hilly smiled, recalling fond memories of a more innocent time. They were on the floor where they had fallen during their love-making. Curtis had awakened and grinned back at Hilly who had her head on his chest feeling the slow rise and fall of each slow breath. He traced figure eights on her lower back wet with perspiration.

"An entire month?" he asked again. "How will you live without me for an entire month?"

Hilly sat up and, feigning a Southern accent, said dramatically, "Oh, my, what will I do for thirty days without you to pleasure me day and night, sir?"

They both laughed, and Hilly planted a kiss on Curtis' mouth. She lingered on his lips before licking the sweat off his chest, tracing the patches of dark hair around each nipple and then to his abdomen. Curtis closed his eyes and sighed. Hilly's tongue played with his belly-button, tickling it before she moved to the dark nest of hair on his lower belly. Curtis moaned. Hilly slid her body between Curtis' legs and softly licked his shaft until it stiffened.

Curtis gasped. Hilly gazed at him, her eyes twinkling with mischief before she guided him into her hot, wet mouth.

"Oh, god!" Curtis called out.

Chapter 4

Alaska

As the plane circled Ted Stevens Anchorage International Airport, Hilly marveled at the beauty of the cobalt blue waters of Turnagain Arm and the deep green forested slopes of nearby mountains. Thin ribbons of roads meandered through vast wild lands—a refreshing contrast to the concrete maze Hilly traveled in North Carolina. She breathed deeply. Despite sitting in the pressurized cabin, she could smell the fresh pine and clean, salt air. As a direct descendant of Stygian, her senses of sight, taste and sound were enhanced. She was no longer surprised by her extraordinary psychic powers which had grown stronger every day since her Revelation at The Nine Muses.

Hilly was returning to her birthplace and anticipated discovering the secrets of her ancient family.

So far, the trip had been a disaster, as if nature was sending subtle warnings to Hilly. After violent weather grounded most flights, she hopped on a plane that safely landed in Seattle, only to remain on the tarmac for three hours due to technical glitches, which caused her to miss her connection. She finally disembarked but had to sprint to the opposite side of the terminal claiming the last seat on the last jet bound for Anchorage. Exhausted, she looked forward to the final leg of her journey—a puddle jumper to Aningan where a comfy cabin awaited her on the outskirts of town. Soaking in a hot bath, drinking wine, and chatting with Curtis on the phone were the only considerations for the evening, but not necessarily in that order.

Shouldering her backpack and scabbard, Hilly grabbed the luggage and walked outside the terminal into the dazzling sunshine. It was five o'clock in the afternoon, and the July sun arced high in the azure sky. Monstrous mosquitoes relished the warm summer temperatures and buzzed around her head seeking a taste of her sweet blood. She furiously swatted at them while searching for the service car that would deliver her to the private hangar. Except for a few individuals waiting for family members to take them home, the taxi lane remained empty. Hilly rummaged in her purse, searching for the itinerary note where she highlighted the name of the person meeting her: Jake Pierson, Pierson Express Flights.

She scanned the area.

Nothing.

Her temper boiled just under the surface. After keeping the company updated on her flight delays, they confirmed they would meet her. But now, she was exhausted, annoyed with the throng of hungry mosquitoes, and angered that this company had forgotten about her.

"Hi ya!" said a squeaky voice.

Hilly jumped.

A small man trotted toward her waving vigorously and smiling a wide toothless grin, save for one tooth on the bottom. A shock of white hair sat atop his brown, round face.

Surely, this isn't Jake Pierson, she thought. "Are you speaking to me?"

"Yep, are you the gal from North Carolina going to Aningan?"

"Umm. Yes, I'm waiting for a service car."

The little man chuckled. "Yep, you're in the right place. I'm Samuel Taylor, but you can call me Sammy. My service car is around the corner," he chirped as he flashed air quotes for the word service. "Security gets upset if I try to park in the taxi lane. I hope you don't mind following me to old Val." He grabbed the wheeled totes. "Boy, these are heavy. I hope we won't have a weight problem on the plane." He dragged the luggage toward his rusted Chevy Valiant idling on the side of the building, blue smoke belching out of the exhaust pipe.

Hilly eyed Sammy as he maneuvered her bags into the trunk. Though small in stature, he was certainly nimble. He coughed the smoke out of his face and turned to take Hilly's backpack and scabbard. "That's okay, I'll manage these myself," Hilly said, already leaning into the trunk. She noticed daylight sneaking in from underneath the base of the trunk's interior. On closer inspection, she saw the pitted asphalt below and realized the trunk's bottom was mostly gone. "Is your car okay? She looks a little under the weather."

Sammy laughed, a jovial chuckle that made Hilly think of a Santa Claus grabbing his belly and chortling over a good joke. "Val is just fine. She may look like shit, but this old girl can kick ass when I need her to."

"I can see the ground through the trunk."

Sammy slammed the lid and guided Hilly to the passenger side. "Yeah, the trunk is almost rusted through. The ice and salt are rough on cars up here. I've got a thick sheet of plywood bolted in there. Your gear will be fine. I guarantee it," he proclaimed with a confident voice.

Hilly reluctantly climbed into the cramped front seat kicking an empty soda can and a box of shriveled fries out of the way before settling in. "Sorry 'bout the mess. Jake didn't tell me you were coming until a little while ago. I would have spruced Val up for you if I'd known earlier."

The car convulsed as Sammy ambled around to the driver's side and hopped atop an immense brown pillow, a sweat-stained cushion vomiting stuffing. The seat was so far forward his chest rested on the steering wheel and his eyes peered just above the dashboard, but at least his toes could touch the gas pedal—barely. Hilly reached over her shoulder for the seatbelt but encountered shredded fabric instead.

"Oh, there ain't no seatbelt. Had to cut it last winter when I ran off the road. Rolled into a snow drift. My leg got wound around the belt, and I couldn't get out unless I cut it. Damn, there I go again. I don't mean to ramble on like I do. I'm a good driver, don't you worry about that. I'll get you to Jake with no problem, we're only driving half a mile." Sammy flashed his toothless grin and Hilly politely grinned back already regretting her decision to climb into "Old Val".

"And we're off!" Sammy yelled while mashing the pedal as hard as his toes could push. Val hesitated with a couple of hiccups before the tires finally gripped the road and she squealed away, leaving black skid marks on the concrete. Hilly grabbed the dashboard and glared at Sammy. The strange little man whistled a tune and tapped his fingers on the steering wheel as though the two of them were out for a leisurely drive. "Almost there!"

Five minutes later, Val screeched to a stop in front of a small hangar. Hilly slammed against the glovebox and yelled. "Shit! Who taught you to drive?!"

Sammy didn't hear her. He had already jumped to the ground and scampered around to open her door.

"There's a little trick to getting this open." Planting his feet and gritting his teeth, Sammy tugged on the handle with all his might. "Doesn't always work the first time." He changed his grip and pulled furiously on the handle, huffing and puffing like a little locomotive. Finally, the door screeched open. "There. It works like a charm every time."

"Let me guess, the door was damaged when you rolled it into the snow drift, right?"

"Exactly!" Sammy agreed and then took her hand and helped her out. Something felt odd about his grip, something unexpected and chilling. She looked at his hand and noticed the tips of three fingers were missing. Sammy noticed her gawking.

"Oh this. Well, I had a new chainsaw. One of those fancy, gas models, and she was a little temperamental and wouldn't cut through some of my logs, so I got a little creative with her and...well let's just say, I don't have the chainsaw anymore, and I just use my axe."

Hilly scanned the area and spied a lone figure standing by a prop plane on the tarmac. The person returned her stare. She shivered, feeling a sense of familiarity. But she couldn't put her finger on it. It's that creepy déjà vu that tugs at your brain, but you can't make sense of what you are seeing.

Sammy hefted the two larger bags out of the trunk while Hilly snatched the backpack and scabbard. "Jake, Jake!" Sammy yelled. "Here's your client. That gal from North Carolina. You should take a look at the cargo she's hauling!"

Jake Pierson waited beside his plane, arms crossed. He stood over six feet tall and was dressed in a green flight suit with a vintage aviator hat straddling his head. Mirrored sunglasses illuminated his tanned face. Visions of a World War I flying ace preparing for his next mission danced through Hilly's mind as she neared. She stared at the images of her and Sammy reflecting in Jake's sunglasses, distorted images you might see in a carnival mirror house—Sammy was tall and lean while Hilly looked comically tiny and squat.

"Hi, I'm Hilly Kemp," she said, extending her hand toward Jake.

Jake tightened his lips, tilted his head to one side, and spat a large gob onto the ground near Hilly's feet.

Who the hell does Mr. Sunglasses think he is? she thought.

"Jake, this is the girl renting the cabin outside Aningan," Sammy interjected.

"How did you know that?" Hilly demanded.

"Er..." Sammy stuttered and stared at the ground. "Um, why..."

"We all know your business up here, miss," Jake responded.

Hilly's voices screamed, and her senses went on alert. Although she didn't like to use telepathy on unknowing people, these two were suspicious, not to mention, bizarre. They seemingly knew too much about her, information they shouldn't know. She probed their minds and stepped into two streams of thoughts.

From Jake, she picked up: *Damn woman doesn't know what she's getting herself into. She's wasting my time. What the hell is she doing?*

The connection to Jake's mind ended abruptly. It was as though someone had erected an impenetrable wall. Hilly frowned and, for a moment, considered the idea that Jake had realized she was reading his thoughts.

From Sammy, she received: *She sure is pretty. Gee, she's got great legs. I hope she's not sore at me for knowing her business, but Jake told me.*

Hilly sighed and took several steps toward Mr. Sunglasses.

"Look, I hired you and already paid you. So the least you can do is attempt to be courteous toward a paying client. All I care about is getting to Aningan. Of course, if you'd rather issue me a refund right now..."

Jake held up a hand. "Now, hold on. There's no need for being nasty."

Hilly raised an eyebrow. She walked inches from Jake's face, and he stiffened like a climber paralyzed with fear while watching an avalanche roar toward him. "*You* refused to take my hand when I politely introduced myself. *You* nosed around in my business and *I* politely ignored that violation of privacy. If there was an award for being nasty, *you* would be holding a trophy right now."

Jake smiled and it was the first time he had shown emotion since Hilly arrived.

The elders had spoken of a newcomer coming to Alaska, a fiery *cheechako*. They had described their prophetic dreams depicting the arrival of two adversaries: one representing good and the other the embodiment of evil. The opponents would meet on Denali, and The Great Mother would test their strengths to determine the outcome. An altercation that would change humanity forever.

Jake had assumed Hilly was just another ignorant climber, woefully unprepared for the Alaskan bush. He might have continued believing that if she hadn't attempted to read his thoughts. This was no ordinary *cheechako*. Curious about her intentions, he would play it cool and learn more before judging her.

"Look Sammy, here's that spitfire *cheechako* we've been told about." Jake smirked. Sammy laughed and snuck a peek toward Hilly to see if she was smiling. She wasn't. Sammy cleared his throat and stared at the ground.

"*Cheechako*?" Hilly asked, staring intently at her reflection in Jake's sunglasses.

"Yeah, it's Alaskan for a newcomer," he replied as he shoved his hand toward Hilly, intending to shake hers. She stared at it before returning to her image in his glasses.

"Ah, but I'm not a *cheechako*. I was born here. I was born in Anchorage." Jake's hand hung in the air. "Please remove your glasses if you want to shake my hand. I like to see whom I'm doing business with."

Sammy slammed both hands over his mouth to stifle the giggle that bubbled up and snuck glances at both Hilly and Jake.

Jake's hand dropped to his side like a wet noodle. Hilly tested his patience, and he didn't like that. She was strong, confident, and spoke her mind. Not the typical woman Jake encountered. Finally, he reached up and whipped off his glasses. His brilliant blue eyes squinted in the bright sunshine. Mimicking a British accent, Jake re-introduced himself, "Madam, you have the pleasure of meeting your pilot for the day, Jake Pierson." He extended his hand and bowed toward her.

Hilly accepted his hand and shook it while replying, "You can drop the attitude Jake Pierson and just be my pilot today." Then, Hilly smiled broadly, showing off her white teeth. "Let's see how you handle the puddle jumper, shall we?"

Sammy roared with laughter. "I like this one, Jake, she's got a great sense of humor."

"If you like her that much, go grab her bags and pack the plane."

"Sure thing, Jake," Sammy said, scurrying off. His bandy legs ran double time on the pitted tarmac.

Hilly and Jake didn't move. They stared at each other, testing each other's resolve, measuring the other person's spirit.

Jake broke the silence. "You need some water?"

"Yes. That would be nice."

They walked into the hangar, a cavernous building engulfing two Cessna planes and an assortment of machines leaking various fluids. The hot, musty air, thick with oil and gasoline fumes, caught in the back of Hilly's throat and she coughed violently. "Nice place you have here," she gasped as she followed Jake to the water cooler in a separate room at the back of the building. Upon opening the door, she shivered thanks to a robust air conditioner.

Jake ignored her comment, grabbed a paper cup, and filled it while the water cooler burbled. He dangled the cup in the air, waiting for Hilly to clear her throat. She took it and drank it slowly. The chemical taste slowly drifted away.

"Can I have another, please?" Jake obliged. This time Hilly closed her eyes, allowing the cool fluid to slowly trickle down her throat, savoring every moment of its sweetness. Jake snatched the opportunity to check her out. She was a gorgeous woman, not just her outer appearance, but a beauty born of confidence and self-assuredness that you can feel. It was as if she was enshrouded in a cushion of energized air. Hilly finished her water and dangled the cup in front of his face. "Did you hear me?"

Jake jerked out of his daydream. "What?"

Hilly rolled her eyes. "I asked if you were ready to leave."

"Sure, sure...just wanted to make sure you had enough water before we took off," he lied. His suspicions returned, and he wondered if Hilly had just bewitched him or hypnotized him for a few minutes.

"Let's go. I appreciate cooling off from that burning sun, but frost is forming on my face in here. I need to get outside and warm up." She left the office and strode out of the hanger. He watched her exit. He was both tantalized and bewildered by this newcomer. He needed to find out more about her: why is she here, and what are her intentions? It's hard to keep secrets in a small town like Aningan and Jake was confident he would get his answers.

He trotted after her. "So, why are you here in Alaska?"

She burst out laughing. "Why Jake, I thought you knew all about my business."

Jake swore under his breath. He realized he had started on the wrong foot with this captivating visitor, and he could kick himself for being such a jerk. "Sarcasm...nice. I had that coming. Let's start over, okay? Aningan is a small community, and *you're* an outsider. Sammy and I belong to one of the native tribes, whose members live all over this area. Sammy's great-uncle owns the cabin you rented, and Sammy's cousin cleans all the properties. Oh, and Sammy's great-aunt maintains the books. So, it's easy to find out information about a stranger. Who needs the internet when you've got the 'family-net'?"

Hilly's eyes widened. This was the most Jake had spoken since her arrival. "Good golly. It's like being back home in Pilot Mountain. Small towns are the same all over."

"Pilot Mountain? North Carolina?"

"Yep, have you heard of it?"

"I may have, sounds familiar." Jake knew more than he shared. Sure, he knew Pilot Mountain. He'd visited many times and hiked to the top of The Knob last year. It's a powerful place, energy-wise, and well-known for its vortex. His suspicions returned and stuck in his gut. "Got family there, have you?"

"Just me and my husband." Hilly turned away and stared at the ground. She chewed her lower lip.

Jake noticed her behavior. Something he said had jangled her nerves.

"All ready to go, boss. Everything's packed!" Sammy yelled, breaking the intense paranoia building between the two. "What's in that leather sheath? Feels like a sword."

"You shouldn't have touched that. I told you I would manage it myself."

"I'm sorry. I forgot. Did I do something wrong?" Sammy shot a weird look toward Jake, and then jerked his head to the side like he wanted to chat.

Jake shook his head and mouthed *later.*

Hilly realized her curt response had caused more suspicion. She glanced at Jake and Sammy who appeared like two puzzled puppies, heads tilted to the side, confused by her reaction. "No, you didn't do anything wrong. I'm particular about who touches my broadsword."

"Sword? I imagine you have a good reason to bring a weapon with you," Jake said.

"I do, but it's none of your business." Hilly forced a smile and narrowed her eyes at Jake, convinced she could not trust him. But she needed to get to Aningan and his plane was the only way. Despite the warnings from her intuition, she decided to remain friendly and, stay alert for the unexpected.

"All right. Are you ready to see Aningan, Ms. Kemp?"

Noticing the switch in Jake's tone, Hilly replied in kind, "Yes, Mr. Pierson, I'm ready."

Jake circled his plane for the last safety check of the tail, wings and propeller. Meanwhile, he kept a wary eye on Hilly who climbed into the back seat and checked her luggage. Hilly placed her hands on the sheath, and Raven, her sword, hummed in recognition of her mistress. Satisfied that everything was safely stowed, Hilly jumped out of the plane.

Sammy leapt into the rear seat. He sucked in a deep breath before stuffing himself between Hilly's two totes, wiggling back and forth, creating as much room as possible. "Whew. This is a tight squeeze," he complained.

Hilly folded into the front seat and watched Jake glide his hand along the plane's fuselage. She noticed the word "LOLA" painted on the side of the nose in bold red and mused on if that was the name of someone special in Jake's life. The disgusting dirt of the hangar hadn't prepared her for what she would find inside the aircraft. The interior was spotless—no dust, no smudges, and the chrome gleamed. It was obvious Jake adored Lola.

Jake took his time inspecting the aircraft, sliding his hand over the metal skin—down one prop blade and up another, along the wings, and then back to the tail. His soft touches and gentle caresses made Hilly think of her interactions with Raven, a close, loving bond that was much more than friendship. Jake's ritual was solemn and conducted with reverence as if Lola was a living, breathing entity.

Hilly had an inkling that Jake was using psychometry. He was seeing with his hands, measuring the energy, noting any flaws in the aircraft, and confirming it was okay to fly. Satisfied with his inspection, he returned to the propeller, faced the plane with his hands at heart center, and bowed. Hilly nodded. She now understood who Lola was.

Jake yanked the door open, and jumped into his seat. "Buckle up. That means you too, Sammy."

"Gee whiz, Jake. It seems so unnecessary. The belt pushes on my belly and gives me heartburn."

"No argument. Do it, now." Jake watched in the mirror as Sammy reluctantly stretched the belt across his lap. He appeared like a sausage bound too tight with rubber bands.

"I can hardly breathe."

"Hold your breath then," Jake said while checking the instrument panel.

"Here we go," he said and, eased the plane forward along the pavement leading to the runway. His head swiveled, keeping an eye on the outbuildings and the clearance to Lola's wingtips. Lola bumped along the rutted concrete before rolling to a gentle stop on the edge of the runway. Jake stared into the distance and revved the engine.

"Here...we...go," Sammy called out from the backseat, gasping for air between words.

Hilly closed her eyes and explored the energy around the plane and the mountains surrounding the airfield. Satisfied, she opened her eyes.

Jake noticed. "Scared of flying?"

"Scared? No." Hilly smirked and peered out the windshield as her thoughts traveled back to the battle on the beach—a screeching beast looming overhead as her siblings thrust their broadswords into her body. "It's all about the adventure, isn't it?" She looked over at Jake and winked.

Jake's eyebrow arched with surprised before he faced forward, and pressed the push knob. The plane sped down the runway. They bumped along, increasing speed before he pulled back on the control wheel and Lola gently lifted into the air.

"Shit, this belt is tight." Hilly heard Sammy cursing under his breath from the back seat. "Damn seatbelt."

Once they reached cruising altitude Jake announced, "Attention lady and gentle....and Sammy. You have boarded the no-frills flight 'Lola Express' to beautiful Aningan. This is an economy trip: no smoking, no food, no drinks, and no bathroom. We also forbid all forms of puking. And, if you must barf, please roll down the window and blow it outside. Thank you for flying with 'Lola Express'."

Suddenly, a loud burp followed by a squishy fart emanated from the back seat. "Sammy!" Jake groaned.

Sammy giggled like a little boy as the stench filled the cabin. "You didn't say anything about burping or farting."

Hilly covered her nose with her hand while Jake retched like a cat tossing a furball. Hilly rolled her eyes. Aningan couldn't arrive soon enough.

Chapter 5

Alaska Triangle

LOLA FLEW NORTH, CRUISING over icy mountain peaks, thick sprawling forests, and meandering rivers. The familiar route to Aningan typically lasted forty-five minutes if the weather cooperated like today.

That hadn't been the case just two days earlier, on Friday. Jake shuddered as he recalled the unnatural events that had forced his disabled plane to spiral toward the ground.

It was an ordinary hot, steamy day and without chatty passengers aboard, Jake's mind wandered. He was looking forward to meeting his buddy at Flanagan's, an Irish pub known for great music, food, and the best stout in town. He'd met a cute girl last week and she'd promised to meet him again. He daydreamed, recalling her lips, her beautiful face, and her incredible body.

A thick bank of unusual clouds drifted from the east, filling the sky like undulating dark-gray earthworms. Storms were common this time of year, so Jake hadn't worried, at first. But as Lola's flight path nudged against the outer boundary of the Alaska Triangle, an expanse of air space known for snatching souls, Lola's warning bells roused Jake from his daydream.

A thick blanket of clouds surrounded the plane, blocking the sun and the sky. Flying blind, he checked the instrument panel—dials spun crazily while the artificial horizon swung between high and low. His mind raced. Just minutes before, everything was fine, but, now nothing made sense. He turned the dials on the radio, which snapped and hissed in response. He gripped the control wheel and stared out the windshield looking for anything, but all he could see were dark clouds, murky and swirling, smothering the plane as he flew onward. Lola shuddered, colliding with a solid object, and Jake tumbled from his seat. Recovering, he gazed out the window, unnerved by what he saw. A pulsing blue light slithered through the clouds like a luminescent snake repeatedly striking the plane's fuselage. The assault escalated with a continuous wave of energy pulses, muddling his mind with intense dizziness. He suddenly realized what was happening—a vortex had snatched the plane and was slowly reeling it in.

He'd heard many tales of vortices opening and swallowing everything and anybody within its reach. These rotating masses of energy were birthed along intersecting ley lines, and Alaska was covered with these magnetic areas. Lola convulsed, flying straight toward the swirling eddy of energy. She moved slowly toward the shimmering lights, hapless prey for the magnetic maw, while Jake fought to remain conscious against the disorientation and pressure building in the cabin. He refused to be another statistic, another pilot who simply went missing without a trace. If he was going to die today, it would be on his terms. The solution had to be just as absurd, just as drastic as the situation he faced—he turned off the engine. He reasoned that removing the energy source might weaken the vortex sufficiently, allowing him the chance to regain control by manipulating the element of air. But he had to act immediately. If he was successful, he'd have a great story to share with his buddy over a pint. If it didn't work, nothing would matter anymore.

A sane person may have considered that action too severe, but Jake was no ordinary person.

Silence filled the cockpit, except for Jake's strong and steady breathing as he focused on his next move. He strangled the yoke as Lola hung in the cloud bank illuminated by static charges sliding along her metal skin. The nose gently drifted up before tilting downward and dropping Lola like a boulder tumbling from a cliff. The force pulled at Jake as he braced himself against the seat and extended his arms. He closed his eyes and recited an ancient incantation his family had used for centuries. His arms rotated in opposite circles as he repeated the spell, circling faster and faster until the movement blurred, and his voice morphed into a vibrational hum like a million honeybees.

Gradually, Lola slowed her descent, and leveled off as Jake pushed his hands forward, guiding the plane away from the Alaska Triangle, beyond the vortex's control. Using his mind, Jake restored power to Lola's engine and the propeller roared to life.

He glanced out the window, relieved to see open water punctuated by spits of land. He recognized they were now somewhere over the Bering Sea, hundreds of miles off course and in the opposite direction from where they encountered the vortex. He gazed skyward, giving thanks to the ancient spirits for saving his life. He turned the plane around and set course for Anchorage where he could stop to refuel before heading to Aningan again. He took care to fly the western route this time, avoiding the Alaska Triangle altogether.

When the plane touched down in Aningan, six hours after the initial take off, Jake looked forward to sharing his story with his buddy but doubted his friend would believe him. Jake chuckled. *I wouldn't believe me, and I lived through it*, he had thought.

Jake scrutinized the landscape for energy pulses and anomalies, vigilant for energy disturbances. The propeller's continuous droning lulled Sammy to sleep just ten minutes after takeoff. "Happens every time," Jake remarked as a low snore drifted from the back seat. "I swear, Sammy can sleep anywhere."

Hilly studied the small man. Sammy's head rested on one of the suitcases, his mouth agape like a fish gasping for air. He breathed deeply in and out, creating noises alternating between high whistles and low rattles. "He looks uncomfortable," she noted.

"Mind if I ask you something?" Hilly took her time responding. Jake glared at her. "Well?"

"I was just wondering how I should answer you. It's a loaded question." She tapped her cheek with her finger, deep in thought.

"Never mind," Jake sighed.

Sammy's snorts punctuated a long awkward stillness. *I wish you would just talk with me,* Jake thought.

To his surprise, Hilly responded telepathically, *I wish you would treat me with respect, and then I might talk with you.*

They looked at each other.

Jake peeked at Sammy who snored happily against Hilly's luggage, which was now soaked with drool. "It's okay to talk. He won't hear us."

"You're telepathic?" Hilly asked.

"Yeah, and apparently you are, too," Jake responded. "I felt you trying to probe my mind back at the hangar."

Hilly blushed. "I'm kinda new at this...three months to be exact. Besides my brothers and sister, I've never encountered another person who had special gifts. Are you part of an ancient family and tribe?"

Jake grinned. He envied this woman for her strength and also pitied her because she knew nothing about her abilities. It was like watching a baby walk for the first time. "You've only been practicing for three months? Where have you been...living in a cave? What about your elders? Your shamans? Your teachers? How did you get to be this age and not know about your gifts?"

Hilly turned away and stared out the window. Wounded by his questions, a deep sorrow filled her heart. Jake's questions re-opened scars from when she was ten years old. Her psychic abilities were completely natural to her as a child, and her mother, Freda, encouraged her to practice them, but only if it was with family members. She had explained that others might not understand her actions.

Hilly had obeyed her mother, but on a day, almost forty years ago, a dear friend was tortured by a bully and Hilly wanted to even the odds. Natasha was feared by all the younger kids at school. She was a known bully who would stop at nothing to make others cry. She delighted in breaking the spirits of people who appeared different whether it was height, weight, hair color or she simply didn't like them, which applied to nearly everybody.

On this day, Natasha had targeted Hilly's close friend, Nathan, a shy boy who shared Hilly's love of nature. Studious and nonathletic, Nathan preferred books and music. He was calm and happy when he read, danced, or walked in the woods. But in the lunchroom, the chaotic noise and bullies like Natasha overwhelmed his senses and he often shut down, speaking to no one and eating like a mouse—attempting to appear small and insignificant while sneaking little bites of food into his mouth.

But, this time, Natasha went too far, sniping around him hunting for ways to upset him. "Look at the baby," she jeered. Tears welled in Nathan's eyes. His reaction spurred Natasha to continue. "Do you need to be spoon fed, little baby?"

Nathan stared at his food, his hands clenched into fists in his lap.

Hilly had enough of the tormentor. She stood across the table and screamed, "Leave him alone, Natasha! Get out of here and leave us both alone!"

Natasha stood her ground and smirked at Nathan. "What a baby, you can't even stand up for yourself, You have to get your babysitter to do your talking!" Nathan looked at Hilly with tears rolling down his cheeks.

Hilly couldn't bear to see anyone cry, much less her best friend. What she said next quieted the lunchroom. "Stop or I'll make you stop!"

"Oh, really? And, what are you going to do about it?" Natasha taunted as she pushed Nathan's milk carton off the tray causing it to tumble into his lap, soaking his pants. "Look at the idiot," she proclaimed to the lunchroom. "He's just peed his pants!"

Hilly ran to the other side of the table, arms raised, hands outstretched as if to strangle her adversary. She summoned her power, despite her mother's warning, and threw a psychic blast toward Natasha, propelling her across the room and slamming her against the far wall.

The fury that had built inside Hilly vented its raw and unchecked emotions directly onto Natasha, and she dropped to the floor in a crumpled heap.

The lunchroom grew quiet. It was the type of stillness that follows an event so heinous that spectators have no words for what they've just witnessed. Nathan stared at the crumpled Natasha and grinned, a smile that only those who have finally witnessed justice understand. Then he turned to Hilly, her hands blood-red, steaming, and still extended toward the wall in the event the bully should arise and try to strike again. He grabbed Hilly's arm, yanking her toward the door as speechless onlookers pointed at the bizarre girl and her friend. Almost forty years had passed, and the incident was as fresh as if it occurred yesterday.

"I've lost you. Did I say something wrong?" Hilly refused to look at him. *What happened? What did I say?* he mentally messaged.

She shook her head, tears welling in her eyes. *I'd rather not talk about it.*

After all these years, she had finally found someone like herself. Her joy at finding a kindred spirit deteriorated into a deep sadness. Because, unlike her upbringing, Jake had flourished under the support of his tribe, knowledgeable and caring individuals who had nurtured him and encouraged him since he was a child. Jake was part of a family that had taught him the ancient traditions and instructed him about the magical ways, which were now second nature to him. Finding Jake was exciting, but she felt jealousy toward the life he lived and bitterness toward her parents for cloaking her memories until Darrius restored them.

She felt lost and alone. She yearned to have Curtis hold her. She wished Darrius was near to advise her, and she longed for her siblings' comfort and encouragement.

"Hilly, tell me how I hurt you. I didn't mean to offend you. I'm not used to meeting magicians from other lands and other families. I didn't know they did things differently." Jake gently took her chin and looked into her eyes. His blue eyes sparkled and swirled with flashes of violet dancing in the pupils. Hilly immediately thought of Darrius and Prasad, and how they had mesmerized her family with their beautiful emerald eyes when they first arrived at The Nine Muses.

"I know what you're doing and you're not going to trance me."

"That obvious?" he teased.

Hilly noticed Jake's hands were no longer on the control wheel, and he hadn't been flying the plane for many minutes. "Oh, my god! Who's flying the plane?" Sammy snorted loudly and mumbled as he shifted his weight to the other suitcase, falling into another rhythmic snore.

"Shh." Jake held his finger to his lips. "Don't wake sleeping beauty. Lola's in command. But she's not on cruise control."

Hilly looked at Jake, eyes wide. "Lola is your spirit companion?"

Jake ran his hand along the dashboard and a soothing vibration emanated from all around the cabin as the plane hummed a greeting. "Lola is my familiar spirit. Or, as you referenced it, spirit companion, magical partner, or whatever you prefer. She is the ethereal being who partnered with me several years ago and protects me. And I'll do anything to defend her."

Hilly nodded. "Raven is my constant companion. She's already saved my life once. She bears the symbols of my family—suns and dragons.

"You're a firewalker?" Jake had heard legends about ancestors who possessed the power to manipulate the sun and light, to open and close portals, and to control fire. But these were tales shared around campfires. There hadn't been firewalkers in his family for decades, ever since Stygian and his Yfel Brethren killed them all. The elders spoke of one soul who rose into the sky to escape the Yfel that night. Jake always figured they were describing a person who died and joined the other spirits in the heavens, but now he wondered if the elders meant someone had escaped. He stared at Hilly. Was this woman sitting next to him that soul who escaped the massacre? If his suspicions were true, this knowledge could change his life and the lives of his family, forever. "You can control the element of fire?"

"Yes. What about you?"

"I thought that was obvious." He chuckled, "I work with the element of air," he said as he swept his arms wide.

When Hilly left Pilot Mountain for Alaska, she hoped to discover the roots of her ancient family. She never dreamed she would stumble upon other individuals who had the same abilities as she and her siblings. She couldn't wait to share the news with her brothers and sister.

"What about Sammy? Does he possess magical abilities?"

Jake glanced into the back seat, finding Sammy curled up in a fetal position, softly snoring. "You know, that's a great question. We're members of the same tribe but I don't know if he has any gifts or represents an elemental family like us. If he does possess magic, he's never used it around me. He's always been my gopher, my buddy..."

Lola's nose dipped suddenly and Jake grabbed the yoke. "Looks like we're making our approach to Aningan."

"Can Lola land without your help?"

"Absolutely, but how weird would that look to the control tower? I want to keep our relationship a secret from those I don't know." He grinned. "So, I guess that means you've gained entrance into my circle of trust."

Hilly liked the sound of that, and her sadness lifted. She now had a second family of sorts and looked forward to learning more about Jake and his relatives.

Lola swept by the control tower and Jake waved. "It's all for show, but I look forward to the day when Lola flies by and *nobody* is at the controls." He laughed. It was obvious he adored his relationship with Lola.

The plane landed and taxied to a small hangar on the edge of the field. "Sammy, wake up!" Jake barked.

With a loud snort, Sammy bolted forward only to be yanked back by the seatbelt. "What...OW...what's going on?"

"We're in Aningan, Sammy. We need to get Hilly to Uncle Aaron so she can get her key. And then you need to drive her out to the cabin."

"Isn't there someone else who can drive me? I'm sure Sammy is too tired—," Hilly protested.

"No problem at all," Sammy interrupted. "I got a great sleep back here and am raring to go."

The last thing Hilly wanted was to travel with Sammy again. His driving left a lot to be desired, and she didn't relish being with him when the next accident happened. "Great!" she lied, stepping out of the plane and stretching. She walked along the tarmac, surveying the area, and watching bald eagles circle overhead while Jake helped Sammy unload Lola.

"Jake, I've got something to tell you," Sammy whispered.

Jake batted him away. "Sammy, stop spitting in my ear. Why are you whispering?"

"I don't want Hilly to hear us."

Jake glanced out the windshield, watching Hilly stroll across the tarmac while looking at the scenery. "She's almost thirty feet away. She wouldn't be able to hear you fart."

"Don't tempt me," Sammy teased with a twinkle in his eye. "But seriously, do you remember I wanted to talk to you before we took off?"

"Yeah, I remember. What about?"

"That sword of hers. It's not your normal slice-and-dice weapon. I think it's alive, like a pet or something."

Jake stopped moving the luggage and stared at Sammy, "What do you mean?"

Sammy looked out the window, keeping an eye on Hilly. "When I stowed it away, it felt light, like a plastic sword. I wanted to check it out, so I pulled back the sheath and looked at it. Jake, it doesn't look like the steel swords we've seen at the festivals."

"Go on."

"The blade is translucent and shimmers, oily-like. It's got all these jewels stuck in the handle and there are suns and lizard creatures on the blade. I touched the blade and the damn thing bit me!"

"Bit you? It's got teeth?" Jake stifled his chuckle.

"Nah, but it felt like it nipped me. It was like a shower of sparks or static electricity."

"Oh..."

"Yeah, she's got something spooky in that case. Want to see it?"

As much as Jake wanted to see Raven, he resisted the temptation and waved Sammy off. "That's okay, Sammy. It's her business, not ours. You're better off not sticking your fingers where they shouldn't be in the first place. You know you always get burned. Remember the chainsaw incident when you borrowed your neighbor's gas chainsaw without his permission?"

Sammy stared at his right hand, recalling the day his fingers were sheared off. "Yeah, but that sword is weird. I'm going to keep my eyes on this woman for sure."

Hilly appeared in the doorway. "You remember that I want to unload my backpack and scabbard, right guys?"

"Absolutely," Jake declared as he threw a tote at Sammy knocking him backwards onto the tarmac. Grabbing the other suitcase, Jake jumped down and motioned for Hilly to climb in. "The plane is all yours, Ms. Kemp."

She climbed in and touched Raven who vibrated a warm greeting. Grabbing her backpack, Hilly cradled the sword and leapt from the plane.

"If you'll follow me, I'll take you to Uncle Aaron," Sammy said pointing to a faded powder-blue station wagon. Faux wood panels peeled away from the sides of the vintage Chevy that displayed similar rust spots to Old Val.

Hilly gulped. "Sammy, do you have *any* newer cars?"

"Ms. Hilly, Stella runs like a charm. She's different than Old Val," Sammy boasted. "Stella's got a lot of speed for her age."

"That's what I'm afraid of," Hilly said under her breath.

"Look, Miss Hilly," Sammy directed as he strolled around Stella and pointed out her other fine features. "Almost new tires, comfortable seats, and she even has seat belts!"

Hilly sighed and glanced at Jake who shrugged. "Don't fight it. He's the best gig in town for getting you to Uncle Aaron." Turning to Sammy, Jake continued, "I'll bum a ride into town. I need to go to the office and get caught up on my paperwork."

"Perfect!" Sammy said as he pushed the luggage into the hatch. Hilly yanked the back door open and carefully placed Raven and her backpack onto the seat before sliding in. "Don't you want to ride shotgun?" Sammy asked.

Before Hilly could respond, Jake blurted, "I already called it. You know I like riding up front so I can keep an eye on the road. One of us needs to." They both laughed, and Sammy punched Jake in the arm.

Jake shot Hilly a side glance. *I figured you could use a break from Sammy,* he mentally messaged.

Thanks. I owe you one! she replied.

Chapter 6

Uncle Aaron

As Stella bumped and lurched along the dirt road winding from the airstrip to Aningan, Hilly gazed out the window. Filled with wonder, her soul plunged into a vast pool of positive energy emanating from the surrounding landscape. The soothing power lovingly provided by the plants, animals, and living things, intertwined with Hilly's spirit, charging her essence with pulses of energetic love. With both her physical and psychic senses fully engaged, Hilly breathed the fresh, damp earth, felt the roughness of the boulder edges, and feasted on sweet berries growing along the creek beds. She flew beside eagles and caught fish with the grizzlies. Her heart galloped with the elk, and her consciousness rested in the embrace of old cedar trees. A feeling of returning home washed over her—a place that mourned her absence and now rejoiced, knowing her energy had returned. A sensation so emotional, it moved her to tears.

"Everything okay back there?" Sammy asked.

Hilly wiped her eyes. "My kidneys will never be the same," she joked, cloaking the well of emotions stuck in her throat.

Jake yelled over his shoulder, "Wait until we get to Aningan...then the fun starts!" A large pothole threw them all into the air as Stella's undercarriage slammed the gravel road and then bounced up again.

"Yeehaw!" Sammy yelled, obviously enjoying the bucking ride. "We're almost there! The road's not too bad right now. You should see it in the wintertime. Best to put skis on the frame and use it as a sled." Sammy chuckled. "I don't do that, but it's a great idea. Maybe I'll do it this winter. What do you think, Jake?" Not expecting an answer, Sammy continued while pointing. "That house over there is my cousin's, and that little store over there is my aunt's..." Hilly wondered if Aningan's population only consisted of Sammy's relatives.

Stella passed a wooden sign constructed from a large, weathered pallet painted with white words: WELCOME TO BEAUTIFUL DOWNTOWN ANINGAN. Visitors inundated the downtown area and Sammy slowed Stella to a crawl to avoid hitting the distracted newcomers wandering into the street while gazing at their phones. Hilly thought of the tiny, North Carolina, mountain hamlets she often visited. Small, unique, artsy, and full of surprises, many of them also used similar handmade signs welcoming strangers to their town.

"Ah, looks like we have a nice crop of wannabe mountain climbers," Jake observed as the street crawled with bodies of every make and size. A group of ten stood in the middle of the road and focused on a map held by their leader. "Let's have some fun and buzz these crazy people," Jake joked before adding, "On second thought, just drop me off here, and I'll walk the rest of the way. I'm too tired to mess with stupid tourists right now."

"Let me just rev the engine, Jake," Sammy begged. "I just want to frighten them a little."

"No, Sammy. They may be annoying, but these folks bring good money into our town."

Sammy threw Stella into park and yelled, "All out for Pierson Express Flights. Next stop is Aningan Properties. Make sure you have all small children by the hand as you exit the car."

"Give it a rest, Sammy. You say the same thing every time you bring somebody here. It's getting kinda old. You need new material." Jake grabbed his bag from the hatch. He passed the side window and waved at Hilly. "It's been my pleasure, Ms. Kemp. Enjoy your stay here in the beautiful land of Denali."

"It's been an interesting trip so far. I hope we get a chance to talk before I head home." Jake banged the side of the car with his fist, signaling Sammy it was clear to pull forward.

Jake watched Stella roll away, narrowly missing the tourists meandering in the street. He didn't mention anything to Hilly, but he would see her again and it would be a lot sooner than she anticipated. He jumped onto the wood plank boardwalk and walked three doors down to Pierson Express Flights—an insignificant office featuring the company name painted in red on a weathered door. Jake picked at the lettering—the "l" flaked away last year making it appear that "F ights" took place inside this cramped building. He had been in a few nasty fights in the past, but he never instigated a single one, at least, that's the story he told anybody who cared to listen.

He turned the key and entered his office. A tiny bell tinkled a welcome as he strode into the musty room illuminated by an angry red glare from the answering machine notifying Jake of messages. He pressed play and heard a familiar voice advising him of her delayed flights and hoping somebody would be waiting for her in Anchorage. Jake hadn't heard Hilly's original messages but knew of her delays. Uncle Aaron made sure Jake was aware of everything concerning Ms. Kemp and his instructions were clear: *Ensure she arrives safely and make sure nothing happens to her while in Alaska.*

Although Jake wasn't privy to the full details, Uncle Aaron also shared another bit of information. He cautioned Jake that The Cererian Prophecy was unfolding right here in Aningan and events were controlled by the arrival of Hilly Kemp. Uncle Aaron's last statement intrigued Jake: *The beast will rip through the vortex, and the battle will change humanity forever.*

Sammy turned off the main street and drove down a ribbon of an alley, which was so narrow that two draft horses couldn't pass at the same time. Sammy stopped in front of a row of gray, dilapidated wooden buildings. Gazing at the clapboard buildings and dusty, rutted road, Hilly saw Aningan as a frontier town that hadn't changed since it was established in the 1890s. There were no distinguishing features in the row except for one office door that was painted a bright ruby-red with printed words in a deep forest green: ANINGAN PROPERTIES.

"I'll drop you here and go park around back," Sammy said as he threw Stella into park and ran around to open Hilly's door. She crawled out and reached back in for her backpack and scabbard.

"You don't need to take those with you, you'll only be in there a few minutes filling out paperwork," Sammy chirped.

"That's okay, I prefer to keep them with me," she said as she shouldered both.

"As you wish," Sammy replied, clearly disappointed. "I'll take Stella out back and will return in a shake. You can go right in. Uncle Aaron is expecting you."

Hilly stood at the base of the wooden stairs and watched Sammy pull away. Exhausted and hungry, Hilly's energy lagged as she climbed the steps to the porch of the tiny building. At the top of the stairs, she glanced both ways. She hoped Sammy was right about the paperwork taking only a few minutes, she was dead on her feet and needed sleep. She was utterly alone, and her intuition kicked her stomach—something wasn't right, something was amiss.

CAW!

Hilly jumped back and looked up. A raven perched on the roof and glared at her. It ruffled its feathers and called to her again.

CAW!

She closed her eyes and attempted to join the bird's spirit—to sense what it could hear and see. But the black bird launched into the air, squawking loudly as it flew north, toward Denali. She followed its flight, instantly realizing the creature posed no threat. It was a messenger, a courier sent from The Great One, Denali.

Home for a few minutes and already The Great Mother reaches out to me, Hilly thought.

She turned back to the Christmas-colored door. What an odd little building—no windows, no outside lights, no extraneous decorations. Just solid walls and a festive door: the perfect portal for someone cloaking a deep, dark secret. She knocked. When nobody responded, she carefully turned the cast iron handle and the wooden door creaked open.

The shaft of daylight stabbed into the darkened room, which was illuminated by a flickering ceiling light. Hilly left the door open, not only would it offer more light, but it would allow an easy escape route if one was needed. Her little voices chatted to her, but she sensed no immediate danger

It was eerily quiet. She stood in the entranceway and scanned the room. It featured several, plain wooden chairs surrounding a large black desk. Its top was bare except for a service bell placed right in the middle. Clouds of dust swirled past the doorway and cobwebs fluttered from the ceiling light. *This is a place of business?* Hilly thought as she ventured further into the room. A hallway led toward the back, and Hilly, peering into the darkness, called out, "Hello? Is anyone back there? Uncle Aaron?"

Silence.

Hilly smashed the service bell. She waited a few minutes and still, nobody showed. Her impatience growing, she slammed her hand on the bell two more times.

DING!

DING!

Nobody. She suddenly noticed a small paper sign, the kind someone would print on an office copier. It was taped to the far wall behind the desk, and in simple black ink it read: "Please have a seat. We appreciate your patience."

"Shit!" she said as she whirled around and marched toward the door. She stopped in the entryway. What was she going to do? Aningan Properties had the key to her cabin, the perfect location for her Alaskan journey, her vision quest. There was no other place to go.

"Okay, we'll play by your rules!" she yelled into the darkness as she surveyed the sparse selection of wooden chairs. Choosing one nearest the hallway, she dropped her backpack onto the floor and rested Raven against it. She slumped onto the hard seat and glared down the hallway, mentally demanding somebody to emerge and give her the key.

Several minutes ticked by and still nobody. In a desperate attempt to reach someone, she grabbed her cellphone to call the office, when an unusual noise caught her attention.

Barely audible, a soft sound whooshed along the wood floors punctuated by a light *tick, tick, tick*. Hilly strained to see what manner of creature produced such a weird sound. Whatever it was, it slowly strolled down the hallway toward Hilly. She perched on the edge of her seat, her hand on Raven, ready to fight if needed. Soon, two emerald-green orbs floated in the blackness, and Hilly tensed, tightening her grip on the sword.

Meow!

Hilly jerked. She was ready to do battle, but not with a cat. She loosened her grip on Raven and extended her hand toward the kitty. "Well, hi there. Where did you come from?" The feline purred in response and stepped into the light toward Hilly's hand. The cat was magnificent—an immense Persian with fur the color of dark ebony. The tail, a fluffy plume, arched upward, ending in a fuzzy question mark.

"Come here, I won't hurt you." Hilly relaxed as she scratched its ears and chin. Switching its tail side to side, the feline gazed at Hilly with its brilliant green eyes which shimmered and pulsed. The purr intensified. A low rumble at first, but the vibration escalated to a louder thrumming like a fast heartbeat. Mesmerized, Hilly leaned closer and the cat responded by sitting back on his haunches and cradling her face with its huge, furry paws. He stared directly into her eyes and his purr grew louder...and louder...and louder.

"Ms. Kemp?"

Hilly shook her head and looked around the room. She was no longer in the front office petting the cat. She was now in a room with a window overlooking the back alleyway.

"Ms. Kemp, are you alright?"

Hilly followed the voice and found a man sitting across from her. Unsure how she got into this room, she stood, her hands balled into fists, prepared to defend herself. "What happened? Who are you?" Scanning the floor for Raven, she barked, "Where are my belongings?"

"Your sword is safe, Ms. Kemp. It's in the front room with your backpack. I'm Aaron Aningan. We talked about the cabin you're renting."

Concerned with the lost time, Hilly's mind raced. *Did I get tranced? Did this guy do it? Can I trust him? I was petting a cat, where is the fucking cat!* "I'm going to ask you a very odd question. How did I get here?

"Why, Ms. Kemp, you walked in. You seem disoriented. Would you like some water?" Aaron strolled to a small refrigerator and grabbed two bottles of water. "I could use some myself," he said, placing the waters on the desk.

Still standing, Hilly grabbed one, unscrewed the top and sipped it while keeping her eyes on Aaron. She wasn't sure about this man standing across from her. Possessing a linebacker's sturdy frame, his muscled arms bulged in his all-black, silk suit. His long, gray hair was groomed back into a ponytail and secured with a multi-colored, braided band. Chakra-colored gemstones fastened to a silver post dangled from his right ear while a simple diamond stud pierced his left lobe. Unusual eyes—one was emerald green and the other opalescent—popped from his tanned face, etched with age creases around his eyes and mouth. His appearance reminded Hilly of an aging hippie.

"I was petting a fluffy cat in the waiting room," she mentioned, checking the room for the feline.

"Ah, Jeffrey. He's a wonderful creature, very curious. Sometimes I think he's better than a dog for ensuring only the right people come into the office."

"Only the right people?" Hilly asked. "Do you get bad people here in Aningan?"

"We get all sorts of people, Ms. Kemp, especially this time of year when Denali beckons, and thousands of people answer her call. Please sit."

"But, how did I get into your office? I don't remember walking in here, and I don't remember meeting you."

"I can only imagine how tired you must be. After all the flight delays and the amount of time it took you to arrive in our beautiful city. Some say the energy in Aningan impacts strangers in the most peculiar way. I've seen some of our visitors walk miles into the valley, transfixed by Denali, but later they can't recall how they got there."

Hilly considered Aaron's words. After all, she was tired and hungry. She still didn't trust him. Everything about him seemed bizarre. She probed his mind and found the path blocked. At least she knew he wasn't human. "Perhaps you're right. I've been awake for almost twenty-four hours. I would love to soak in a hot tub and relax in my cabin." For now, she'd play along with this strange man until she could figure things out for herself. Perhaps later, after she's rested, she'll come into town and check out the locals, check out Aaron. She smiled politely. "Is it a coincidence that your last name and the name of the town are the same?"

"No coincidence." Aaron's eyes twinkled. "My family has been revered in this city for generations. You might say, we made this town what it is today."

"Very interesting. So, do I owe you anything right now?"

"No, I have your card on file and won't process it until you're satisfied with your stay. As requested, you've rented our most remote cabin closest to Denali. I hope you don't mind sharing your home with our wild creatures. The isolation makes it one of my favorites. During the winter, the long, dark nights are remarkably meditative. When you look at the heavens, your gaze is met with thousands of eyes peering back at you. Some believe that our ancestors maintain a watchful eye on us." He winked, or at least, Hilly thought he winked. She wasn't sure if he winked or if it was a facial tic.

"I'm quite familiar with the ways of nature and can take care of myself. Did you arrange with the shaman to lead my vision quest?"

"Yes, he is a much-revered local shaman who has successfully conducted many vision quests. As we discussed on the phone, he can't guarantee what you will encounter, but your journey will be unique and full of the answers you seek. He will visit you tomorrow morning."

"I'm looking forward to it. If there is nothing else you need from me, I'd like to get to my cabin and relax a bit. How far out of town is it?"

"It's about thirty minutes away. Sammy is standing by to drive you there."

"Ah, yes, Sammy told me he would take me there."

Aaron abruptly stood and led Hilly to the front office. "As you may be aware, Sammy is my great-nephew. He's a character, but he's an excellent *human.*"

Hilly found it odd that Aaron would emphasize *human.* She asked him, "That's an odd thing to say, are there other beings here besides humans?"

Hilly instantly regretted her question. Aaron stared at Hilly, his face expressionless. "My child, you understand less than one-percent of the forces that roam this world of ours. The universe is vast and so are the life forms that inhabit it."

Confused and a little embarrassed, Hilly feared she had offended Aaron with her question. She was sure he was something more than Sammy's great-uncle. But she couldn't sense his abilities, and she couldn't probe his thoughts. It was like looking into a void—he emitted absolutely no vibrations. Although he reminded her greatly of Darrius, Aaron was completely different. She felt Aaron was hiding something because he spoke in riddles. "Have I offended you, Aaron?"

"Not at all, Ms. Kemp. I find you fascinating. We'll have more opportunities to chat and I look forward to hearing about your adventures here in Alaska."

Hilly stood in the doorway, "I look forward to spending time at your cabin and sharing my experiences."

Suddenly Stella belched a loud honk. "Ah, my great-nephew awaits his passenger." Hilly turned and offered to shake his hand. He stared at it briefly before bowing toward her. "The pleasure is all mine, Ms. Kemp." He then guided her toward the steps leading down to the road.

"Sammy, take care of our precious cargo." Turning to Hilly, Aaron gripped her hands tightly and whispered, "Walk cautiously, child. Alaska can be a dangerous place."

Stunned by his statement, Hilly asked, "What danger?"

Uncle Aaron gazed at her with his mismatched eyes, sparkling and shimmering. A loud buzzing filled her head and then...

"Hilly? Are you awake?"

Groggy, Hilly shook her head. She was in the front passenger seat with her arm draped outside the window. She stared at the landscape whizzing by as they sped down the smooth gravel road. They were no longer in Aningan. "Where are we? How long have we been driving?"

"We've been on the road for over fifteen minutes now. You asked about my family and next thing I know it looked like you dozed off. Everything okay?"

Something was amiss. One minute she's talking to Aaron, the next minute she's sitting beside Sammy. Maybe Aaron was right about the strange energy in this area. "I'm just tired, I guess."

Sammy laughed. "I wish all my passengers were like you." Sammy tapped his fingers on the steering wheel and hummed an unfamiliar tune. "Yep, you've been a perfect companion."

Denali loomed in the distance, observing them as they wound through the Mat-Su Valley, passing colorful carpets of wildflowers, rushing rivers and extraordinary rock formations. "Wow, we really are going out into the wilderness, aren't we?" Hilly said, leaning back into her seat. "The beauty is indescribable."

"In my opinion, you've got the best cabin, especially for your vision quest."

Hilly rolled her head to look at Sammy. She was no longer surprised he knew about her plans in Alaska. Jake had called it the "family-net," a much better connection than the internet for quick information. She shook her head. She couldn't wait to tell Curtis about this strange little town and its inhabitants.

Fifteen minutes later, Stella stopped in front of a log cabin flanked by trees and an unobstructed view of Denali. "We have arrived at your new abode," Sammy announced as he exited and ran around to Hilly's door.

"She's beautiful," Hilly said, taking in the rustic charm of the cabin. She noticed a small outbuilding and a stone structure. "What are those?"

"That stony thing is a well for clean water. Some visitors have used it as a wishing well, so I'm still fishing out coins—mostly pennies. The wooden shack contains a lot of supplies you may find useful like tools, chairs, and a charcoal grill."

"I'm guessing there's no running water."

"Yep, but we stocked the cabin with bottles of drinking water. You only need the well water for a bath or to clean the dishes." Hilly sighed, realizing that the long-awaited soak in a hot tub was not going to happen. "You do have electricity and a phone. Your cell phone won't work out here so the landline is your lifeline." Sammy grinned at his pun.

Hilly grabbed her backpack and scabbard while Sammy struggled to carry the large luggage, dragging them along the stony ground. Opening the cabin door, Hilly stood in the doorway. It was exactly as she envisioned it—rustic, small and cozy. The thick pine logs retained a smoky scent from a recent blaze in the fireplace. "It looks perfect, Sammy."

Sammy smiled his toothless grin, extremely pleased with the positive comment. "Uncle Aaron will be happy to hear the news." Hilly held the door as Sammy brought the luggage inside.

"Just drop my bags on the floor over there if you would," Hilly requested as she carefully placed Raven on the dining table. Sammy guided her around the cabin, pointing out the essentials: phone, light switch, bathroom, linens, cleaning supplies, and how to operate the fireplace. "I think that's everything. Don't forget, if you need anything, call. I placed a list of numbers beside the phone. Uncle Aaron's is at the top of the list. You can call him day or night. Seriously, he will pick up."

"Thank you, Sammy, I appreciate all your help," Hilly said, hoping Sammy wouldn't linger much longer.

"No problem. Remember if you need anything..."

"I know, just call Aaron."

"Yep. That's right." Sammy jumped into Stella, waved at Hilly, and peeled out of the front yard, leaving a cloud of debris in his wake.

Hilly sighed. Aaron's warning cast a dark shadow over her homecoming. And, then there was the raven, the messenger from Denali Most of all, she wondered about Sammy. Uncle Aaron called him human, but Hilly felt something else, a nagging anomaly as if he was a puppet in a bizarre play. She hoped her dreams that night would reveal some answers.

Sammy sped away, still zipping along on Hilly's glorious comment about the cabin. He had worked diligently to ensure everything was perfect for her stay, and her compliment made him feel appreciated, like a valued person. He liked Hilly. People weren't always nice to him, but Hilly was different. He hoped Uncle Aaron would send him out again...and soon.

Chapter 7

Astral Travel

PEACE AT LAST. HILLY pushed the heavy door closed. She fiddled with the handle, probing for the lock. Not finding one, she noticed two massive surface bolts, foot-long black iron fastenings thick and sturdy enough to deter a hoard of intruders from entering the cabin, secured at the top and bottom of the door. The locks reminded her of hardware used on old dungeon cells. But this cabin wasn't a prison, it was her sanctuary, and for the next thirty days, she planned to recharge her energy and unearth the secrets of her ancient family. Still, she wondered why such impressive hardware was installed.

Sammy was long gone, a distant dust trail followed him out to the main road. Hilly stood in the living room and surveyed the explosion of 1970s paraphernalia—blue and purple tie-dyed cushions bunched on one end of the orange futon, which sat on a lime-green shag area rug. A lava lamp burped red blobs within a discolored liquid, and a black, vintage rotary phone sat on a tiny wooden end table. Threadbare paisley print curtains with hues of pink, gold, and brown covered the front window.

She wiped a film of dust off the glass and peered outside. Acres of vegetation, rocks, and dirt met her gaze for miles—ten acres actually—and she yearned to explore the area, to reconnect with the land.

But first things first—she needed to cleanse the cabin and prepare it for her stay. Negative energy resulting from arguments, sadness, sickness, and gloomy thoughts adheres to all surfaces like spaghetti thrown against the wall. You can scrape most of the food off, but the tomato sauce seeps into the paint, reaches for the drywall, and festers. Destructive energy acts similarly—it always finds somewhere to take root and multiply, unless it's properly dispersed.

Every culture has its traditions and methods for clearing negative energy, but Hilly had developed her style in tune with her elemental magic beliefs. She grabbed her backpack, rifled through, and withdrew sandalwood incense and a box of matches. Her father had taught her that matches were more reliable than a butane lighter. Striking the match on the side of the box, a slight sulfur scent wafted up and tickled her nose reminding her of the many evenings spent with her mother learning to cast spells and understanding the ways of magic. Sandalwood, known for its powerful protection properties, would deter unwanted energy and entities during her stay.

The cabin filled with the pleasant aroma of the incense and reminded Hilly of Curtis and how much she teased him about his daily ritual, lighting several cones of sandalwood throughout their home.

"It's like an obsession with you, isn't it? You can't even have breakfast until you light these cones," she had poked at him.

"As a witch, I thought you would understand the importance, but if you're just going to mock me, then just fly off on your broom and let me do my job," he had joked, shoving her aside.

"Just try and stop me," she had squealed while stealing his matches and incense and racing away.

"Hilly, I swear...."

Not one day had passed and she already missed Curtis, terribly. Of course, she would never tell him that because he would say, "I told you so!" It was almost nine o'clock at night, Anchorage time, so it would be one in the morning in Pilot Mountain. She had promised she'd call him when she got settled, so, before she finished cleansing the cabin, she would ring him.

Hovering over the antique rotary phone, she shook her head in disbelief. She had used a similar phone when she was a kid; and remembered how the cord always wound around itself like a snake, twisting into an unforgiving knot. She picked up the receiver, relieved to hear the buzz of a dial tone. Now, for the hard part—dialing each number, one at a time, by inserting her finger into the corresponding hole and whirling it to the finger stop. The dial responded. *Click, click,* click. Then it moved back into place, ready for the next number. Hilly laughed, it was taking forever just to key in all eleven digits. Using this old clunker of a phone made her appreciate the swiftness of cell phones. Finally, the last number was dialed, and Hilly held her breath hoping to hear the familiar ringing as the connection was completed. Her excitement soon turned to disappointment when her call was redirected to Curtis' voicemail: "Hi, you've reached Curtis. Leave a message or not, the outcome is up to you." *BEEP.*

Hilly understood. Curtis was in bed. A shipment of curiosities was set to arrive at their shop early in the morning, and he needed to be there to ensure all the items were okay. She masked her disappointment in her message.

"Hey, honey, I'm finally in the cabin. I have so much to tell you about the trip. I'll call you tomorrow around nine o'clock at night your time. Love you!"

She placed the receiver onto the cradle and stared at it. She felt very alone. If only she could have chatted with Curtis. She sighed. Her logical voice suddenly burst through the sadness: *Come on, Hilly. You're just tired. Tomorrow will be a better day. Finish clearing the cabin.*

Every practitioner has a unique style for cleansing a space—there is no wrong way, but there are many preferred methods—and Hilly preferred to use her spiritual breath and incense to remove unwanted energy and seal the space for her magical work. Starting at the door, she gently blew the sandalwood smoke around the door clockwise and then moved to the window before moving around the living room to her bedroom which possessed a curious porthole window, and finally returning to the front door. Hilly closed her eyes and mentally assessed the cabin. Satisfied it was thoroughly cleansed, she returned to the living room and unfurled a grass mat.

She sat on the mat and pulled her backpack closer. One by one, she retrieved her ceremonial tools—petrified wood, a censer, a small bowl (which she filled with water from her bottle), and a white candle. First, a match was struck to light the candle and the fresh cone of incense, which she placed in the censer. All the tools were then carefully positioned—petrified wood in the north, incense to the east, candle to the south, and water to the west. The circle was ready for Hilly to meditate and astral travel, allowing her spirit to travel the physical plain.

Sitting cross-legged, she formed the gyan mudra by touching her index finger and thumb together before resting each hand on each knee. Clearing her mind, to allow it to freely wander, she recited a sacred mantra and entered a trance, letting her soul lift away from her body. Hilly's spirit drifted through the dusty windowpane and hovered in the front yard considering the directions for exploration. Finally, she headed northwest, toward Denali.

In the astral realm, the spirit feels and senses all life forms they encounter, but they are not seen by living things outside the spiritual veil. Thus, Hilly was free to explore the area undetected. Hovering above the Mat-Su Valley she gasped in awe at the diverse wild spaces and the clean, fresh air. Barbed-wire fencing denoted the edge of the property. Aaron had suggested that she find a location suitable for her vision quest within the boundaries—a place that resonated with her energy and identified with her soul. She floated over a vast field of purple lupine, and noticed a large boulder with symbols carved along its side. In the distance loomed Denali. *This is a perfect spot for my vision quest,* she thought as she deployed psychic markers into the land. Hilly would be able to easily find this remote space with the shaman.

She flew closer to Denali, drawn to the granite rock's energy as though a magnetic cushion of air held her aloft while floating over the mountain's sprawling glaciers and wondrous peaks.

A soft glow in the distance snatched her attention.

Aningan was calling to her.

She drifted toward the tiny town, intent on learning more about the unusual city and bizarre inhabitants, especially Jake, Sammy, and Aaron. This time of year, Aningan was a flurry of activity, as climbers and tourists, who considered it the ideal location to catch glimpses of Denali and enjoy the outdoor activities during the continuous daylight hours, descended upon the town. Hilly boldly walked the street, amazed by the astral spirit's ability to be among the living undetected, shoulder to shoulder with crowds of humans rushing to restaurants, bars, and stores. She was but a shadow in the crush of humanity as she strolled down the boardwalk searching for one business in particular. Pierson Express Flights.

Outside the weathered door, Hilly giggled at the missing "l" in the word "Flights." "If it's a fight he wants, I can certainly provide him with one," she whispered as she silently slid through the window glass and stood inside. Muffled noises came from the back room where she found Jake and Sammy watching a game show on an old television. A bulbous tube protruded from the back of the TV while rabbit ears, swaddled in aluminum foil, decorated the top.

With his long legs propped on a windowsill, Jake sank into an ancient stuffed chair that appeared to have been assaulted by a clowder of cats. He nodded to sleep while Sammy stuffed a sandwich into his mouth between gulps of soda from a large red cup. Hilly wandered closer to them.

Jake snorted and sat upright. "What was that?" he asked searching the room.

"What was what?" Sammy exclaimed.

"I thought I heard something," Jake said, walking to the front window, the same one Hilly had passed through earlier. Watching the tourists march by his nose twitched. Sniffing the air like a bloodhound, he turned toward Sammy. Hilly stood between them.

"Damn, Sammy, I smell sandalwood."

Hilly tensed. Could he smell the incense on her clothes? That didn't make any sense. She's just a shadow in the ether, he shouldn't be able to see her or sense her. Jake took a big step forward and sniffed the air again.

"What's going on, Jake?" Sammy asked, finishing the remnants of his sandwich.

Jake didn't answer. Hilly's heart pounded, she didn't dare move. Jake was only a foot away and stared right at her. Leaning forward, he slowly smiled. "Nothing, Sammy. I must be *seeing* things."

Hilly mentally catapulted herself back to the cabin, back to her mat. Her heart hammered in her chest. *He could smell me. He could see me.* She grabbed a bottle of water from the fridge and stood in front of the window, sipping slowly. "That son of a bitch saw me!"

Chapter 8

The Shaman

Hilly grabbed only snippets of true sleep after the astral adventure went awry, dozing on the futon while her mind replayed the events of the night. A feeling of inadequacy crept in again as she mulled over how easily Jake used his psychic gifts. Like a little girl learning ABCs for the first time, she felt like a novice using her magical abilities and she hated that. Her exhilaration while soaring over the Mat-Su Valley plummeted into embarrassment when Jake sensed her presence in his office. Witnessing the beauty of a magician wielding his power effectively and efficiently stoked the fires of her jealousy.

Sipping coffee, she brooded over last night's folly and considered canceling her morning vision quest. Aaron had made special arrangements with a native shaman who would arrive that morning, and she wrestled with her emotions—would she feel worse canceling at the last minute or going through with it?

She stood and looked out the front window as her conscience nagged at her. *Come on, Hilly, put on your big girl panties and just do it. You've looked forward to this vision quest for months, and now you're thinking about cancelling it just because of your pride?*

"What an idiot," she said out loud. Her heart-to-heart internal chats always helped her see the big picture. "Why would I cancel the most important experience in my life just because someone else is better at magic? It makes me sound insecure."

The appointment with the shaman was at 9:00 a.m., one hour away, so she scrambled to pull herself together—a bath at the kitchen sink with cold well water (extra splashes in her eyes to wake up), gathering up the gear and jumping into her hiking clothes. With only fifteen minutes remaining before the shaman's arrival, she devoured two granola bars and an apple. She would be fasting for the duration of the vision quest and needed something in her stomach.

The vision quest was a trek not to be taken lightly, and was described as a twenty-four-hour journey in the Alaskan wilderness where the wanderer would discover his or her true purpose and uncover elusive answers to all their questions. Many souls, initially fascinated by mysticism and traditions, eventually succumb to hardships, abandoning their quests out of fear, doubt, or an unwillingness to accept the truth about themselves.

Hilly was ready. She had planned this adventure for the last three months. She scanned the checklist provided by Aaron, ensuring she had all the essentials including water, a blanket, a jacket, and a hat. Another critical component of the quest was a knife or spear, a valued partner while wandering in the wilds where humans are insignificant in the vastness of nature. Hilly touched Raven which hummed in anticipation of the journey with her mistress.

A strangled honk surprised Hilly, and she dashed to the window. Sammy was waving vigorously beside Stella, the station wagon. Anxious to meet the sacred healer, Hilly trotted outside and stopped in her tracks. Her smile melted into a frown upon seeing Jake stroll around the front of the car, mirrored glasses on his face.

"Were you expecting some tiny Inuit with a brown, round face, and serene smile?" Jake joked.

But Hilly wasn't amused. "I wasn't expecting *you*!"

She returned to the house and slammed the door.

"She seems disappointed, Jake," Sammy said as he shuffled toward the cabin with Jake following behind.

Knock, knock, knock.

"Hello, Hilly? It's Sammy."

"I bloody well know who you are. Go away!"

"She seems mad, Jake. Whatcha think that's about?" Sammy raised his fist to knock again.

Jake gently grabbed his arm and pulled him back. "Wait here for a sec." Facing the door, he placed his palms on the wood, closed his eyes, and mentally reached out to Hilly. *We come in peace, Hilly. Please let us in.*

Inside, her hands clenched into fists, Hilly narrowed her eyes on the door and returned his message. *It's better if you just go away. Leave me alone.*

Nope, I'm not going to leave. It's not wise to let things fester. They only get bigger and nastier. Let's just talk, Jake replied.

Moments passed while Hilly considered her options. The stubbornness that propelled her to victory battling Stygian could sometimes be a detriment, especially when it served no useful purpose like refusing to talk with Jake because he punctured her pride. Taking a deep, cleansing breath, she threw the door open.

"Well, hi there!" Jake smiled warmly. "Mind if Sammy and I come in?"

Hilly glared at Jake and then eyed Sammy who stood to the side grinning like an eager puppy. Rolling her eyes, she acquiesced, holding the door wider so they could enter. "Sure, I guess."

Jake strode into the living room, breathing deeply. "Ah, there's that sandalwood I smelled yesterday."

Hilly suppressed her rising anger, shocked at how quickly it materialized. "Did you see me? Or, could you just pick up on the scent?"

"It was more intuition than anything. But sandalwood is a strong scent. I reckon I caught a few whiffs as you strolled through the office. You were floating in a different dimension, so there was no way for me to see you."

Hilly's anger subsided. It was evident Jake wasn't going to ridicule or embarrass her about last night's encounter. She bit her lip, upset that she had catapulted to crazy conclusions about Jake's intentions. She had a reputation for doing that. Curtis called it Hilly's "'fist of fury" referencing her ability to go from serene wife to wicked warrior in seconds. Hilly relaxed and went into the kitchen to get everyone water. When she returned, a warm smile replaced her scowl.

"There's the Hilly we know. Thanks for the water," Jake said, taking the bottles and passing one to Sammy.

Hilly sat down. "So, your intuition alerted you to my presence, and the sandalwood drifted into your dimension from mine?"

"When it comes to magic, it's not black and white. There's a rainbow of possibilities. However, my intuition is very strong, and I listen to it. I have learned the hard way that bad things will happen if I ignore them." He rolled up his right sleeve, exposing a long scar running from the elbow to his wrist. "Like this, for example. If I had listened to my voices, I wouldn't have almost severed my arm in a hiking accident."

Hilly's eyes widened as she explored the white line snaking down his tanned arm. "What happened?"

"When a friend dares you to jump from one boulder to another and you're slightly inebriated, two thousand feet above a river, you should listen to the voices screaming in your head, pay your friend the fifty-cent wager, and call it a day."

"Fifty cents? He only bet you fifty cents to risk your life? That's insane!"

"Hearing you say it out loud does make it seem a little crazy. But, at the time, I thought I could do it."

Jake and Hilly burst into laughter, lightening the room's mood.

"I'm glad you didn't lose the arm," Hilly said gazing into Jake's eyes. He appeared so different today. He wore dusty blue jeans, weathered boots, and a long-sleeved, light blue Henley, laced with sinew, revealing his chest tattooed with black symbols. The trappings of a shaman had replaced

Jake's pilot persona, softening his appearance in a serene and mystical way. "What are those?" Hilly asked, pointing to the markings.

"These are my calling card...my ID. When somebody ascends to shaman status, the entire family plans an initiation ceremony. The markings represent spirits who possess the power to protect me in my shamanistic work, and my psychic or physical travels. The elders performed dreamwork, a sacred ritual in which they elapsed into meditative trances, and received messages from The Great Spirit who resides in the heavens. They were told to use ancient techniques to tattoo the symbols onto my chest. It's a very spiritual ceremony." Hilly gazed downward, a hint of tears welling in her eyes. "What's wrong?" Jake asked.

"It's not you." She sighed and looked at him. "Every time you share a piece of your magical life, I get sad. I yearn for that family connection. Three months ago, I discovered I was the shaman of my family, but I'm the last descendant. Nobody can perform the initiation ceremony. I don't even know what my role is, or how to use my powers. Walking the path of the ancient shamans is supposed to unlock all the answers I seek. That's why I contacted Aaron and requested a local shaman who could assist me."

Jake stared at Hilly, convinced that the woman sitting before him was the lost soul who escaped the massacre that had decimated an entire family. He felt as though he was in the presence of royalty, gazing upon the warrior The Cererian Prophecy described would arrive and change the course of humanity. He felt a mix of reverence and pity for this woman wearing the title of firewalker and shaman, yet she wanders the earth without understanding the responsibilities of either.

"Jake? Anyone home?" Hilly poked.

Jake shook the cobwebs from his mind. "Sorry, you caught me daydreaming. I was just thinking of your situation. It's not right that you haven't been initiated into your official role. Perhaps Uncle Aaron can figure out a way to correct this injustice."

Sammy chimed in, "Yeah, Jake, Uncle Aaron knows everybody. I bet he can make things right for Hilly."

The warmth of an extended magical family is what Hilly yearned for. Growing up in a loving, non-magical household, her adoptive parents had protected her and her siblings, but her mother and father could never provide the mystic traditions of each of their ancient families. Reconnecting with her tribe, learning the ancient ways of her family and thriving in a nurturing environment have always been her biggest wishes. Hilly hoped she had finally found the link to that mystical community.

"Wipe your tears and erase that frown," Jake announced in a booming voice. "We've wasted too much time already. It's time to get this vision quest on the road. Hilly, grab your gear. Do you have everything on the checklist?" Hilly and Sammy jumped up as though being poked with a cattle prod.

"Yep," Hilly replied, grabbing her backpack and displaying the water, blanket, jacket, and hat. She opened the closet door and gently removed the leather sheath. "For my knife, I'm bringing this." Laying it on the table she unfastened the straps and extracted her broadsword, Raven. The etched dragons and pentacles gleamed in the light.

"Wow," Sammy squealed (as if he had never seen Raven before). "Look at the size of that sword." He moved closer to touch it.

Hilly pulled it away, and Sammy scowled. "Please don't touch it. It's a very personal item of mine."

"Sorry, Hilly. I wasn't going to hurt it," Sammy said, backing away.

"Alright. Let's go. We have a vision quest to get underway," Jake barked, pointing toward the door and circling his arm like he was herding cattle.

Heading toward Stella, Hilly excitedly rambled about the perfect location she had discovered during her astral travel. "I can't wait to show you. It has a tremendous view of Denali. It's so ideal, and it's located at the outer boundary of the property in the middle of a wildflower meadow with...." She realized that Jake and Sammy were no longer walking beside her. "Come on, guys, let's get going," she said, yanking on the car door.

Jake held up his hand and stopped her. "Hold your horses, Hilly. For a proper vision quest, you have to walk into the arms of nature, no cars." He gestured northwest toward Denali which loomed large in the distance. "We'll hike to your wildflower meadow."

"But, it's like two miles away," Hilly complained as she shouldered the backpack and scabbard.

"Great. So, not far away at all. Let's get walking." He swung a large pack onto his back and headed out into the shrubby vegetation.

"What about Sammy?"

"He'll hang out in the cabin until we get back. Sammy, if we're not back in twenty-four hours, come looking for us."

Sammy grinned at Hilly. She was unsure about him staying in the cabin alone even though she had gridded the inside with crystals and cloaked her magical tools. She convinced herself all would be okay unless Sammy knew magic. Hell, even if he did know magic, he wouldn't be able to undo her protection spells.

"Hilly!" Jake was already one hundred yards away.

"Coming! She trotted to Jake and, together, they hiked into the wilderness toward Denali.

Sammy watched them until they were bobbing heads in the distance. Then he strolled back to the cabin. “Now, we’ll see what we can find out about Miss Hilly,” he said. He stole one more look over his shoulder, confirming they were out of sight and closed the door.

Chapter 9

The Vision Quest

JOGGING, HILLY STRUGGLED TO keep pace with Jake whose long stride equaled two of hers. Ascending the rocky hills and maneuvering down slippery slopes took its toll on Hilly. "I admire your determination," Jake said. "Do you want me to slow down?"

Panting, she replied, "Nope, I'm good."

She pushed herself to run slightly ahead of Jake, which made him walk even faster.

The purple lupines reached out to Hilly with a sweet fragrance floating on the breeze. She breathed in the clean, aromatic air. "I can smell the flowers. We're almost there." They followed a dirt track toward the meadow and soon encountered the boulder Hilly had seen on her astral flight. Her psychic markers, deployed last night, still pulsed like spiritual signposts. The chunk of granite, about the size of a small car, guarded the entrance to the field of flowers. Jake tenderly stroked the symbols decorating the side and mouthed inaudible words. When he finished, Hilly dared to ask, "Were you casting a spell?"

Jake shook his head. "No, not a spell. I was saying hello to an old friend. I was offering him a simple prayer."

"A prayer?"

"When you walk in nature and encounter elemental spirits, what do you do?"

Hilly pondered his question. "I've never thought about it. I love to touch everything, but I've never formally offered any kind of greeting."

Still stroking the rock, Jake replied, "This boulder is as familiar to me as my family. Within it's hard exterior beats a heart of the millennium. It tells me how it was formed from the bowels of the earth, how it was pushed to the surface by the friction and force of the tectonic plates; and how it was carved from its mother during a volcanic explosion to finally come to rest here as the protector of the meadow."

Hilly carefully listened, noting the passion in Jake's voice. While he spoke, he gently caressed the cold granite as though it was a loved one. This was not the same arrogant pilot she had encountered in Anchorage. This was a sensitive, kind soul, a magician at peace with his surroundings and connected to the land of the elemental spirits. She envied Jake's advanced knowledge of nature. She could learn so much from him if she could keep her emotions in check. She was born here, but she felt like a stranger, having lost connections to the land and to Great Mother, Denali. "I wish you could download all your knowledge and experiences into my head right now," she said, smiling.

"I know it's frustrating, but I grew up here, learning for decades from my elders and teachers. You've returned after a long absence, a child returning to her mother, a mother you no longer know." He faced Denali and raised his hands in homage.

Jake's metaphor upset Hilly. She knew Jake meant Denali when he said "mother," but Hilly never knew her biological mother who, along with the rest of her family, was massacred by Stygian. Hilly would have perished as well if it hadn't been for Prasad who saved her and delivered her to the Kemps, her adoptive parents. Hilly often wondered what it would be like to talk to her real mother. What would she say, what questions would she ask? "I never knew my real mum," Hilly replied softly.

"I'm sorry, Hilly. I didn't mean to conjure up any bad memories. I was talking about the mother of all native Alaskans: Denali."

"I know you didn't mean any harm. It's just so hard thinking of all those lost years—what I could have experienced, what my mother and father could have taught me..."

"I've got an idea. Let's start with an easy lesson." He grabbed her hand and placed it on the boulder. "See if you can pick up on the rock's energy flow."

Hilly closed her eyes, allowing her mind to wander, to bump into any entity that happened to be hovering around. Jake added, "His energy is subtle. Like a ground swell from a spring, it starts low and roils toward the surface."

Hilly opened her mind and found herself standing in the meadow, alone and facing the stone. Its surface had become warm from baking in the sunshine all day. Beneath the welcoming warmth lay a coolness like a calm pool of water. A blue opal flashed in front of her eyes and disappeared just as quickly. A low vibration rumbled to the surface as if a heartbeat struck low in the ground and rippled upward.

Thump, thump.

She placed her other hand on the boulder, caressing the stone in circles, each hand moving counter to the other. The vibration intensified and the heartbeat increased.

Thump, thump, thump, thump.

Soon the boulder shared its secret with Hilly.

Jake tapped her on the shoulder and Hilly woke from her trance. She looked at Jake, tears of joy running down her face. "He spoke to you?"

"Yes, he told me—" Jake held his finger against his lips before she could say more.

"Don't say anything else. What he shared with you was intended only for you." Jake smiled. "You can do this. All you need is a little guidance, and a little patience."

"But there was one thing," Hilly pressed. "A blue opal flashed in front of me but immediately disappeared. What does that mean?"

"A blue opal? Curious. It's a gemstone used in emotional healing because of its powerful energy. It induces peace in the one who possesses it. Perhaps the boulder sent a vision gift. Hold on to that image. It will serve you well throughout the coming days."

"I noticed the symbols carved into the rock's surface when I flew over last night. What do they mean?" Hilly asked, kneeling beside the boulder.

"They're too ancient for me to understand. My great-grandfather once told me that the star visitors, who roamed this land for thousands of years, used this location for special rituals, and that the markings represent a code meant to open another dimension. But you need a special key to unlock that secret."

Hilly traced the carvings with her finger and thought of her brother, Kai. "My brother has a specialized role in his family. He is the Keeper of the Keys. He has physical and spiritual manifestations that can be used to unlock anything in the universe. I wonder if he would be able to unlock it?"

"I've never heard of such a title. But I'm still learning the history of my tribe. We were scattered all over the earth during the dark period, when hundreds of magicians, including entire clans and families, were hunted and killed. It's been a struggle to stitch the lineage together. Hell, most people are still in hiding, afraid to reveal their location lest the Yfel Brethren find and kill them."

Jake spoke of a history that was familiar, yet foreign to Hilly. "You mentioned clan. What is that? I've only been aware of the four tribes and the elemental families within each tribe."

"My understanding is that there were four original tribes located all over the world. Each tribe was composed of families which represented the four natural elements of earth, air, fire, and water. Within each family were numerous clans containing both magicians and the Folk, which are nonmagical individuals."

Hilly squinted her eyes and wrinkled her forehead.

Jake could see Hilly was confused. "Think of the tribes as being continents. On each continent, you have countries that represent the elemental families. Within each country you have cities that represent the clans.

Hilly nodded. "I see." She mulled over his words. Darrius and Prasad shared that she and her siblings were the last descendants of their individual families, but now she wondered if they may have meant *clan* instead of *family*. If so, then she still had a chance to reconnect with more relatives, perhaps even some who knew her biological parents. Jake's explanation buoyed her hopes for reconnecting with her lost past.

Peering into the distance, Jake changed the subject. "Time is passing quickly and Denali calls. You need to prepare for your journey." Gathering his backpack, Jake patted the huge boulder before heading down the dirt trail leading to the fragrant meadow. Now that she understood the rock's secret, Hilly also caressed the granite before following.

Jake brushed the lupine heads as he passed. "Are the flowers speaking to you?" Hilly asked, noting his peaceful face whenever he touched the blooms.

"Yes," he replied. "They provide insight on the surrounding area. I asked them to help me choose an appropriate place for your vision quest. I'm being drawn toward the center of the wildflowers." He pointed toward a large, flattened area. "This is where you will begin your spiritual journey. A great moose laid here last night—a sign from nature that this area is the natural center for your vision quest."

"What's the significance of the moose?"

"The moose stands for strength, wisdom and magic."

Hilly nodded and unpacked her items, carefully unfurling the blanket onto the ground. Sitting cross-legged in the center, she faced Denali and unsheathed her broadsword, laying it in front of her. The lupine reached above her head and swayed in the gentle breeze, making her feel protected and loved. Jake removed a small bowl and a sage stick from his backpack. Lighting the sage, he circled Hilly as he chanted ancient, mystical words and blew smoke onto and around her body while performing a cleansing ceremony. He placed the bowl on a flat rock in front of her and added dried leaves from a small pouch.

"What herbs are you using?" Hilly asked, fascinated by Jake's preparation.

"My special blend," he answered, winking at her. "Listen, Hilly. It's important that you know I'll be with you the entire time. You may not always see me, but I will be with you. I'll have your back. For the next twenty-four hours, you'll meditate in the shadow of Denali. If she calls for you, don't hesitate to answer. When you meet The Great One, be prepared to ask your questions. If you hesitate, she'll dismiss you. If you want to rise and explore the area, follow your intuition. There's nothing to fear."

"Do you think I'll need Raven?"

"It's always wise to bring a weapon when you're in the Alaskan wilderness. You're an intruder in this land owned by the beasts. This is their home, not yours. They should leave you alone, but if you need to defend yourself, you'll be ready." Jake struck a match and lit the leaves, softly blowing until pungent smoke wafted up. Hilly breathed deeply and soon became drowsy. Her eyes slowly opened and closed like butterfly wings.

"Jake, these herbs smell familiar and..." her words trailed off as she entered a deep trance.

Strange sensations swept over her. Her limbs grew heavy and unresponsive, yet her body floated upward above the flowers. A sense of peace washed over her, and she felt no fear. Carried on a current of air, she drifted toward the mountain, Denali, which pulsed an energetic greeting, sending shockwaves tumbling over her in familiar, sweet caresses. Far away, native chanting accompanied by a low drumbeat echoed in her brain. She gasped, recognizing the language of her ancient ancestors. The sweet-smelling lupine danced with joy, swirling colorful patterns across the meadow. The aurora borealis shimmered around her, transforming her skin to luminous neon-green. Fireflies joined her, tiny points of light swirling clockwise, rising upward, engulfing Hilly in a net of warmth. Tranquility and serenity filled her completely as she held her arms up to touch the fireflies swarming in the midnight sky, but they metamorphosed into twinkling stars. Hilly was aware that darkness did not come to Alaska this time of year, but her visions made perfect sense to her. Rising into the chilly Alaskan night, Hilly ascended into the ether surrounded by stars, planets, asteroids, and moons. A comet passed by, it's long tail of dust engulfing her, welcoming her.

A loud thump rocked the land. A vibration from the base of Denali raced toward the lupine meadow. The energy tsunami collided with Hilly. The concussion shocked her heart, causing it to palpate. Regaining her senses, she hovered her hand over her heart, calming it with healing energy.

"Hilly, my lost child. Come to me," an elderly woman spoke. Hilly hesitated and mentally scanned the meadow, searching for someone who might have spoken. The voice called out again, "Come to me, my daughter."

"Open your mind and walk the path that stretches before you," Jake instructed from beyond the vision veil. His voice, a whisper carried on the wind, encouraged Hilly to rise and begin her quest to Mother Denali.

Hilly nodded. The mother beckoned and she must obey. Floating on electromagnetic energy, Hilly drifted along the slopes, marveling at the immense glaciers slicing through the peaks, spilling toward the tundra in the foothills below the mountain.

Ascending higher and higher, she circled up the slope like a raven, easily reaching the summit lashed by snowy winds and ice. But Hilly was not cold, nor did she feel the sting of the sleet. She sat cross-legged in the snow and meditated, mouthing a sacred mantra, her thoughts focused only on Denali.

Soon, The Great Mother spoke, "Child, what is it you seek?"

Hilly carefully considered this question, remembering Jake's caution. *If Denali asks you a question, make sure you are ready. If she senses any hesitation, she will dismiss you.*

"I seek the truth, Mother," Hilly responded. "I seek the truth of my family. Who am I?"

"Your family lived in my shadow for a millennium. I know them intimately. Native families sing of their accomplishments. Nature recognizes their compassion and love for all living things. They brought balance to the land, they worked as one with the forests and beasts, and they respected all life and each other. Then the wicked ones arrived. The elders welcomed them with open arms, but they were soon betrayed. Nature was raped, and the balance was lost. Walk cautiously, young one, for there are those that will disguise themselves as friends. They are mirror images of who they really are. They seek to destroy you, to feed from your powers."

"How do I avoid them, Mother?"

Denali quieted. The wind whistled, carrying snow and ice in its arms, covering Hilly in an icy veil. Soon The Great One answered, "My child, we cannot avoid the evil in our lives...no one can. But you can be prepared by allowing all actions, good and bad, to wash over you like the ocean's cleansing waves. Unwanted debris shall be removed by the outgoing tide, and true blessings and happiness will cling to you, and protect you. Your intuition is your strongest ally, and it will never betray you. This is my guidance, instructions that will serve you well for the rest of your life. As an added protection, I bestow upon you a spirit animal, my messenger, who will always be with you. From this day forward the magic of the raven will keep you safe, it will bolster your courage and open your mind as you continue your path to discovery."

"I am honored, Mother, to accept your gift."

CAW!

A large raven, shiny and black, descended from the heavens and landed on the ground in front of Hilly. Hopping onto her shoulder, it peered into her eyes and squawked once more. Hilly recognized it as the raven that greeted her at Aaron's office.

"When the raven speaks, listen, my child, for it brings you the wisdom of the universe. It will reveal the imposters who seek to do you harm. As you walk the path of the ancients, you will only find truth by living yours."

"But, Mother, I don't know my truth," Hilly countered,

Denali sighed. The winds shifted and blew directly into Hilly's face. "You must complete the path and endure the hardships before you can live your truth."

The blizzard gales lashed at Hilly, knocking her over and catapulting her into the air as though The Great Mother had spat her out sending her back to complete her journey. Hilly wailed into the blizzard, "Mother, please. I still have more questions!"

The Great One remained silent and shifted under her snowy mantle. A low rumble rose from the depths with one final comment. "Remember, daughter, I will always be with you. You will feel my heartbeat when you are on the true path."

Hilly launched into the cosmos. Shooting stars and galaxies welcomed her with dazzling displays. Soon, she was pulled downward, descending toward the wildflower meadow which swirled against her body in a happy homecoming.

She awoke, standing near the fence line staring at The Great Mother looming in the distance. A thin trail of icy tears cascaded down her cheeks, still chilled from the frozen summit. The lupine comforted Hilly, brushing her legs with their fragrant heads. But she was sad, feeling rejected by Denali before receiving all her answers. Hilly sighed. Disappointment was becoming a familiar friend.

A screech broke her reverie. An abrasive, sickening caterwaul like dried bones tossed into a wood chipper. Hilly searched the landscape, anxiously looking for the source of the noise.

Screechhhh!

She recognized the blood-curdling howl as one she'd heard before on the beach near The Nine Muses. It had come from the oil black beast, Stygian, when he had attacked her and her siblings. Hilly's heart quickened. Whirling around, she spotted a dragon approaching from the east, its massive wings pumping the air, propelling miniature tornadoes across the valley. It raced toward Hilly.

Soulless, black eyes burned in a coal-black head. Her heart hammered in her chest. *How can this be? I banished Stygian to an interdimensional prison. How can he be here, now?* She frantically searched the ground looking for her broadsword, Raven, to defend herself, but it no longer lay near the blanket.

Screeeeech.

The beast soared toward Hilly who ripped at the flowers anxiously looking for Raven, but the sword had vanished. *It was right here on the ground. It couldn't have disappeared!*

The dragon screamed and spewed a blast of stale, hot breath that swirled around Hilly's body like the unwelcome advances of a predator. She shivered, feeling dirty and violated...and angry.

Hilly's fury exploded as she whirled to face the beast with her hands stretched forward. Her palms glowed red hot as she pushed her psychic energy toward the dragon. Using the words of her ancient family she screamed a protection spell, and steeled her gaze on the black eyes of the beast. It hung in the air, momentarily stunned by her powerful magic, then it snorted, reared its head back, and snapped at Hilly with its enormous fangs.

She dodged its attack and followed the beast with her palms raised. This time she conjured fire magic. Her hands vibrated as steam drifted from her fingertips. An orange ball of fire appeared suspended between her hands. As she prepared to propel it toward the dragon, the monster heaved a gust of fetid wind that swept the fireball into the distant horizon.

Disarmed, HIlly faced the beast.

It crept closer. She raised her hands in defense but she could no longer channel energy through them.

Out of nowhere, the flash of two translucent blades snatched Hilly's attention. Jake stood in front of her, holding two battle daggers, one in each hand. The dragon lunged for him, and he leapt into the air above the creature. As he catapulted over its head, he thrust both blades into the eyes of the beast and withdrew the daggers before landing safely on the ground. The dragon screamed and clawed at its face. Hilly joined Jake as they watched the beast writhe in agony.

As swiftly as it arrived, the beast suddenly vanished.

Hilly jolted awake. Her hands were outstretched in front of her. She panted—a rapid, raspy breath that burned the back of her throat as though she had inhaled intense heat and smoke. Still on high alert, she frantically scanned the skies and landscape around her, but there was no sign of the black beast nor of Jake. She remained on the blanket in the meadow, Raven still lying on the ground before her. Checking her hands, they appeared rosy-pink, but hadn't retained the severe heat as in previous altercations.

The sun hung in the sky in the same place as when she embarked on her quest, so she had no idea how much time had transpired. Puzzled, she rose and searched the area but found nothing and nobody.

She was alone. There were stories about travelers who became mired in their quest, not being able to find a way out. Like a continuous loop, they languished in another dimension, retracing their steps, continuously searching for the path back home. Fear suddenly gripped Hilly. She wondered if she was still on her journey, or if she was now lost on another plane, destined to walk the wilderness forever.

"Did you have a good journey?"

Hilly jumped upon hearing the voice, and she whirled ready to defend herself.

"What the...?" Hilly exclaimed.

"Jumpy?" Standing before her was Jake, smiling and offering her a bottle of water.

"A little. Where did you go? You were nowhere in sight when I woke up."

"I've been here the entire time. Like I told you, you may not always see me, but I have your back. Did you get your answers?"

"Most of them." Remembering Denali's caution about those who profess to be her friend but are actually mirror images. She suddenly grew suspicious of Jake.

"That always seems to be the case with The Mother," he said as he turned to look at the mountain. "She likes to give you bite-sized pieces of information but prefers you figure out the rest of the meal." He chuckled.

"She likes speaking in riddles."

"She veils the truth in her statements. You have to read between the lines."

Still wary of Jake, Hilly asked, "So, if you were here the entire time, where were you when I stood up and looked around?"

"Funny thing about spiritual quests, they can play with your mind. You don't always know if you're living in the present or walking in your dream. But, to answer your question, I was always here. I watched you dream. Once you shoved your hands out in front of you, they glowed red hot. That's an interesting trait. Do you know if everyone in your family has that gift?"

Hilly sensed Jake was getting nosy again and decided to keep her answers vague. After all, only her siblings and Darrius knew she shared blood with Stygian, which gave her powers well beyond the typical magician. "Perhaps. I don't know."

He knew she was withholding information. "Okay. No need to answer my questions. I'm just curious about your abilities. It's not every day I get to meet someone from a different family."

Remembering a detail from her quest, Hilly blurted, "You were in my quest."

Jake turned toward Denali, his back to Hilly. "Oh?"

"A beast was flying in the air—" she began.

"Which direction?" he interrupted.

"East. Why?"

"Just curious. Please continue." Hilly grabbed the water bottle and took a long slow drink. Jake was interested, and she wanted to keep him on the hook. She put the bottle down. Jake followed her every move and anxiously asked, "And?"

"Oh...yes, the beast was flying toward me. Everything was turning dark. I reached for my sword, but Raven had disappeared."

"What else?"

"The beast flew toward me and its wings propelled tornadoes ahead of it."

"What did you do?"

"I was frantic and raced around the meadow looking for my sword. Then I held up my hands toward the beast."

"Damn."

"Finally, I found Raven just as the dragon raced toward me, and I plunged it deep into its heart!"

"Liar!"

They both stared at each other. Jake realized he had blundered. He had contradicted himself.

"I *knew* you were in my vision."

"Wait a minute..." Jake stammered. "I mean..."

"Exactly!" Hilly proclaimed.

Guilty as charged Jake hung his head resigned. He couldn't back pedal nor could he go forward. It's best to roll over and expose his belly and hope she wouldn't plunge the blade in too deep. Hilly narrowed her eyes at him. Despite her suspicions about his true intentions, she was curious about his ability to penetrate her vision quest. "How did you pop into my dream?"

"It's just something I can do." He added, "I can jump in and out of dimensions at will. Like with your hot hands, we each have unique gifts."

"And, why did you need to leap uninvited into my vision?"

"Because it wasn't exactly a vision." Hilly stood before him, her hands on her hips, anger darkening her face. "It was a real event conjured by your subconsciousness." She scowled at him.

"You're saying I brought the beast to me?"

"In a way. I can't imagine that you've encountered such a creature in your lifetime, but your subconscious thought it was important to replay it. It must have a special meaning for you."

Hilly didn't answer him. That was family history best left on the beach of Manchester-by-the-Sea. "So, if it was a figment of my imagination, why did you have to jump in? It wouldn't have killed me if it wasn't real."

Jake shifted on his feet. "Vision quests are very real—everything you feel, see, smell, and experience is real. This beast entered your quest because it is a living entity, meaning it's something that's not yet dead or vanquished."

Hilly shuddered. The beast was Stygian, and Stygian was not dead, which allowed the monster freedom to roam. Or, had Stygian sent the dragon to Hilly?

"Did I say something wrong?"

"No. This is all so new to me and bizarre. It's so hard to figure out." Jake's demeanor abruptly changed. His eyes flashed and the corner of his mouth jerked up in a smirk.

"You know the beast. You've seen this beast before." He probed.

Hilly changed the subject, fearing that she would divulge too much about her history, her lineage. "What I want to know is *how* you killed the beast. What did you use?"

Jake grinned. Hilly was diverting from the truth for a reason. But why? He was certain Hilly had encountered this monster before and her reaction proved him right. He decided not to press the issue right now. "You mean these?" he said, producing two short swords from the sides of his backpack. He flipped and twirled them in the air before catching them. Their translucent blades shimmered. Their hilts were made of golden bronze with dragonflies etched into the handle and adhered to each hilt was a gold medallion featuring the head of a black wolf—a symbol of bravery, protection, and wisdom. Jake lovingly gazed at them as if they were extensions of his own hands. "Beauties, aren't they?"

"Yes. They are. I've never fought with two blades. Is it easy to learn?"

"It takes a little practice, but I'm sure you can quickly grasp the basics. My right hand mastered the maneuvers quickly, but it took almost a full year before my left arm became proficient at wielding the blade."

"Maybe one day you and I will have a sparring match. Raven versus your two tiny blades." Hilly held Raven in front of her and grinned at Jake. "Do your fighting daggers have names?"

Holding them aloft, he replied, "Cathal and Cadmar."

Hilly laughed. "Big names for such tiny swords."

"They get the job done. Cathal is Celtic for 'strong in battle,' and Cadmar is Irish for 'brave warrior'."

Now that the tension had eased between them, Jake asked Hilly to gather up her items so he could formally close the circle he'd cast for the vision quest. More than twenty-four hours had passed since Hilly closed her eyes and took flight into the universe, and Jake grew concerned that Sammy hadn't driven out to collect them, especially since it was well past the allotted time. Tired and hungry, they would now have to hike the two miles back to the cabin.

"Did I ever tell you about my uncle's mishap with magic?" Jake asked as he crested a hill.

"Nope," Hilly panted as she followed behind.

Jake chuckled as he recalled his uncle's account. "Uncle Bob was just a young kid, no more than ten. He'd been flexing his magic muscles on teleporting..."

"Teleporting?" Hilly interrupted.

"The ability to physically move from one location to another. It's usually done via dimension manipulation like when I entered your vision." Jake looked at Hilly over his shoulder and flashed a smile. "Anyway, Uncle Bob had dressed in his swimming trunks and focused on appearing in the pool in his backyard."

Jake giggled, and then snorted. "Poor Uncle Bob. He did materialize in water, but it was in the middle of a lake fifty miles away." Jake laughed hard.

Hilly giggled, caught up in Jake's infectious laughter.

"Thank goodness nearby boaters pulled him to safety or he'd have a long way to swim home!"

They both giggled for a long time before falling silent again with only the sounds of their boots scuffing through the vegetation.

"My brother Chance can burp the ABCs," Hilly remarked matter-of-factly. "He sucks a can of soda down, and then the magic begins." Jake stopped walking and looked back at Hilly. She raised her eyebrows and shrugged. "Everyone has a gift."

They laughed all the way back to the cabin.

As they approached the house, Jake went on alert, and withdrew his daggers. Hilly followed his lead and swung Raven in front of her. The front door was wide open but there was no sign of Sammy. "Something's strange," Jake cautioned.

They crept closer, using their intuition to explore the area for intruders.

"Where's Sammy?" Hilly whispered raising Raven in defense, and edging toward the front of the home. Likewise, Jake held Cathal and Cadmar in each hand. He arced to the right as Hilly went left, both keeping an eye on the house and surrounding landscape.

"Hello..." A weak voice hailed them. "Is someone there?"

Jake looked at Hilly and mouthed *"Sammy?"* Weapons ready, they crept closer to the door.

"Is somebody out there?" Louder and shaking, the voice was stressed and nearly panicking.

"Sammy? Is that you?" Jake replied.

"Jake? Damn, I'm glad you're back. I'm Sorry I didn't come get you. You might say I got a little hung up."

Jake shrugged at Hilly, and they both peered in through the doorway. Sammy was dangling upside down from the ceiling by silken threads spun into a cocoon that engulfed him except for his head, which was blackened, an unfortunate result of triggering an explosive protection spell. It looked as though a giant spider had spun a monstrous web inside the living room and then ensnared Sammy as its prey.

"What the hell..." Jake said, lowering his weapons.

Hilly's reaction was quite different. "Damn it, Sammy, you weren't supposed to touch anything!"

Jake glanced at Hilly. "This is your doing?"

"Your *friend* strayed into my conjured web, because he was snooping in my things. Isn't that right, Sammy?" Sammy swayed like a cotton pendulum, his eyes bulging from the blood that had rushed to his head.

"Gee, Hilly, I'm sorry. But my head is going to explode if I don't get down. Would you please release your spell?"

Hilly scowled at Jake, and then glanced at pitiful Sammy swinging like a beetle in the sticky web. She rolled her eyes. "Men! Between you and Jake, I don't know who's worse!" She said a few words while waving her hands, and Sammy plummeted to the floor with a loud thud.

"Oww!" Sammy rolled around on the floor trying to free his arms, and then he tried to dislodge the sticky fibers from his clothes.

Hilly surveyed the interior. Her spell had worked all right but goo covered everything in the living room as though the house had vomited sticky taffy. Irritated with both Sammy and Jake, Hilly mumbled under her breath while she plucked web strands off the furniture.

Jake sighed. "Um, I guess we should go and leave you alone." Hilly ignored him. Jake snatched Sammy by the collar and shoved him out the open door. "I'm sorry, Hilly. Sammy was just curious. He can't help himself sometimes. Honestly, he didn't mean anything by it."

Hilly said nothing and continued cleaning. If she opened her mouth, she would only lob a litany of obscenities at Jake, and she didn't want to spoil what was left of the beautiful afterglow from her vision quest. She just wanted them to leave and get out of her life. Snatching a pile of sticky goo from the futon she flung it at Jake. He ducked just in time, but the glob flew out the open door slamming against Sammy's head.

"Oww!"

"I guess we'll go. I'll touch base with you tomorrow, okay?" Jake said.

Her back to him, Hilly continued silently collecting sticky fibers from the walls. Jake sighed and exited, closing the door behind him. Sammy finally freed his arms and revved Stella into life. Jake slid into the passenger seat and stared at his partner behind the steering wheel. "From my point of view, Sammy, you look like a turd rolled in a dust bunny." They both snorted and laughed.

"Gee, she's awfully mad, Jake. I was only doing what you told me to do."

"Shut up, Sammy!" Jake growled. He glanced back toward the house. "Get us outta here. I've got a lot to think about." Sammy gunned Stella, and she squealed down the gravel road. "I think Uncle Aaron has a lot of explaining to do."

"Whatever you say," Sammy said as they sped toward Aningan.

Chapter 10

The Package

Now that Sammy and Jake had finally left her alone, Hilly could deal with the monstrous mess in the cabin. Sticky strands stretched everywhere, and long tendrils of glistening goo dripped from the ceiling. She had intentionally used her spider spell to thwart anyone snooping for her magical tools. It was effective magic, but messy—very messy. Part of the trick for this particular conjuring was to arrange clever decoy locations that would lure an intruder into her snare. Meanwhile, her ritual paraphernalia lay cleverly hidden in plain sight, but also fortified by a protection incantation. Chuckling, she remembered Sammy hanging upside down, swaddled in a cocoon. Yes, very effective.

After more than a day exploring the great outdoors, she stunk and felt grubby. Time for a hot bath—Alaskan-bush style. When she first arrived, Sammy had proudly pointed out an artesian well. It produced ice-cold water, one bucket at a time, and it was one hell of a workout retrieving enough water for a sixty-two-quart pot. A lot of the water spilled as she lugged the huge container onto the stove. While it heated up for her bath, she undressed.

Bolting the front door, she peeled off her shirt on her way into the bedroom where she removed her jeans. One leg had three ragged tears, as though gigantic talons had swiped at her. She studied the rips, poking her fingers through the holes, and thinking back to her vision quest. Maybe

Jake was right, maybe the beast had visited her. But if Stygian was still imprisoned in his interdimensional cell, who was the monster, and how did it materialize in her quest? A follow-up conversation with Jake was needed. Their mutual distrust of each other was like an elaborate, slow dance, where sometimes she would lead, and other times, he took control. However, they kept stepping on each other's toes.

Standing naked in the kitchen, she methodically dipped her face cloth into the steaming water before applying liquid soap and slowly scrubbing her body—starting at her head and moving downward, careful to dislodge the caked-dirt between her fingers and toes. The entire process was meditative, allowing her to dwell on her vision quest—Denali's words (and what she didn't say), the interaction with the cosmos and universe, the black beast, and Jake. It was time to wash her hair. As she leaned over the kitchen sink, she used a bowl to pour water over her head and then shampooed the day's grime away. It was not as satisfying as lounging in a bathtub, but the quick sponge bath accomplished the same result, and Hilly soon felt warm and clean.

Towel around her head and wearing a bathrobe, Hilly placed the tea kettle on the stove for some hot water. Tea and sweet biscuits sounded wonderful and Aaron had been kind enough to leave a welcome basket full of treats including teas, biscuits, assorted cheeses, and dried fruits. Relaxing was the only thing she wanted to do at that moment, but she caught sight of the mess in the living room, which was now a pigsty. Before she could rest, she needed to clear out the space. There was only one solution—reverse the spell. Raising her hands toward the living room she prepared to recite her incantation backward—a technique she learned from a green witch she befriended in North Carolina. It's a simple method, but extreme care is required to ensure every syllable of every word is uttered in the exact reverse way from the original spell, or you might create an even bigger mess.

She closed her eyes, allowing herself to visualize the words of her original incantation, and slowly, and purposely, recited the words backward. When she opened her eyes, the room was pristine and the sticky web strands were gone. Hilly smiled. She loved when a spell goes well. Of course, she had experienced some bad magic in her lifetime like when she asked the spirits to knead the bread while she picked herbs from the garden. When she returned, a gooey, doughy mess dripped from the ceiling and walls. She hadn't been specific as to where the kneading should occur. She still wasn't perfect, but as magicians go, she wasn't bad. And, she didn't mind failing on occasion.

The kettle whistled, and Hilly poured the hot water into a huge mug containing a bag of black tea. She picked through the basket of goodies and settled on some water crackers and wheat biscuits. Sitting on the futon, she sipped the warm tea and gazed out the dirty front window. The mid-morning sunshine was bright despite the gritty film on the glass. It was difficult to imagine that twenty-four hours earlier she was sitting in the middle of the lupine meadow staring up at Mother Denali. Now, after a warm bath, sleep demanded to be heard. Finishing her tea, she placed the cup on the end table and reclined back into the cushions. Eyelids heavy, she stared at the ceiling, and moments later she was sound asleep—the sleep of the adventurer, the slumber of a warrior.

Bang, Bang, Bang!

Hilly awoke to the loud pounding on the front door and sat upright, gathering her robe around her. Awakened from a sound sleep, nothing made sense just yet.

Bang, Bang, Bang!

The assault on the door continued. "Who is it?" she yelled, jumping to her feet and searching for her sword Raven.

"Sammy," came the reply as a little brown face and toothless grin appeared in the bottom pane of the front window. "I have a package for you."

Hilly rolled her eyes. "Hold on." The irritating pest had just left, and now he was back. "I need to get dressed."

She trotted into the bedroom, snatched a suitcase from the floor, and flung it open on the bed. Rifling through the bag, she grabbed the first pieces of clothing that looked halfway suitable: a blouse and a pair of shorts. She padded bare-foot to the front door, unlatched the bolts, and opened the door.

"Hi Miss Hilly," Sammy chirped before launching into his machine-gun banter. "I was knocking for quite a long time, but you were sleeping so peacefully, and I could see you through the window, but I didn't want to wake you, and this package arrived today, and it was an immediate delivery, we don't get these very much up here, and so I thought I better get it out to you right—"

"Stop!" Hilly shouted, holding up her hand. Sammy shut-up mid-sentence and stared at Hilly with his puppy dog eyes, awaiting his next command. "I'm sorry, Sammy. I just woke up and don't even know what's going on yet. Didn't you just leave here an hour ago?"

"An hour ago?" Sammy asked. "Miss Hilly, I haven't seen you in two days, you know when you caught me in your big old spider web? When you and Jake did the vision quest—"

"Stop!" Hilly shook her head. Sammy's words made no sense. "What do you mean two days? I just laid down a little while ago."

"Maybe you did, but I haven't been to your house in two days and—"

"Okay, okay..." Hilly stopped him from rambling. "I guess I was really tired." She mulled over Sammy's words. Had she been sleeping on the couch for two entire days? It didn't make sense. It was as though time moved at a different pace in the Alaskan wilderness. Sometimes it fast-forwards and sometimes it rewinds, creeping slowly. "You said you had a package for me?"

"Yes, ma'am!" Sammy held a small box, cradling it with reverence as if it was a holy relic. "Here it is. See, it's marked urgent on the top. We don't normally get deliveries like that up here. Everyone at the depot said it must be something important."

"Okay. Let me see it."

"You need to sign for it first." Sammy held a clipboard with a document and pointed at the X for her signature. Hilly sighed at the amount of red tape surrounding the delivery of one little package but reluctantly scribbled her signature and took the parcel from Sammy.

"Are you gonna open it now?" Sammy asked, his fingers twitching in anticipation, hoping she would reveal the contents of the package.

"No," she replied flatly. "I appreciate you driving it out to me." Reaching into the pockets of her shorts, she realized she didn't have money in her pants. "Hang on, I'll get my purse."

"That's okay Miss Hilly. I don't need a tip. I love driving out here and seeing what you're up to." Sammy stopped. His eyes darted between the floor and the door, before he blurted, "Er, I mean, it's my pleasure to help you." Before Hilly could respond, he twirled and trotted for the old station wagon. He jumped in the driver's seat and pulled the door shut.

What an odd man, Hilly thought as she watched him race away. She wondered if he ever accelerated slowly anywhere. Sammy appeared to have only one speed—fast. Hilly followed the car's dust trail until it disappeared near the edge of the property, and then shut the door carrying the package to the couch.

Her mind reeled. She wondered how two entire days had passed without her knowledge. The last thing she remembered was taking a sponge bath and sipping tea before falling asleep. Something didn't make sense. Had Aaron spiked the black tea? If so, he went to a lot of trouble to cellophane wrap and seal one box of tea. Had the spiritual journey taken such a physical and mental toll on her that it thrust her into a deep sleep? Perhaps she's still in a dream, like in her vision quest, and Sammy was just a figment of her imagination. But her hands still held the small package, and that was real. It barely weighed anything, as if someone sent her a box of air. Her name was printed perfectly in black ink on the top of the package and a thick black line underscored it. The shipping label also included Aaron's name and address but no return address.

She sat down and slowly unwrapped the package, which was double-wrapped in brown, kraft paper. Each fold was perfect—sharp edges and just enough tape to seal the flaps—a method Curtis would have used. Their anniversary was only three weeks away, and Hilly grew excited thinking it was a surprise from her husband. Mentally checking the package, she envisioned total emptiness as if the parcel contained nothing at all. Hilly tossed the brown paper aside, revealing a blue box, the color of a robin's egg. It was a sturdy package with black lettering on the top that read TIFFANY & CO.

Curtis had sent her jewelry! Hilly removed the lid and threw it to the floor, then removed the fluffy cotton. She gasped.

With trembling fingers, she lifted out a white gold wedding band, with four different stones: emerald, sapphire, amber, and amethyst. Curtis possessed a similar ring. Rotating it in her fingers, she noticed tiny drops of blood on the inside. She probed the ring with her psychic powers to determine if it belonged to Curtis. But, she could gather no information on the piece, as if someone had cloaked the ring. She noticed a white card visible through a single layer of light-blue tissue paper and picked it up. The message was simple:

Consider this a token of what is to come if you do not deliver Stygian to us.
- Yfel Brethren

"Curtis!" Hilly screamed, and ran to the phone. She twirled the first number on the vintage rotary phone, as fast as possible, and anxiously awaited its return to position before dialing the next number. "Shit!" she screamed when she realized she chose a number out of order and had to start from scratch. Finally, completing all the numbers, she held the receiver in a death grip up to her ear, counting the rings as if each one was the heartbeat of her husband.

She heard Curtis' voice as he chirped, "Hi..."

"Curtis? Curtis are you there? Are you okay?"

"... you've reached Curtis, leave a message, or not, the outcome is up to you."

Hilly slammed the receiver down causing the phone to tumble onto the floor with a loud ring. Was Curtis okay? Had the Yfel Brethren kidnapped him? Maybe he had stepped out. Maybe he was taking a shower. She decided to call back.

She snatched the phone off the floor, and carefully redialed the number. It droned through the rings, and she impatiently thumped her fingers on the arm of the futon. "C'mon. Curtis. C'mon!"

Again, his cheery voice asked to leave a message. Hilly pleaded, "Curtis, please...please call me as soon as possible. I'm worried. I need to talk to you." She slammed the receiver down.

On the verge of tears, she bit her lip and a drop of blood fell onto her blouse. What should she do? She didn't want to overreact and she didn't want to frighten anybody else. Then again, if this was an emergency, she didn't want to wait too long.

She had an idea. She'd call her new neighbors, Ben and Alicia. There would be no harm in having them check to see if Curtis was home. He'd answer the door for the new neighbors.

They had known Ben and Alicia for a few months. They realized they were sweet retirees looking for ways to keep themselves busy. Alicia loved to garden, and Ben yearned to play golf, something he gave up while working in the corporate world. Pilot Mountain was the perfect town for both hobbies. When they had first met, Hilly sensed the two neighbors were kindhearted souls whose own children had flown the coop, so Curtis and Hilly represented a new outlet for their parental doting. Alicia had even offered to cook for Curtis while Hilly was on her month-long journey into the Alaskan wilderness. Offering to keep an eye on Curtis and the house, Alicia had reminded Hilly, "If you ever need anything, please don't hesitate to call me. I'm here for you, honey." It couldn't hurt to ask Alicia to check on Curtis, just in case his phone wasn't working. Hilly dialed Alicia's cell number and crossed her fingers.

"Hello?"

"Hi Alicia, it's Hilly."

"Hi, Sweetie," Alicia greeted. "How are you? Are you enjoying yourself?"

Hilly melted into the futon, relieved to have reached a live person. Home seemed too far away, but now she had a connection to Pilot Mountain. Hilly tried to remain calm and sensible in her words. "I'm doing great, just did some hiking near Denali yesterday."

"That sounds beautiful but dangerous. Did you encounter any grizzlies?"

"Nope, no wild critters. Alicia, can you please do me a favor?

"Sure, pumpkin."

"Will you go see if Curtis is home? I've left messages for him, and he hasn't answered. I'm sure he's busy...or maybe his phone is busted again."

"Oh, sure. Do you want me to go now?"

Hilly wanted to scream, *Of course, I fucking want you to go now.* But she took a deep breath and calmly said, "Yes, that would be great. I'm getting ready to go out again and I don't want to miss Curtis' call."

"Sure, honey, walk with me as I go over..." Hilly heard thumping and scuffling as Alicia grabbed her keys and other items before she headed out the door. "Ben, I'm going next door to check on Curtis. Do you want to come?"

Frustrated with Alicia's meandering, Hilly wanted to scream, *Alicia, get your ass over to my house now and see if everything is okay with Curtis!* But, she didn't. She sighed and took a long deep breath.

More scuffling ensued as Alicia hugged Ben and the two of them finally headed next door to check on Curtis. Suddenly Hilly heard the dial tone. "Oh, no," she wailed, slamming the receiver down and looking for her neighbor's number to call her back. Before Hilly could dial, the old phone rang and Hilly answered. "Hello? Hello...Curtis?"

"Hi honey," Alicia replied in her sweet voice. "It's just me. I dropped the phone, and I must have lost you."

Ben chimed in, chuckling at his wife, "You know she can't do two things at the same time."

"Don't mind Ben. We're almost to the door. I'll ring the bell."

"No, Alicia, don't press the button!"

It was too late. Soon the jingle from *The Addams Family* floated over the intercom. Hilly hung her head. Why had she allowed Curtis to change the pleasant ding, dong to *The Addams Family* melody? He had a brilliantly twisted sense of humor, but that's why she loved him so much.

"What the?" Alicia said, bewildered by the creepy tune. "Honey, did you know your doorbell is broken?"

Hilly suppressed a chuckle at her neighbor's naivety.

"Ben can help Curtis get that fixed."

"Did he answer?"

"No, I'll ring..."

"NO! Don't touch the doorbell again. Get the spare key from under the garden gnome holding the lantern."

"Hilly, you sound worried. Should I be concerned about anything? Ben, help me, the key is under the little gnome, and he won't budge." Hilly heard scuffling and the word "shit" a couple of times before Alicia got back on the phone. "We have the key."

"Great!" Hilly was ecstatic that someone would finally get into the house and check on Curtis. Hilly listened as Alicia unlocked and opened the door, which creaked.

"Curtis!" Alicia yelled.

"Hey buddy, it's Ben and Alicia." Ben called out.

"Honey, we're walking into the house. I hope you don't mind," Alicia said. "Nobody seems to be here."

"What's that over there?" Ben asked.

"Hilly, there's some sort of package on the floor in your sitting room."

"A package?" A weird feeling punched Hilly in the gut. Her husband was missing, and another mysterious package had appeared. She feared something malicious had occurred. She frowned at the thought Curtis had been taken against his will. But, by whom?

"Ben, don't touch it! It could be booby-trapped!" Alicia snapped.

"I doubt Curtis would leave an exploding package in the sitting room," Hilly interjected. "What does it look like?"

"It looks like a little present. It's got purple wrapping paper and a big white bow on the top. Ben, I said, don't touch it!"

Ben snatched the box from the floor and held it in his hands. "It's light as a feather. I bet there's jewelry inside."

Hilly scrambled to make sense of what was going on. She hated being over four thousand miles away and reliant on her elderly neighbors to be her eyes and ears.

"Ben, stop shaking the package. You might break something. Hilly, I have the box in my hand. Ben was going to break it for sure. Do you want me to open it, honey?"

"Why would Curtis leave a gift in the middle of the sitting room? Are you sure he's not there?"

Hilly waited while Ben checked the house, going upstairs and checking every bedroom. "Neat as a pin," Alicia responded. "Nobody's here. Maybe he went out."

Hilly frowned, Curtis wouldn't randomly place a gift in the sitting room and then leave the house. After all, Hilly wouldn't be returning for three weeks. Her voices nagged at her, and her stomach lurched. Something was terribly wrong.

"Alicia, will you please open the package?"

"Sure, honey. Ben, hold the phone while I unwrap the present." Hilly heard scuffling and swearing as Alicia handed the phone to Ben. Seconds passed and finally Alicia shouted into the phone, "I'm opening the present now! Ben, hold the phone closer. I think I'm screaming into Hilly's ear."

Hilly closed her eyes. Listening to Ben and Alicia was like hearing an old vaudeville comedy act on the radio. Her intuition screamed at her, *Hilly, something is wrong!*

"Here I go, Hilly. I'm carefully unwrapping the paper so you can save it for another day."

"For God's sake, Alicia, just rip the fuckin' paper!" Ben yelled.

Hilly shook her head. If only she was there. But she was at the mercy of her aged neighbors and their eccentricities.

"The paper is off. Look there's a beautiful purple box." Purple was Hilly's favorite color so part of her still imagined that Curtis had bought her something for their anniversary. But why would he leave it on the floor, and why now? More scuffling was heard as Alicia maneuvered the top off the box. "Look, Ben, Curtis put crinkly purple confetti inside. Honey, it's getting all over the floor, but we'll pick it up." Hilly smiled, Curtis knew she hated crinkly confetti, and so putting it into a gift was a sign of his warped sense of humor. Maybe this was a random gift he left for her...but three weeks early? "I just pulled out a purple cellophane bag but it has a weird smell to it," Alicia said.

"Maybe Curtis threw in some herbs," Hilly suggested, feeling nervous.

"Oh, look, Ben. There's a tiny label on the bag and it says 'open me carefully'. Should I open it, Hilly? I don't want to spoil any surprise Curtis intended for you."

"Go ahead, Alicia," Hilly said, and held her breath.

"I'm opening the bag—."

There was a scream and the phone thudded to the floor. Hilly heard Ben whimpering, "Oh my God! Oh my God!"

"What is it? Hello?" That nagging fear exploded in Hilly's brain and she knew something must have happened to Curtis. "HELLO!"

"Hilly?" Ben had picked up the phone.

"Ben, what was it? Tell me!"

"Hilly, I don't know how to say this."

"Ben, just tell me...please."

Ben sniffed, obviously crying, and said, "There was a finger in the bag."

Hilly clamped her hand over her mouth, stifling a scream. She bit her lip to regain her senses and a drop of blood fell onto the floor.

"Honey, I'm so sorry...are you still there? There's something else—there's a note. I'll read it to you:"

> *Every day Stygian is not freed, you will receive another reminder from your husband.*
> *Don't contact us, we will contact you.*
> *-Yfel Brethren*

Silence.

"Hello, Hilly? Are you still there?"

Hilly couldn't respond to Ben. She was too busy screaming into a cushion.

Chapter 11

Curtis

CURTIS AWOKE TO AN uneasy stillness. His eyes were open but he could see nothing because of the suffocating blackness that swirled around his body. He lay prone inside a cramped container, his arms wedged by his side. The lid hovered so close to his face that his breath bounced back across his eyelashes. Visions of lying inside a coffin pierced his brain and his heart quickened at the sudden flood of adrenaline surging throughout his body. He panted as anxiety rose from the pit of his stomach. His left hand rested in a puddle of viscous fluid and throbbed for attention. Nothing made sense.

The last thing he remembered was answering the door. When he had checked the security camera, Curtis had seen the familiar brown uniform of a delivery driver and expected his shipment of medicinal herbs had finally arrived. When he threw the door open, he was surprised to find three men.

The one in the brown uniform had asked, "Are you Curtis Dawson?"

"Yes, why?" he had replied. And it was the last thing he recalled before waking up in his darkened cell. A slow, rolling vibration rattled his prison with a constant thump, thump, thump. He imagined he must be on a vehicle or a train, but why? The stale air and rhythmic thumping lured him into drowsiness. He would have drifted to sleep had it not been for the oppressive confinement. Blackness—an unbearable inky void where fears manifest and steal your sanity.

Curtis was close to losing his.

Not long after he awoke, the rolling motion stopped, and he heard metal scraping on the side of his box as the padlocks were unlocked. The lid flew open, and he was greeted by the same three men who met him at the house. Grabbing his legs and arms, they pulled him roughly from the coffin and dragged him toward a cabin. Pain exploded in his hand.

Glancing downward, he noticed something was terribly wrong. He counted his fingers. One, two, three, four. FOUR? The ring finger was missing and a blood-soaked rag covered the gap between the digits. Struggling against his abductors, he demanded, "Who are you guys?"

One of the men suddenly punched Curtis in the head, who quickly fell unconscious into the arms of the other two men.

"That will keep him quiet," Everild growled.

"Be careful, brother, you might kill our bait before we have the fish on the hook," Thane cautioned, half-joking.

"So, what? His body will still provide the bait we need to lure the female magician to us and force her to release our lord from his prison." Everild kicked the unconscious Curtis in the side and laughed. "Weak, stupid human. That's all he is to me."

The remote cabin lay safely hidden in a thick pine forest at the end of a dirt mountain trail winding up the switchbacks of Pilot Mountain. The rustic, log house was a traditional hunting lodge surrounded by three hundred acres of pristine woodland. Like many cabins in the mountains, this home had no physical address, so nobody knew it existed except for four people: the three abductors and the owner of the home, Aaron Aningan.

The three men pulled Curtis into the house and chained him to a bed in a back bedroom. "Thane, you and Benedict seal the location so that the meddling witch won't find us through her husband," Everild commanded. They nodded and bowed to their leader before heading outside to protect the property with magical spells.

Everild assumed control of the Yfel Brethren three months earlier after Stygian was tricked by Hilly and locked away in his interdimensional prison. It had been an opportune moment to seize control of the group as Everild had become weary of Stygian's obsession with Hilly and her magical family. He believed Stygian had abandoned the group's primary mission to eradicate the magicians from the face of the Earth. He chuckled, realizing the sorceress had done all the hard work for him. Stygian was ignorant, thinking he could easily slip in and out of Hilly's mind without betraying his secrets. The witch had bested him at his own game, and now Everild was in charge.

Thane and Benedict were obedient followers. They wouldn't cause any trouble and were happy to have order in their troop again.

There were moments, however, when Everild wondered if he should follow through with his plan to release Stygian. *Why not let him rot in his interdimensional hell?* But, although he thirsted for power and control, he was dependent on his leader. Stygian may have been sloppy dealing with the Kemps, but he was extremely clever in keeping the Yfel's secrets all to himself. Everild hated to admit that he needed Stygian now more than ever so he could locate and kill the magicians that still roamed the world. He closed his eyes and imagined how it would feel to consume all their magical powers.

Stygian would reward him handsomely for releasing him from his prison and applaud his cunning and devotion to the cause. Everild smirked while thinking, *Stygian will acknowledge all my hard work even up to the final moment when I kill him and assume ultimate control.* He chuckled maniacally.

Thane and Benedict walked in opposite directions around the cabin, speaking the words of the ancients while weaving a veiling spell. To those on the inside of the veil, it would appear as though they were gazing through a water globe. They would see everything including the trees, the animals, people, but the images would shimmer as though they existed through a watery filter. On the outside of the veil, an intruder would merely see the forest, all other elements would disappear. If an unlucky soul inadvertently walked through the boundaries of the veil, his body would not withstand the pressure of passing from one dimension into another. It would immediately disintegrate into nothingness.

"Do you think Everild's plan will work?" Benedict asked as he made his final pass around the home.

"I think it will get the magician's attention, but I'm not sure he'll ensnare her. She's crafty. She imprisoned Lord Stygian and that took tremendous power and resolve. She's more than a sorceress. I believe there's more to her than what we know." Thane slapped Benedict on the shoulder. "We should go in. Everild is not a patient man." Benedict nodded. They surveyed the area again, ensuring their spell had deployed successfully. Satisfied, they entered the cabin.

Curtis awoke groggy. His right hand was chained to the bed's metal headboard. His head pounded from where he had been punched. Lifting his shirt, he found a deep purple bruise spread along his ribs. Unwrapping the bandage from his left hand, he grimaced in horror at the mangled flesh that had once been his ring finger. A piece of bone protruded through the tip of angry, red tissue. Realizing the wound would need to be cleaned to prevent infection, Curtis gazed about the room, which was empty except for a toilet and a small sink near the bed. It was just within reach, and he was forced to use his injured left hand to turn the four-pronged faucet. The searing pain pushed him to the brink of blackness, but he managed to crank the spigot until it belched a small trickle of cold water. The last thing he wanted to do was thrust his hand under the stream, but he sucked in a deep breath, sharply exhaled, and pushed the bloody flesh under the tap. The ice-cold water briefly numbed his hand before a burning, throbbing sensation raced toward the ragged, fleshy edge of the amputation. Curtis bit his lip, suppressing the scream begging to be released.

Swaddling his hand in a dirty towel, he leaned back onto the bed and thrust his arm upward, hoping to calm the throbbing and leakage. The gray light filtering through the small window above the sink magnified Curtis' gloomy mood. Hours earlier, he had been anticipating a busy day at the herbal shop, but now he had been plunged into an insane situation, and for what reason? What did these men want?

He longed for Hilly. She always managed to lift his spirits and make things right. Although he wasn't a magician and didn't possess special abilities, he tried to mentally message her. Squeezing his eyes, he reached out, *Hilly, if you can hear me, I'm in a little room chained to a bed. I'm alive, but I don't know for how long. I don't know where I am. I saw a cabin and thick woods before they knocked me out. I hope you can hear me, babe. If I don't make it out of this, know that I've always loved you.*

The door burst open. "Surprise, Romeo," shouted the man who had punched him. He strode into the room flanked by two other men—the one who had worn the brown uniform at his house, and another who was very tall and pale-looking. "I forgot how stupid the Folk are really when they don't have their magician counterparts with them."

Curtis recoiled. "What do you want? Why did you do this to me?" he asked, thrusting his wounded hand toward them.

The apparent leader peered directly into Curtis' eyes. "Why? To capture your bitch witch bride. That's why." He snatched Curtis' wounded hand and squeezed hard. Curtis screamed in agony. Laughing, the man continued, "And, guess what? We picked up every little word you messaged to your sweetheart. I hope she hears you because that will make her come to us sooner than expected."

Curtis refused to cry. His anger simmered just under the surface, but his common sense told him retaliation would be the worst thing he could do right now. He gripped his sore hand and cowered by the headboard.

"You see, human, we can pry into your psyche anytime we want to. We can pick out any interesting memories to lure the sorceress to us. As a matter of fact, you've already helped us set the trap twice. We couldn't have done that without your intimate knowledge about your wife."

"What do you mean?" Curtis asked.

The men glanced at each other before they all pointed and laughed, mocking Curtis in his misery.

The leader placed his hand on Curtis' shoulder, causing him to cringe. "My dear boy. We've been leaving presents for the witch—personal gifts from you." He pointed at Curtis' hand. "In the first package, we sent her your wedding band in a blue Tiffany box, an image we pulled out of your deep memories from when you both went on a trip to New York City. In the second present, we sent your second offering, your ring finger in a purple box with purple accoutrements just like Hilly prefers. We can extract any of your memories and use them against you or anyone you know." Narrowing his eyes, the leader disdainfully looked at Curtis. "But, it's impossible for humans like you to understand our brilliance." He howled with laughter. His cohorts joined him in mocking Curtis, pointing at him as though he was a caged animal in the zoo.

Curtis' mind raced. These men obviously possessed magical abilities, yet they weren't anything like his wife. They were evil and meant to harm her even if that meant killing him. Chained to the bed, his best defense was to simply shut down. He entered a deep meditative trance, an easy transition since he used his pain to focus his thoughts. At least if the leader chose to punish him, Curtis wouldn't feel the blows.

Infuriated by Curtis' actions, Everild raised his fist in anger before lowering it and turning to the others. "I'm getting a message. We can deal with the human later."

The Brethren filed out of the room and went into the main living area. Everild stood in the middle of the room, raised his arms, and closed his eyes. Thane and Benedict observed his actions with curiosity and a little envy. Unlike Everild, they hadn't perfected the ability to transmit and receive long-distance messages. They admired their leader's ability to talk with their informant located on the other side of the continent.

When the message was complete, Everild lowered his arms. "Our present has been delivered. We will have our answer shortly." He looked toward the back room where Curtis sat meditating. "We may not need the human anymore. Pity. I enjoyed watching the terror in his eyes while I carved on him. I may still hack body parts off for the sheer thrill of it."

"What if the witch says no?" Thane asked.

Everild glared at him with brilliant, green eyes. "Then we need to make an important decision, my brothers. What should be our next gift to the sorceress? An ear? An eye? Or, perhaps we should present her with the most important part of all—his manhood."

The three men nodded in agreement, devilish smirks spreading across their faces.

Chapter 12

Darrius Arrives

HILLY FLUNG THE CUSHION at the front window. She growled obscenities and softly sobbed. Her tirade continued for several minutes until the voice of an angel interrupted her. Hilly stopped crying and tilted her head, straining to hear the soothing sound. The sugary sweet voice of Alicia drifted up from the receiver sprawled on the floor. "Hilly? Are you still there, dear?"

In the aftermath of talking with Ben, Hilly had thrown the phone to the ground. Now, Alicia's monotone sweetness seemed oddly comforting to her, and she snatched the receiver. "I'm here, Alicia. I was talking to Ben. Is he okay?"

"He's so upset, hon. We both are."

"I don't know what any of this means, but I'm going to get to the bottom of it." Tears welled in Hilly's eyes, and she tensed her body, hoping to push the sadness away. *This is a time of action, not emotions*, she convinced herself.

"Hilly, something obviously happened to Curtis. We should get the police involved," Alicia pressed.

Hilly clenched her fists. Poor, sweet, kind-hearted Alicia. She had no idea what mess she shuffled into. How do you explain to someone that evil aliens have abducted your husband, and now you must use your magical powers to find him. He may even be in the bowels of some dark dungeon in another dimension. *Do you think the police would understand all of that, Alicia?* Hilly took a deep breath. "Alicia, remember how I told you I came to Alaska to explore the Alaskan wilderness? Well, I need to let you in on a secret."

"Oooh, a secret, I won't tell anybody," Alicia cooed. At seventy-nine, she didn't have many people in her life.

"You must promise you won't tell anyone. You and Ben could get into a lot of trouble."

"Yes, yes, I promise, but please tell me you're not involved with the mob or their hitmen. Is that what happened to Curtis? Did the mob get him?"

Hilly wanted to scream at Alicia, *Shut up, you stupid bitch, and let me talk so I can save my husband!* But, she didn't. She took another deep breath and crossed her fingers (she still believed telling a fib while crossing her fingers wasn't lying.) "I'm with the government on a secret mission. That's ALL I can tell you, but adversaries have taken Curtis and now I need to find him. That's why you can't call the police. This situation is so far above the police department, it would make your head spin."

Alicia was silent, which was odd for the usually chatty woman. "You're like a secret agent. For whose side?"

"You know darn well who." Hilly thought it clever of her to not admit anything else. It was bad enough she had lied about being with the government.

"Oh, honey, you're right. How silly of me. Your secret is safe with me."

"What secret?" Ben bellowed, joining his wife.

"Ben, be quiet. I'm talking to Hilly about her secret..."

"ALICIA STOP TALKING TO BEN!" Hilly screamed.

"I'm sorry, dear. My lips are sealed." Alicia drew her fingers across her freshly lip-sticked mouth, closing an imaginary zipper.

"Why are you zippering your lips?" Ben hollered.

"Because of Hilly's secret! Oh no, I did it again. I'm sorry, Hilly. No more, that's it. Perhaps we should get off the phone. I'm feeling a little frazzled."

"Of course, Alicia. Remember, not a word to anyone, not even Ben. Or your lives could be in jeopardy. Can I count on you?"

"Absolutely, honey. I promise. Not another word. But, please call me if you find dear Curtis. You're such a precious couple, and you've been so kind to me and Ben.

"I'll let you know what happens. For right now mum's the word."

"I have one more question."

Hilly sighed. "Yes?"

"What do we do with Curtis' fing—, uh, the package?"

Hilly squeezed her eyes at the mental image and steeled herself to respond. "Alicia, please put it into our freezer. If I do find Curtis, and, if we can save his finger, maybe they can reattach it." Hilly knew chances were slim of finding Curtis, but she needed to keep that glimmer of hope alive. "Just put the entire package in the freezer for now."

"Okay, dear. I'll have Ben do that. Please take care and call me with any updates." Alicia abruptly hung up.

Hilly slammed the receiver down and hung her head, exhausted from the conversation with her neighbor. Alicia meant to be kind, but her memory sucked. Hopefully, the old, sweet couple will stay out of harm's way. Taking another cleansing breath, Hilly prepared for the second part of her plan, contacting Darrius.

Dealing with the Yfel Brethren would not be easy and she needed an ally who knew the group intimately and who could easily communicate with them. Hopefully, she could mentally contact him. The distance between Massachusetts and Alaska was farther than she'd ever attempted before. Perhaps, Mother Denali's power would assist her in magnifying the communication vibration.

Hilly walked outside, greeted by brilliant sunshine and a cloudless blue sky, reminding her of the recent vision quest. Her mood lifted as though the elements of nature welcomed her with compassion and warmth. The Alaskan summer baked the landscape in eighty-degree temperatures, an ideal environment for a relentless swarm of mosquitos, bigger than any she had ever seen. To ward off the hungry pests, she cast a spell, surrounding herself in a protective bubble. The persistent insects continued to jab at the invisible barrier producing a sound much like a gentle rainfall. Denali loomed in front of her and Hilly held out her hands toward The Great One to connect with the energetic ley lines leading to the mountain like a psychic runway. Hoping to tap into Denali's wisdom, Hilly closed her eyes and whispered, "Mother, I need your guidance."

THUMP. THUMP.

Denali's heartbeat raced across the valley toward Hilly, pulsing in her chest, creating a union between mother and child. The intensity of the psychic connection surprised Hilly, and she gasped as the mountain's spirit joined her soul. When they were joined, Hilly heard a distant chanti-ng—the song of her people—reminding her of her ancient roots. She lapsed into a deep trance, floating between the spiritual and physical realms.

"Child, you summoned me." Denali whispered.

"Mother, I seek strength and wisdom to deal with magicians much stronger than me. They have stolen my husband, a precious, innocent soul who has harmed no one. Mother, I need the strength to contact my ally, Darrius, across the continent."

"Child, you ask for that which you already possess. Look deep inside and find the answers you seek."

"Mother, these magicians have tremendous power—"

"My child, just by uttering those words, you empower your adversaries," Denali interrupted. "Does the salmon submit because the bear is more powerful? No, the fish leaps out of harm's way. Does the cedar surrender to the storm's fury and fall to the ground? No, its power lies in the knowledge that bending with the gales disarms the storm's strength. Yet, you cry to me that you don't have the ability. Insolent child!"

Contrite, Hilly whispered to The Great One, "I have a lot to learn. I doubt my abilities, but I will do as you ask."

Falling into a deeper trance, Hilly reached out to Darrius, requesting his presence, hoping he would join her soon. The connection was faint, but Hilly felt a familiar ripple from her old friend as he responded. He would come as soon as possible. Hilly turned back to Denali. "Mother, you are wise. I will never doubt my abilities again."

Denali shifted under her rocky mantle, sending a vibration rolling toward Hilly, washing over her like a sweet caress. "My child. The ancients walk with you at all times and sing secrets into your ear. The elemental beings watch over you and provide signs that shouldn't be ignored, and I, your earth mother, am always a part of your soul. Go now and complete your journey. I will wait for you at my summit."

Denali separated from Hilly and retreated into her granite home. Hilly nodded, understanding that even when she stands alone in the world, she is never truly by herself. Slowly, she emerged from her meditative trance. Tears trickled down her cheek, a testimony to the emotional energy forged by the special union.

"Hilly?" Slowly she opened her eyes and saw someone walking toward her.

Thinking Denali had assumed human form, Hilly held out her hands and whispered, "Mother?"

"Hilly, wake up." Hilly shook her head, clearing her mind, and squinted into the brilliant sunshine, into the dazzling green eyes of Darrius.

"Darrius?" Hilly lightly touched his face to confirm it was actually him. "Darrius, it's you!" Swinging her arms around his neck, she held him in a bear hug. He bent down and kissed her lightly on the cheek. "I've missed you so much. How did you get here?"

"You forget that I can teleport anywhere in the world. When you messaged me, I dropped what I was doing and transported right away."

"I have a huge problem. Curtis is in trouble, and I need your help."

Darrius folded his hands in front of his chest. "Yes, I know. Brother Aaron reached out to me."

"*Brother* Aaron? Aaron is a Cererian? I *knew* there was something odd about him. But how? What does he know?"

"Aaron contacted me when he received the package addressed to you," Darrius replied. It didn't take him long to mentally scan the contents of the box and trace the origin back to the Yfel Brethren. Humans leave evidence behind like fingerprints. Cererians impart psychic proof of their actions on anything they touch, which allowed Aaron to recognize the owners of the invisible markers on the box."

"How did they know I was in Alaska? And, how did they know where to ship the package?"

"Cererians have special powers that allow us to scan human minds. It's an easy technique that can be accomplished in a matter of seconds. The human has no idea the action is being performed. The Yfel Brethren probably used this method on Curtis. Since the location of your cabin is only known to Aaron, the Yfel sent the shipment directly to him." Darrius studied Hilly. Worry lines deepened around her eyes, and her cheeks were wet from recent tears. "You're exhausted. Let's go inside the cabin and talk about how we're going to bring Curtis home safe and unhurt."

Hilly threw her arms around Darrius and hugged him tightly. She buried her face into his chest and breathed deeply. A mixture of herbs and floral scents swirled about Darrius, and Hilly thought back to Prasad's healing potions, calming concoctions that had saved many lives. Darrius' presence comforted her, and she knew all would be okay, and Curtis would soon be home. "You've had such an impact on my energy already," Hilly said, clinging to Darrius, afraid to let him go.

"And, you've had a positive impact on me as well," Darrius responded. "Prasad would be proud to see how you've progressed. One thing I've learned from your family is that hope is the true magic. Hope has the ability to shift dimensions and re-order future events. This is not the Cererian way, but I have witnessed this phenomenon in your family. Hilly, I dare to hope that Curtis will be saved." The two friends hugged again before turning to enter the cabin. Suddenly, Darrius stopped and scanned the tundra surrounding the area.

"What is it?" Hilly asked, concerned that the Yfel Brethren had arrived.

Lying in the middle of ten acres with only one access road, the cabin was in a secure location. However, the thick forests provided several opportunities for unsavory types to hide. "I thought I heard someone walking through the grass," Darrius replied. "But I didn't detect any humans or Cererians."

"Aaron guaranteed my safety out here," Hilly said, opening the door. "Grab a seat on the futon and I'll bring you some water."

Darrius chuckled. "Just three months ago, alcohol was the chosen refreshment for you to get through the stressful times."

"Seems more like three years. So much has happened since then." They sat in silence reflecting on the memories of the battle and of the sacrifice. "Prasad has been on my mind lately," Hilly said as she showed Darrius a photo she had secretly snapped of Prasad and Fen. "I'm sure the two of them would still be together if he hadn't sacrificed his life for mine." Her eyes misted, but she didn't cry. She couldn't shed tears for a valiant soldier who had paid the ultimate price so she could live and continue the battle. But she would always remember and honor his accomplishments and sacrifices.

Darrius changed the subject. "The Yfel Brethren are led by a complicated fellow by the name of Everild. If Stygian could clone himself, Everild would be it. He's not nearly as powerful as Stygian, but he is a nasty adversary. He shares Stygian's thirst for brutality as you've already witnessed by the packages you received. His second-in-command is Thane. Prasad and I were disappointed when Thane decided to join Stygian's soldiers. He was a kind-hearted soul but was better equipped to follow and not lead. Stygian tempted him with promises of power. The third and final member—"

"Three? There are only three soldiers?"

"Yes, their group may be small, but don't underestimate their collective power. As I was saying, the third member is Benedict who, along with his father, Andee, arrived with our exploration group. Alas, Andee was surprised by a tiger, and was mortally mauled. Benedict was suddenly alone, and Stygian realized the potential in the young man. Or perhaps he recognized Benedict's vulnerability and loneliness and took him under his wing. At first, it appeared as though Stygian was kind and benevolent. But when Stygian insisted Benedict participate in the murders, Benedict refused and ran away. Stygian found him and ordered Everild to formally forge him into the Brethren with binding magic. He is more a slave than a soldier."

"How do we find them?" Hilly asked.

"They will reach out to you. My suggestion is that we travel to Aningan and talk to Aaron. Since the Yfel Brethren know how to reach him, he's our best point of contact."

"What do I say, Darrius? I won't release Stygian, and I can't have my husband killed."

Darrius gathered up Hilly's hands and gazed into her eyes. "When times get rough, I've always found that the Kemps do better when family comes together."

"What are you saying?"

"Chance is here in Aningan. We decided it would be prudent for him to maintain a low profile until we had a plan. He's thrilled to share some important news he found in the family records, which reveal there might be a crack in the armor of the Yfel Brethren. And, if so, this information would be vital in successfully retrieving Curtis."

"When do we leave? I can't wait to give my brother a big hug." Hilly's eyes danced with excitement, anticipating the family reunion.

"Now. I can teleport us there. First, we'll meet with Aaron and then eat dinner with Chance afterward."

Hilly grabbed her backpack. "That works for me. I'm ready to get this done, Darrius." Darrius wrapped an arm around Hilly, pulled her close, and rapidly mouthed a Cererian incantation. They vanished.

Outside the front window, Sammy hunkered down and peered in, catching the moment Darrius and Hilly jumped into another dimension. "Uncle Aaron will love my report on these two. Maybe he'll even reward me." Grabbing the black, Cererian quartz pendant swinging from his neck, Sammy pressed a black switch on the clasp and he, too, vanished.

Chapter 13

Aaron's Meeting

ANINGAN BUSTLED WITH ACTIVITY. Tour buses belching diesel fumes filled the dirt streets as lines of outdoor enthusiasts climbed aboard, eager to see the beautiful views and wildlife of the Mat-Su Valley. Amid the throng of visitors milling about in the street trudged Jake and Sammy. Like an icebreaker in the North Atlantic, they sliced through the sea of humanity, carving a pathway as they hurried to Uncle Aaron's office. Still the height of the mountain climbing season, most of the mob roaming the streets were climbers assembling with their guides to travel to the base camp located on Kahiltna Glacier. "Keep up, Sammy! You were late meeting me, and now you're making *me* late!" Jake yelled above the noise.

"Sorry, Jake. I had another meeting with Uncle—" Sammy clamped his mouth shut and peered at Jake who marched onward, unaware Sammy spoke.

Earlier that morning, Uncle Aaron summoned them for a very important meeting, emphasizing that everyone will be there and not to be late. Jake was tired of Aaron's demands and no longer hid his displeasure. He felt like a dog responding to his master's whistle, and he detested it. Yet, to disobey Uncle Aaron was not an option, unless one didn't mind the painful punishment that followed disobedience. Bottom line, Jake was losing a ton of money bending the knee to a man who gave him nothing but grief.

Today's paying customers, climbers bound for Denali, couldn't wait for Jake. Time was of the essence when planning climbs to the summit, and Denali waits for no one. Reluctantly, Jake had surrendered his clients to his competition, Plane to Mountain Tours, knowing full well, that the courtesy would never be repaid. *Uncle Aaron doesn't give a rat's ass about me losing money,* Jake thought as he pushed through the crowd.

Sammy trotted after Jake. "Jake. I can't keep up!" Sammy deflected off bodies like a steel marble bouncing inside a pinball machine, and soon fell behind.

"You know where we're going!" Jake yelled above the cacophony of guides shouting instructions and the hisses from motor coaches releasing their brakes to begin their journeys. Jake was pissed at the world right now, and Sammy's antics were pushing him to the breaking point. *Fucking Uncle Aaron snaps his fingers and we come running.*

The sea of humanity parted at the narrow alleyway leading to the non-descript offices, including Uncle Aaron's. No businesses on this quiet dirt lane attracted vacationers, so it wasn't unusual to find this section of town vacant. Jake leapt onto the wooden boardwalk, his boots thumping on the planks as he made his way to the red and green door of Aningan Properties. He scanned the street. Sammy was nowhere to be seen. "Where is that little shit?" Jake hocked a gob of phlegm onto the dirt street and wiped his mouth with the back of his hand. "Fuck him, maybe I'll get points for being early." Glancing at his watch, he decided to go in.

As his hand touched the doorknob he heard Sammy yell.

"Jake! Jake! Wait for me!" Sammy sprinted as much as his bowed legs would allow. Lurching with each stride, he reached the bottom of the steps, breathless, sweat cascading down his brown face. He grinned up at Jake who looked at him with contempt.

"Come on, Sammy. You know Uncle Aaron doesn't like it when we're late." Still breathless, Sammy began climbing the steps like a four-legged animal, using his hands as support. Jake reached down, grabbed Sammy's collar, and swung him up onto the boardwalk.

"Thanks, Jake!" Sammy coughed, recovering from the collar's pressure on his throat. He adjusted his shirt, which had twisted halfway up his body in the violence of being lifted.

"Don't mention it. Now let's go in," Jake directed, opening the door and shoving Sammy into the dimly lit room.

Teleporting great distances is a skill requiring accuracy and timing. The sensation of the trip is akin to standing in the middle of a tornado, observing the world swirl around you as you travel faster than the speed of light to your destination. The goal was to land at an exact point without disturbing any existing matter while avoiding materializing in a solid structure. The motion could make a person violently ill unless you've teleported for thousands of years like Darrius. The fluttering images overloaded Hilly's senses, and she closed her eyes to the chaos. It felt as though she and Darrius passed through multiple dimensions for hours, but in reality, their trip took less than three seconds. The couple materialized just outside of Aningan Properties, barely missing Sammy and Jake.

Hilly held her stomach and asked, "How did you avoid missing those two?"

Darrius chuckled. "Keeping your senses about you when you teleport allows you to see and feel where everything is, including the people. It takes a lot of practice, but it is an efficient tool of travel."

"I wouldn't have minded landing right on their heads," Hilly growled.

Darrius folded his hands in front of him and asked, "Do you know those two gentlemen?"

Recalling the web spell and the resulting mess, Hilly responded, "Gentlemen? I wouldn't use that word. We've met on several occasions. My gut tells me not to trust either one of them. But I'm trying to keep an open mind." Hilly flashed an exaggerated smile at Darrius, a known advocate for not judging others too quickly.

A loud squawk from above snatched her attention and she glanced up to the eaves. A raven pecked at the shingles and stared at Hilly. She recognized that bird. It was Denali's messenger, the gift to Hilly from The Great Mother. The large corvid appeared agitated and repeatedly stabbed the roof with its beak. The raven had greeted her in a similar manner when she first arrived in Aningan. She considered Denali's caution that the raven may identify imposters and anyone who meant to do her harm.

Darrius looked upward. "A friend of yours?"

"You might say the raven was a gift from a family friend," Hilly replied, smiling at the black bird. As quickly as it arrived, the bird departed and flew west toward the mountain.

"We should go in. Aaron awaits us," Darrius said as he opened the door for Hilly.

A sense of foreboding swirled through the dingy room, making the hairs on the back of Hilly's neck stand at attention. "I had an odd experience here on my last visit, and now my intuition is screaming at me." She rubbed the gooseflesh on her arms while mentally scanning the room for any unsavory sorts who might be lurking nearby.

Aaron appeared in the hallway. "Darrius, my old friend!"

"Aaron! Has it really been over a hundred years since we last talked?" Darrius embraced Aaron, kissing him on both cheeks before standing back and studying him. "Let me look at you, brother. You've changed, you old explorer. The jewelry and silk suit are excellent touches."

"I see you still wear your Italian suits and flamboyant ties," Aaron poked as he fiddled with the knot of Darrius' electric blue tie spilling down the front of his white linen shirt. "Is it possible that you've become more handsome?"

"You're too kind, Aaron. If I was younger, I might fall prey to your compliments. But now I wonder if you're buttering me up because you desire something from me."

Aaron slapped Darrius on the back. "Come on, let me introduce you to the team who will help us with our little problem." Aaron shot a piercing glance of contempt at Hilly as if to imply she was the problem.

Before Hilly could respond to his insult, the two friends were walking down the hallway toward the back office.

Hilly remained alone. Something was up with that old man. His weird behavior was unwarranted and bothered her, especially since Denali had warned her about those who are not as they appear to be. As a precaution, Hilly deployed a protection spell around herself to prevent a recurrence of her last visit when she awoke in Sammy's car missing a chunk of time. Satisfied with her magic, she walked toward the back office to join the others.

Hilly stood in the doorway observing the occupants: Jake, Sammy, Darrius and Aaron. "Please join us Ms. Kemp," Aaron said as he walked toward her, extending his hand. He grinned wide showing his brilliant white, perfectly aligned teeth. Hilly shuddered, thinking he would be an ideal actor for a commercial selling toothpaste to vampires. Allowing him to take her arm, she accepted a chair opposite Sammy and Jake. Aaron continued, "Darrius, allow me to introduce you to my friends, Jake and Sammy."

Darrius first shook Jake's hand and then took Sammy's. "It's a pleasure to meet friends of Aaron's."

"Friends?" Jake whispered out the side of his mouth. The words were barely audible but did not escape Aaron's profound sense of hearing. Aaron glared at him, and Jake winced as though he'd been slapped.

"Nice to meet you too," Sammy chirped. "I hope you'll find Aningan to your liking. If you need help getting around, I have a service car, and—"

"Sammy, enough," Aaron said, holding up a hand.

Poor Sammy. He only wanted to be helpful, but his motor mouth always got him into trouble.

"Jake and Sammy are instrumental in making sure things operate smoothly here in Aningan. Recently they've helped Ms. Kemp to get settled into her cabin and assisted with her vision quest."

"Is that what you call it?" she said, looking directly at Jake.

"Insolence!" Aaron stood, without warning, and pounded both fists on the desk. His outburst caught everyone by surprise, including Darrius who instinctively raised a hand in a defensive posture. "I will not tolerate this insubordination for another minute. Do you all understand?" Jake and Sammy sat rigid, eyes forward, lips sealed.

"Insubordination?" Hilly stood, fists clenched, and walked closer to Aaron. "I am not your soldier nor your slave. How dare you bark orders at me!"

Darrius quietly joined Hilly. "Hilly, will you please do me a favor and return to your seat? I believe Aaron spoke out of turn and didn't mean what he said. Isn't that right, Aaron?" Hilly and Aaron stared at each other until slowly—very slowly—Aaron sat down and turned his gaze to Darrius.

"My apologies to everyone in the room and especially to you, Darrius. I meant no disrespect. And I certainly didn't mean to imply that you, Ms. Kemp, were insubordinate." Flashing a sneer at both Jake and Sammy, Aaron exhaled loudly before clasping his hands in front of his chest.

Darrius guided Hilly back to her chair. He straightened his tie and remained standing. "Aaron, if you'll allow me, I'd like to say a few words first." Aaron nodded approval to his friend and Darrius continued, "I appreciate that all of you agreed to meet today. We have a serious matter to address. Hilly's husband, Curtis, has been kidnapped by the Yfel Brethren and is being tortured in the hopes that Hilly will release Stygian from his prison. Two packages have already been received—one containing his wedding band and the other containing his amputated ring finger. Although they chose an evil path, the Brethren are brothers to Aaron and I. Hence the reason they reached out to Aaron to deliver their message to Hilly. We are assembled today to discuss a course of action to safely return Curtis before the Yfel mangle him further, or worse, kill him."

Hilly stared at the floor recalling the horrific images described by Ben and Alicia after they discovered the contents of the package left in her North Carolina home. She wanted Curtis home more than anything in the world, but she couldn't fathom releasing Stygian from his interdimensional cell. Freeing him was akin to unleashing a plague upon the world. She would be responsible for the murder of thousands of magicians. She couldn't bear to have those deaths on her hands, and she couldn't allow Curtis to die slowly and painfully. There was no clear path to a solution.

"The answer seems simple to me," Aaron began as he rose to address everyone. "Ms. Kemp, you need to release Stygian from his prison and then the Yfel will return your husband."

Hilly bolted out of her chair. "Are you nuts?!"

Jake's eyes widened at Hilly's fury. Sammy flinched, attempting to appear even smaller in his seat.

Aaron gritted his teeth and gripped the edge of the desk, attempting to rein in his fury. The desktop splintered as his fingernails dug into the soft wood. "Darrius, I suggest you calm Ms. Kemp. Cool heads are needed right now."

Before Darrius could respond, Hilly demanded, "Why don't you talk to me, Aaron? It's *my* husband who is being tortured, and it will be *me* who ultimately determines what will be done. Don't dismiss me like I don't exist." Aaron narrowed his eyes at Hilly, and they shimmered and danced. Hilly felt the room lurch and she averted her eyes, realizing Aaron was trancing her.

"Aaron, stop!" Darrius demanded as he stood between his two friends, hands outstretched toward each one. "This is no way to behave. Both of you." A long awkward pause followed before Hilly and Aaron finally sat down, continuing to glare at each other. Darrius studied them, concerned about their heated exchange. Aaron, his long-lost brother, exhibited negative emotions he would expect from the Yfel Brethren. Hilly's swift anger shocked him. Stygian's blood coursed through her veins, and now he wondered if Hilly was changing, becoming more unpredictable like her evil relative.

"If we continue to bicker among ourselves, Curtis will definitely die," Darrius said, addressing the room. "From this point forward, all comments will be civil and focused on the matter at hand. Are we all in agreement?" Heads nodded around the room except for Aaron who continued glaring at Hilly. Darrius positioned himself in Aaron's line of sight and asked, "Are we in agreement, Aaron?"

Aaron mentally messaged Darrius, *This impudent witch is trying my patience, Darrius. She knows what she must do. We are all wasting our time talking about anything else but the inevitable.*

Darrius sighed. Aaron was right. There was only one clear way to prevent Curtis from being hacked to death, but he could sense Hilly's struggle with the alternative—unleashing evil upon the magicians of the world. *I know what you say is true, Aaron. But, perhaps there's an alternative plan.* Aaron nodded his approval. The two men carried on their conversation telepathically, oblivious to the others in the room.

Jake observed them, knowing full well that Aaron and Darrius were discussing the situation and purposely omitting the rest of them as if they were children who couldn't understand the important decisions adults must make. Because the conversation was cloaked, neither Hilly nor Jake could eavesdrop, which frustrated them even more.

Jake mentally messaged Hilly, *Hilly, I'm your friend and would never hurt you, but—*

What do you want, Jake? Hilly replied.

A truce. We made a mistake at the cabin, but we were only following orders.

Orders? Who would order you to snoop in my personal belongings?

"Jake?" Uncle Aaron growled.

"Yes, Uncle Aaron," Jake replied nervously, concerned he overheard him mentally talking with Hilly.

"Darrius and I have reached an agreement. Your services will be needed."

"What?" Hilly asked, standing and facing Darrius. "This was supposed to be a meeting between all of us, not just you and Aaron."

Darrius pulled her hands into his. "Hilly, listen to me. We have a plan. It's dangerous, but if you're able to pull it off, Curtis will be saved, and Stygian will remain in his prison. Are you interested, warrior?"

"Go on," Hilly relaxed. "I'm listening."

Addressing the room, Darrius continued, "Aaron and I have conceived of a clever plan. Aaron will contact the Yfel Brethren and arrange a meeting. We will agree to their demands to release Stygian in exchange for Curtis." Hilly shifted nervously in her seat but resisted challenging Darrius on his plan. "We'll allow the Brethren to choose the meeting location, day, and time. Of course, they'll insist that Hilly come alone, but Jake will be nearby, cloaked so their psychic senses will not detect him.

"Jake, your cloaking power is not strong enough to avoid detection, so Aaron will use his Cererian magic to ensure you're properly hidden from the Brethren. That way you can enter the meeting circle and assist Hilly.

The next step is critical—so important, that if your timing is off by even one second, the plan will fail." Jake and Hilly leaned closer. "Hilly, as you open the dimension in which Stygian is contained, the Brethren will be distracted, anticipating the return of their leader. Those few seconds allow Jake to snatch Curtis and leap into a portal that you will open for their escape. The timing is critical. First the dimension, followed immediately by the portal. The moment Jake is in the portal, you close both openings."

"What about the Yfel? They won't be too pleased," Hilly stated.

"That is the risky part. You'll be left alone with the three soldiers. One against three is bad odds, but I've seen you battle and capture a Cererian."

"Yes, but I had help from three other people. Darrius, this plan is ludicrous. If I'm off by one second, all of us may be killed."

Darrius faced her again. "I have faith in you, Hilly. You're powerful. And, Aaron believes you can do it, isn't that right?" Darrius directed his question to Aaron who sat with a bemused look on his face.

"That's right, Ms. Kemp," he said impassively. "I believe you can take on the Yfel. They're not nearly as powerful as Stygian." His robotic reply was as if he had read the words from a script.

Jake pressed, "Is there a way for me to return through the portal? You know, leave Curtis, and return to fight with Hilly?"

"No. Besides, when was the last time you were actually in a battle?" Aaron replied condescendingly.

Jake sank back into his chair and fumed. Aaron was doing what Aaron does best—seizing control of the entire situation. He may have Darrius duped with this charade, but Jake was going to make sure Hilly knew the dirty truth about Aaron Aningan. After the meeting, he would share all of his secrets.

"Then it's agreed?" Darrius surveyed the room. Everyone was quiet. "Aaron, please contact the Yfel Brethren and let them know we are ready to meet their demands." Aaron smiled broadly like a cat eyeing a mouse.

"Excellent. I'll do that after our meeting. Thank you, dear friend, for bringing sensibility to our discussion." Jake shook his head in disgust. It was just like Aaron to throw more crap on the shit pile and make it stink. Jake met Hilly's gaze and messaged, *We need to talk.*

Hilly looked at Jake but he was already up and leaving the room. She watched him pass by and she messaged him, *Sure, I'll contact you later.* His head still down, eyes on the floor, Jake smiled at her reply.

Sammy jumped up to follow Jake, but Aaron barked at him, "Sammy, stay. I have something for you to do."

Hilly and Darrius stood to go but Aaron called out, "My dear Darrius, can you stay a while? I would love to catch up like old times."

"What a wonderful invitation, but alas, I've already got an engagement. Hilly and I had planned to spend the evening together. But I would love to come by your office early in the morning, if that works for you."

Aaron studied Hilly and Darrius. For thousands of years, he had bettered his life by maintaining the upper hand, and not trusting people. His intuition shouted at him and even though they were brothers, he realized he could not trust Darrius anymore. Yet he continued with the endless dance of pleasantries by replying, "Ah, yes, I'm sure you two have a lot to talk about. Don't let me keep you from your date." He forced a smile. "I'll keep you informed if I hear anything from the Brethren."

"Wonderful!" Darrius replied as he linked his arm with Hilly's. "I'll come by the office tomorrow around eight and you can regale me with your tales about your beautiful city and state."

Darrius and Hilly exited the room. Aaron watched them leave, listening for the closure of the front door. Then he turned to Sammy. "Sammy, keep an eye on those two. I want you to tell me everything and anything they do. Is that clear?"

"Yes, Uncle Aaron. Anything you say." Sammy trotted off and cracked the door, watching Darrius and Hilly who were just walking onto the main road, joining the crowd of vacationers. Silently closing the door, Sammy followed them, keeping the couple in sight as he ambled close behind.

Aaron sat at his desk, peering into the darkness. His eyes twinkled and the corners of his mouth twitched into a smile as he pondered the results of the meeting. His plan was developing nicely, and he appreciated Darrius' unwitting assistance in duping the sorceress to agree to the terms. The Yfel Brethren will reward him handsomely for returning Stygian, and they'll be especially thankful to have two powerful magicians delivered right into their arms.

Pity, I have to sacrifice Jake. He's been incredibly helpful in convincing the others to follow my orders. But he's been acting out. I sense he may attempt to overthrow me. I'm sure another young magician is willing to replace him.

Chapter 14

Nothing is as it Appears

DARRIUS USHERED HILLY ALONG the dirt street, determined to reach the Aningan Hotel without detection. "Keep walking swiftly just in case we're being followed," he advised as he gently guided her through the throng of people.

Darrius' friend had changed and was no longer the man he loved and respected. Aaron's behavior had been eratic. Proper Cererians don't express negative emotions, as it's considered wasteful of energy. What could have happened in the last one hundred years that would have impacted Aaron's actions toward others? Not that people don't change over the years, but the viciousness of his words reminded Darrius of the Yfel soldiers' demeanors—ruthless and inconsiderate.

"Where is Chance staying?" Hilly asked.

"The Aningan Hotel. The front entrance is just off the next street. But we'll enter via the side entrance. I have a sense that we're being followed."

Hilly tensed. "What? Somebody's following us? I haven't felt anything out of the ordinary."

"Ssh," Darrius whispered. "Follow me." They turned left at the next alley, and entered a dark, dusty avenue that smelled of fresh vomit and urine. Hilly held her nose against the offensive odor while Darrius wrapped his arm protectively around her. They turned right at the next lane, a busier street that led to a set of stairs sweeping up into the hotel. Darrius gazed up and down the lane searching for the shadow he detected earlier when they left Aningan Properties. But he saw nobody. He sensed no tricksters. Entering the side door, they followed the corridor past the kitchen and laundry before exiting through an unmarked door into the main hotel lobby.

Darrius surveyed the busy lobby, taking particular notice of a gentleman hunched in an overstuffed chair, a newspaper spread wide, hiding his face. Darrius slowly walked toward the man, stood in front of him and pulled the paper downward. “Mr. Kemp, I presume.”

A wide smile spread across his face as Chance Kemp stood up and grabbed Darrius in a bear hug. “Easy, Chance. Remember your super strength.”

“I’ve missed you, Darrius,” Chance laughed, squeezing Darrius even tighter and spinning him around as visitors gawked at the two men embracing.

“Put me down, Chance. I can hardly breathe!”

Glancing over Darrius’ shoulder, Chance spied Hilly, tears welling in her eyes. “Well, there’s my little sister. Come here, baby girl.” Hilly ran into Chance’s arms as he gripped her tight and lifted her from the ground. She squealed as he swung her side to side. “Everything’s gonna be alright. I’m here, now.” When Darrius had notified Chance of Curtis’ kidnapping, he didn’t hesitate to fly out to Alaska. After all, that’s what family does. But he also had important information about the Yfel Brethren, a critical detail he found in the family records—a massive tome containing the history of the Earth tribes and families. It was sensitive information that should be shared only in person.

“Upstairs, you two,” Darrius interrupted their brief reunion. “We’ll continue our conversation in Chance’s room.”

“Follow me,” Chance said as he led them by the elevators and down the hallway to the stairs. “This is a more secure way to get to the room. No security cameras.”

"Just like your father," Darrius observed. "He never liked technology."

"Yep, go figure. Despite my bellyaching about Dad, I end up more like him every day." Chance paused. "I miss him."

Hilly patted his back. "We all do, Chance. Maybe one day, we'll all be together again." She smiled broadly at her brother, a mischievous twinkle in her eye. "Last one up the stairs, pays for dinner!" She suddenly sprinted up the steps, gripping the railing to pull herself upward.

Chance laughed. "This is gonna be an easy race," he called out and chased after Hilly, taking three steps at a time, his strong thigh muscles bulging under his chinos. "Having superhuman strength has its advantages!" he yelled.

Darrius watched the two siblings, remembering their nasty bickering and loving reconciliation just before they battled Stygian on the beach. *It was a wise move to bring Chance to Alaska. Exactly what Hilly needed.* Darrius stood at the base of the stairs, listening to the giggles and curses as Chance pursued Hilly. Closing his eyes, Darrius mouthed a Cererian incantation and disappeared.

Chance could easily overtake Hilly, but he loved toying with her. "I'm gonna catch you, Hilly. And, when I do, I'll make you pay!" Hilly squealed as she ran up the stairs. She glanced back. Chance marched up the stairs, three steps at a time, easily closing the distance between them. "Here I come," he growled

Breathless from running, she refused to give up, her inner competitor wouldn't allow her to lose to her big brother. Panting, she neared the fourth-floor landing just as Chance clamped his hand on her shoulder and yanked her back. "Oh, no you don't!"

"Nooo!" she cried out. Chance passed her and jumped on the landing, pumping his fists in the air like a victorious boxer. Hilly soon joined him. "Okay, big brother. You won. But I'm not last. There's still Darrius."

"If you want to be technical, I was here first," Darrius said, his voice floating from behind them, making them both jump. "Cererian teleporting powers have their advantages," he said, winking at both of them. "Now let's get to Chance's room and talk."

The apartment was strategically located on the end of the building allowing for unobstructed views of the main street and side alleyway. Promoted as the "Corporate Suite", there were two spacious bedrooms, a living room, and a palatial bathroom featuring a spa tub, massage table and big screen television mounted on the wall. "Wow," Hilly exclaimed as she examined the scented lotions in the bathroom. "How is Janet? How are the kids?"

Chance held up his hand. "Take a breath. We have time to talk. I know it's only been a few months, but I miss you and the others. Forbidden to communicate because of the Yfel Brethren grinds my gears." He scooped her up in a warm hug.

"Okay, but we do need to talk about the furry elephant in the room...what's with the beard?"

Chance ran his fingers through the long, graying hairs on his face. "Oh this scruffy thing? Can you believe this is three months' growth? I decided I would go incognito for a while. Janet doesn't seem to mind the beard...much." They both laughed.

Darrius had been staring out the front window. His head swiveled back and forth as if he was searching for someone. "What's going on, Darrius" Hilly asked as she joined him.

"Our elusive shadow followed us here," he answered. He pointed to the crowds below. "Just as I psychically locked on him, he scurried away like a cockroach. He vanished into thin air."

"You've been followed?" Chance pulled the curtains aside and boldly stared at the window. The vantage point offered a clear view of everyone and everything for a city block.

A deafening roar floated up from the building across from the hotel. Flanagan's Irish Pub, one of the more popular bars, hosted a hoard of climbers celebrating their successful ascent by singing karaoke...drunk karaoke. A lone figure caught Darrius' eye. Leaning against the side of the pub, arms folded, the person stared back. The mystery man wore jeans and boots. An ancient leather aviator cap straddled his head and mirrored sunglasses covered his eyes. The figure, a smirk on his lips, brazenly locked eyes with Darrius who asked, "Anybody know that fellow?"

Chance and Hilly followed the direction Darrius pointed. Hilly sighed.

"I know who that is. Not too many people wear that kind of get-up in Aningan."

Before she could say anything else, she received a mental message, *Hi there, beautiful.*

"Who the fuck is it? Is he here to fight?" Chance asked, already balling his hands into fists.

"Simmer down, big brother. His name is—"

"Jake Pierson," Darrius said, finishing Hilly's statement. "I can sense him easily now. He's a magician just like you and Chance. He's not the one that worries me though. The shadow I sensed on the main street is lurking in the alleyway now. I can't determine who or what it is. I only know that it follows us everywhere. I suspect Jake is watching it too," Darrius said, pointing to the street below where Jake had left the pub and was pushing his way through the mob of people keeping his mirrored eyes trained on something in the distance.

Chance grabbed his broadsword from the closet. Darrius put a hand on his shoulder.

"I don't think you'll need that, Chance. But I could use your super strength power. Hilly, remain up here while Chance and I go downstairs."

"Nope, not an option. If there's a fight, I'm going to help," Hilly proclaimed.

Darrius faced her and gently spoke, "Listen Hilly, we know the Brethren are interested in you and if this is a trap, I need to be sure you're as far away as possible. Promise me you'll stay here."

Reluctantly, Hilly looked into Darrius's emerald eyes. "Don't try to trance me Darrius," she began, "I'll do what you ask, but if you're gone longer than fifteen minutes, then I'm coming down after you. Deal?"

Darrius grinned. "Deal. Besides, we can take the stairs much faster than you." Hilly feigned shock before punching Darrius in the arm.

"Go on...get outta here, before I change my mind."

"Let's go, Chance. Let's keep a low profile and see what this shadow is up to."

"I'm ready," Chance replied.

A sudden banging on the door startled everyone, causing them to jump back with their hands up ready to defend themselves. Darrius closed his eyes, and then remarked, "I sense Jake alone is on the other side of the door."

Looking out the peephole, Hilly saw Jake's face with the mirrored sunglasses staring back at her. She swung the door open to greet him and was surprised to see Jake and Sammy standing in the hallway. Sammy struggled under Jake's tight grip around his collar.

Pushing Sammy into the room, Jake explained, "This fat beetle has been following you since Uncle Aaron's office."

Darrius grabbed Sammy by the arms and stared into his eyes. Sammy stared back, smiling his toothless grin. "I can't penetrate his mind. It's as though he's made of nothing." Darrius pushed him back and studied Sammy who continued to smile at him in a goofy, contented way. "I don't believe it. I knew Aaron was attempting to create such a being for over a thousand years, but he finally succeeded." Turning Sammy to face the others, Darrius continued, "Sammy is a nawiht."

"You mean a half-wit," Jake growled.

Darrius gazed at Jake like a patient parent with an unruly child. "A nawiht is nothingness, not having substance or value. I don't know how Aaron constructed the body, but for all intents and purposes, Sammy doesn't exist. He is not here—he is nothing. My psychic powers detect only traces of natural energy in front of me."

Everyone circled Sammy, studying him head to toe as the happy fellow gazed back at them. Jake spoke first. "Sammy, did Uncle Aaron send you to spy on us?"

Sammy was so happy to finally speak. "Well, not you, Jake. He asked me to follow Darrius and Hilly and report back on what I found."

Darrius interjected, "Were you at Hilly's cabin this afternoon?"

"Sure, I saw you all disappear into thin air. Uncle Aaron was keen to know what you two were up to." Darrius reached into Sammy's shirt and pulled out a black, Cererian crystal. "Look at this. Aaron set him up with a teleporting device. If you press this switch, Sammy will zoom back to Aaron. Like a yo-yo, Aaron has been sending Sammy out into the world to spy on people, and then bringing him right back."

Jake shook Sammy violently. "You little snitch. What have you been telling him about me?"

Darrius intervened and shepherded Sammy to his side. "You're wasting your time on this little fellow. Haven't you ever wondered why he always smiles and never gets upset? It's because he can't feel emotions. He has no idea that he's betrayed your trust or that he's spying on you. He only knows that he's been given a command by his master, and he must fulfill it. If he doesn't complete his task, not only will Aaron know something has happened, but I believe Sammy may disintegrate."

"Literally burst into pieces?" Chance asked, fascinated by the little brown man smiling at him.

"That's my understanding based on the early prototypes Aaron had created. Sammy's been programmed like a computer. But with a nawiht, the coding goes further. If they don't complete their mission within the specified time, they'll burst apart—nothingness into nothingness." Darrius turned to Sammy. "Sammy, when does Uncle Aaron want you back in the office?"

Sammy studied the watch on his wrist. Not an actual timepiece, but a device that was similar in shape and possessed a second hand circling lit numbers in the middle of the dial. Currently, the digits 20:05 appeared and counted down. "Looks like I have a little over twenty minutes."

Darrius cautioned the others. "We have to get Sammy back to Aaron immediately before he explodes. I have no idea if it would be a violent concussion or if he gently disappears like a ripple in a pool."

Jake was visibly upset. "We can't let that happen. He's seen all of us together, so that's exactly what he'll tell Uncle Aaron. There's more to Uncle Aaron than you realize. If Sammy reports that he's seen us all together, I'm a dead man."

"Why would Aaron want to kill you just because you were seen with us?" Darrius asked.

Jake exhaled loudly. He grabbed Sammy by the collar and dragged him in front of the closet and opened the door. Grabbing Sammy's stubby hands, Jake plunged a finger directly into each of Sammy's ears. Then he removed the Cererian crystal from around Sammy's neck and tossed the medallion to Darrius who pocketed it. Satisfied he'd covered all loopholes, Jake shoved Sammy against the far closet wall and slammed the door. Jake faced the others who looked at him with astonished faces. "Why did you throw Sammy in the closet, and why stick his fingers in his ears?" Hilly asked.

"I didn't want him to overhear what I'm going to tell you about Uncle Aaron." Jake opened the minibar and withdrew two nips. "I need my two friends, John and Jack, with me right now." He opened the Johnny Walker Red Label bottle and tossed it back. Then he unscrewed the Jack Daniels nip, but Chance snatched it from his hands.

"This friend likes to hang out with me," Chance said, drinking the whiskey in one gulp. "Hi, I'm Chance Kemp. I'm Hilly's big brother. What can be so bad that you need a sip of courage first?"

"I'm Jake Pierson. I flew your sister to our fine town, Aningan. I would have been flying climbers up to Denali today if Aaron hadn't ordered me to his office for his meeting." Scowling, he grumbled, "You have no idea how much money I'm losing today." Jake stopped talking and stared at the floor. He took several deep breaths before continuing. "Haven't you ever wondered why we call Aaron, *Uncle* Aaron?"

"I thought you told me he was Sammy's great uncle," Hilly responded.

"Yeah, that's just the story we continue to weave around these parts. But, in reality..." Jake paused and took another long breath, carefully choosing his next words. "Uncle Aaron is not related to anybody. Darrius, didn't you wonder why everyone called him uncle?"

"Honestly, I took it as a term of endearment." Hands clasped in front of his chest Darrius listened intently to Jake's words.

"Term of endearment?!" Jake shouted. "It's no damn endearment, it's an order. Aaron demanded we always call him "Uncle Aaron" to demonstrate our reverence for him as head of the family."

"Ordered you? What purpose would Aaron have to order you?" Darrius' eyes darkened and his brow furrowed as he stepped closer to Jake. Jake took two steps backward, his hands raised to defend himself. Darrius realized Jake's fear. "I mean you no harm at all. I'm only curious why Aaron would demand you use that title. Cererians only function as observers in your world. Our duty is to watch and report, not demand anything from humans, nor interfere in your private affairs."

Jake walked closer to Darrius and lowered his voice, "When was the last time you saw your friend, Aaron?"

"Over a hundred years ago, but I don't see what that has to do with anything."

"A hundred years ago, Aaron may have still been your friend and followed your Cererian rules, but before I was born, about forty-five years ago, he made an arrangement with the elders. But years before that treaty was signed, the members of our tribe were slaughtered by Stygian and his soldiers. Despite cloaking our whereabouts, the Yfel Brethren located families with uncanny accuracy. It was as though they had received the information from a source." Darrius exchanged worried glances with Hilly and Chance, refusing to believe Jake's implication that Aaron was involved with the Yfel Brethren. "Our elders spoke of a pact made with the star visitor, the one we now know as Uncle Aaron. In exchange for safety, the tribal members would pay tribute to Aaron and do his bidding. Since then, there have been no more killings, but we are basically slaves to Aaron's whims." Jake looked at Hilly. "At the time the treaty was signed, all of our firewalkers had been destroyed. Yet the elders spoke of one that flew into the night sky. I believe that lost soul is you, Hilly. Once I found out you were a firewalker *and* that you were born in Anchorage, I reckoned it couldn't be a coincidence."

Darrius studied Jake's face and then scanned his thoughts. He had no reason to doubt the young man's story. But Aaron was his friend. His friend had changed, but to what extent? After witnessing Aaron's unexpected outrage in the office, Darrius was torn. Darrius would not be quick to judge at least not yet. "What proof do you have besides your personal interactions with Aaron?" Darrius asked.

"I can arrange a secret meeting with the elders, and they will describe what our people have endured for decades and even for centuries. There you can scan their minds and determine the truth." Jake shifted his weight and scuffed the floor. "There is one thing you should know," he said, looking at Darrius with intense seriousness. "In the song of the firewalkers, the words speak of a star visitor leading other star visitors to the 'final family'. When I first heard the song as a boy, it was only a legend, something from long ago. But, now, I think Aaron directed Stygian to Hilly's family, the final family of firewalkers. But why?"

Before Darrius responded, Hilly blurted, "Because I share his DNA. Killing my family, especially me, would rid the world of this dark secret, and Stygian would be rid of a descendent that might grow more powerful than he."

"What?" Jake looked at Hilly as though she was a hideous monster. "You're related to Stygian?"

Chance moved in front of Hilly. "Look buster, Hilly is first and foremost my sister, and she has *nothing* to prove to you. She's the strongest warrior I know, regardless of her relation to Stygian."

Hilly placed a gentle hand on Chance's shoulder. "You don't need to defend me, Chance. But I do appreciate your brotherly love." She smiled warmly at her brother before scowling at Jake. "What happened to your tribe and your family members have nothing to do with me even though Stygian killed them. My link to him is our advantage to erase his evil in the world."

Darrius quietly observed the interaction between the three. Chance and Hilly were a power to be reckoned with, and the speed at which Chance defended her honor was admirable. But Jake was visibly alarmed by the news and appeared withdrawn, suspicious of his companions. Darrius spoke, "Jake, I understand your hesitancy. This type of news is quite unnerving. But I assure you that Hilly is nothing like Stygian. She may exhibit many of his powers, which is to our advantage, but she did not inherit his temperament."

"I should have known something was different about you when you encountered that dragon on your vision quest," Jake said. "That's never happened to anyone before."

"Are you implying the beast was Stygian?" Hilly challenged. "The dragon could have been many other things."

"Previous visions of the black beast always pointed to Stygian," Darrius added.

"Stygian is locked up," Hilly argued. "If that dragon in my vision quest was a warning from the Yfel, then I can easily take care of it."

"With my help," Jake butted in.

Hilly shot him a nasty look and continued, "And, the beast could represent me. It flew in from the east, which I did, and it is the symbol of firewalkers."

"Have you had a recurrence of the vision?" Darrius asked, concerned for Hilly's life.

"Nope, that's why I believe it represents my birth family. I came to Alaska to discover and to learn about their history and traditions."

Darrius interjected suddenly, "We don't have much time remaining. Sammy needs to return to Aaron. However, we don't want him divulging any information about our meeting." Darrius opened the closet door. Sammy stood against the back wall, his fingers in his ears, smiling his toothless grin. "Come on, Sammy, let's chat." Darrius guided him into the middle of the room. "You can take your fingers out of your ears, Sammy."

"Gee, thanks! I was wondering why Jake shoved my fingers in my ears. I couldn't hear anything, not a single th—"

"Sammy, stop!" Jake and Hilly said in unison.

Darrius bent down and gazed directly into Sammy's eyes. "Sammy, I'm going to ask you some questions but I want you to keep your answers brief. Do you understand?"

"Sure, sure!"

"Can you tell a lie?"

"Nope." Sammy shook his head for emphasis.

"What directions did Aaron give you?"

"He ordered me to follow you and Miss Hilly."

"So, he didn't ask you to gather information on Jake or Chance?"

"Nope."

"When Aaron asks you about what we did, what will you say?"

"Easy. I would tell him that you and Hilly met Chance and Jake at the hotel."

Jake groaned and shook his head.

"I expected that answer but wanted to be sure. So, Sammy, can your orders be changed?"

"Yep! I like this game, Mr. Darrius."

"How can your orders be changed?"

"Uncle Aaron can change them."

"Only Uncle Aaron?"

"Yep!"

"Come on, just let him explode somewhere. This is getting us nowhere fast," Jake barked.

Darrius ignored Jake and continued drilling Sammy. "So, if Uncle Aaron gave you new orders, you would follow them, is that correct?"

"Yes, sir!"

Darrius immediately mentally messaged everyone in the room except for Sammy. *I have a plan. Jake and Chance will leave, I suggest going to the bar across the street and waiting for my signal. I'll shape-shift into Uncle Aaron and provide Sammy with a new directive. After that, Hilly and I will sit at the table and discuss innocuous things that we've encountered in Aningan. Basically, we'll fill Sammy with useless information. Does everyone understand?* Everyone nodded in agreement, and Chance and Jake hurried out the door.

"I'll be back in a little while, I just need to pick up something," Darrius announced as he exited the room. He returned as the spitting image of Uncle Aaron, down to the earrings, long hair, and suit.

"Uncle Aaron!" Sammy hailed, trotting over to him. "I'm so glad you showed up." Glancing at his watch, he continued, "I have ten minutes left, so do you want me to report what I found out now?"

In the perfect gravelly tone unique to Aaron, Darrius acknowledged Sammy. "Go ahead and tell me what you know." Sammy spilled out words as if the floodgates opened, yammering nonstop until he completed his report several minutes later. "Excellent, Sammy. Now I need to give you a new order and be quick about it!"

"Sure, Uncle Aaron, what do you need?"

"I understand Darrius is meeting Hilly for dinner. I want you to observe them and tell me exactly what goes on. Is that clear?"

"Absolutely!" Sammy glanced at his watch. "I only have eight minutes left on my watch, so I'll be quick!"

Darrius went into the hallway, closing the door behind him. Not having enough time to call room service for a real dinner, Hilly gathered food items from around the room and the mini bar. She assembled some bags of peanuts and potato chips as well as assorted candy bars into the middle of the table. "Sammy, do you want to join me?" Hilly asked as she pulled out a chair for him.

"Sure. I can sit for a little bit," he replied.

Darrius re-entered the room, smiling from ear to ear. "Did I miss anything while I was out?"

Sammy stood up. "You missed Uncle Aaron. He could only stay a few minutes, but what a shame you two missed each other and—"

"Sammy, enough!" Hilly shouted, holding up her hand. "Darrius, I put some food on the table. Would you like to join me for dinner?" Hilly was struggling to maintain her composure and not laugh at the meager offerings.

"Sounds wonderful," Darrius grinned, pleased that his plan was working perfectly. He sat down but declined to eat any of the sugar or carbohydrates offered by Hilly. "Thank you, Hilly, I think I'll just have something to drink for now." He poured a glass of wine for Hilly and himself.

"I am famished," Hilly exclaimed, grabbing several candy bars and chomping on them as though they were perfectly broiled filets of steak. "It doesn't get any better than this."

"Here's to good friends!" Darrius lifted his glass and toasted. They clinked glasses and continued drinking and eating while rambling about mundane things and useless information, per the plan. Sammy sat in silence, his hands folded in his lap, observing them eat and drink. He smiled continuously, soaking in every detail. Soon, a high-pitched tone made him jump to his feet.

"I gotta go!" Sammy reached for the Cererian quartz necklace and panicked when he couldn't find it.

"Here you go, Sammy. I was holding it for you," Darrius said, carefully placing the crystal around his neck.

"Whew! I thought I lost it. Uncle Aaron would have been really upset." Sammy turned to leave. His thick finger fidgeted with the little switch on the side of the crystal before it finally clicked and Sammy vanished.

Darrius grinned. "Well, I thought that went well. What do you think?"

Hilly burst into laughter before raising her glass for another toast. "Here's to Sammy, the best decoy we've ever known. Now, if you don't mind, I'm going to order *real* food. I'm sure the boys are starving, too." Hilly called room service, requesting steaks, chicken, and shrimp with all the sides and a big basket of bread and butter.

Across the street at Flanagan's Irish Pub, Jake and Chance leaned against the windowsill sipping their drinks, glancing up at the hotel window, and watching for Darrius' signal. Jake conjured up a myriad of bad things that could go wrong with Darrius' plan—they could have mentioned Jake's name; or like voicemail, Sammy might repeat his first report because Darrius didn't completely erase it; or maybe Sammy won't make it back to Uncle Aaron on time and simply explode, alerting Aaron that something was amiss. Jake smiled at the last thought. He wouldn't miss the little guy, but he also didn't want to invite the wrath of Uncle Aaron.

He glanced up at the hotel window. No sign yet. Better to remain patient and await the "all-clear" signal before jumping to conclusions.

Suddenly they received a telepathic message from Darrius: *It's okay to return. Come through the front door and take the stairs back to the room.*

Jake smiled and replied, *Great, I can't wait to hear how it went.*

The men lingered near the front door of the pub before carefully venturing across the street to the hotel entrance. They inspected the entire area before finally entering. Chance and Jake strode across the lobby, and then took the stairs up to the fourth-floor room. Hilly opened the door.

"You missed a great show. It was a brilliant plan to feed Aaron fake news. Speaking of *feeding, we*'ve got plenty of food. Sit down and help yourself."

Jake whipped off his jacket and wrapped it around the chair.

"Red or white?" Darrius asked.

"I can't stand that stuff. I drink beer or whiskey," Jake replied.

"How about bourbon?" Chance reached into his luggage and produced his private bottle carefully rolled in his jacket. He lifted it as though it was a priceless antique. "I present the smoothest fluid that will ever pass your lips." He raised it into the light and the two men gazed at the bourbon as though it was a holy vessel. "You want ice?"

"Nope. Straight will be fine." Chance poured the bourbon and Jake sipped it, savoring the taste before finishing it in an audible gulp. Chance poured him another drink and clinked his glass with Jake's. Jake leaned back in his chair, feeling mellow from the bourbon's warmth. "I wish I had seen your portrayal of Uncle Aaron," Jake spoke to Darrius.

"Aaron's voice is quite unique, but I think Sammy was convinced. Hopefully, Aaron will be happy with his report." Darrius sipped his wine.

"What's our next steps, Darrius?" Jake asked. "We can't trust Uncle Aaron, yet he's our contact with the Yfel Brethren."

"Because of the details you shared about Aaron, we can be certain he will betray us. I need more information before I can create a plan."

"How? Hilly blurted. "How can you get more information?"

Darrius' eyes danced with excitement. "I'm going to take a walk. And, if I find myself over by Aaron's office, I just might listen in and see if I can learn anything."

"He'll be suspicious of your motives. Aaron will kill to protect his assets," Jake warned.

"I can handle myself." Darrius rose to leave.

"Where ya going, Darrius?" Chance slurred. The bottle was half empty. Chance's eyes slowly opened and closed as his head bobbed.

Darrius recalled when he and Prasad had witnessed the human demonstration of the "tipsy" a few months ago. "I'm stretching my legs. I won't be gone very long. I suggest you watch the alcohol consumption so you're as sharp as can be tomorrow.

Darrius didn't wait for a reply, instead he slipped quietly out the door. Hilly arose and stood at the window, watching for Darrius to exit via the alleyway. After several minutes, he still hadn't appeared, so she walked to the front window and examined the throng of people on the street below. Still no Darrius. Somehow, she missed him. She raked her hair with her fingers.

Jake joined her. "Are you worried?"

She looked at him, and then returned to the people in the street. "Darrius knows how to take care of himself."

A black cat carefully picked a path among the sea of humanity walking along the main street. Pyewacket, brilliant green eyes gleaming, hurried along, weaving between humans and animals alike. Finally, he reached the quiet lane leading to Aningan Properties. He hesitated, searching for any trace of humans or Cererians. Upon seeing none, the feline ran into the side alley and glanced up at the window, illuminated by a faint light from the back office. Bounding atop a wooden barrel underneath the window, the immense black cat crept closer, listening with its keen sense of hearing as two men spoke—one man was Aaron, noticeably irritated, and the other was unknown, yet had a distinct accent, native to ancient Cererians.

Pyewacket switched his tail, eavesdropping on the conversation between the two men discussing a despicable plan, a heinous proposition that was beneficial for them yet deadly for Hilly. The feline realized that the stranger talking with Aaron was Everild. And, if their plan was successfully executed, nobody would survive the meeting atop Denali's summit except the Yfel soldiers.

Chapter 15

Another Gift

THE WARM RAYS OF the morning sun shone down on Curtis and Hilly who lay naked in a meadow of wildflowers, their bodies glistening with sweat from their recent lovemaking. Hilly gazed into Curtis' brown eyes and stroked his dark, curly locks while she assured him, "Everything will be just fine." Curtis sighed, content to lie in her arms. He gently touched her cheek, but Hilly grabbed his hand and squeezed hard. He cried out in pain.

"Why are you hurting me?" Curtis searched his wife's face, devoid of emotion. He fought to pry her fingers from his hand, but she clamped harder, refusing to let it go. The agony was unbearable.

"Everything will be just fine...everything will be just fine..."

Curtis bolted straight up, his eyes wide and full of fear. Traces of the hallucination lingered as he struggled to get out of bed only to be yanked back into reality by the manacle chained to the headboard. Sweat streamed down his face as the fever, which had overwhelmed his body, finally broke. His left hand tingled and burned as if a thousand ants were stinging him.

"Everything will be just fine," the tall, pale man said as he held Curtis' hand between his palms. "My name is Benedict." The man thrummed a low chant and rocked as Curtis closed his eyes and whimpered like a hurt animal. Soon, an intense buzzing filled the room, a strong vibration that penetrated deep into Curtis' soul, rippling throughout his body.

"What are you doing?" Curtis asked in a hoarse whisper. He tried to look at Benedict, but was so weak from the fever and blood loss that his eyelids were too heavy to hold up.

"I'm removing the infection. Plunging your hand into the water from the sink was not a good idea. That water comes from a cistern infested with bacteria and feces. My leader, Everild, won't allow me to heal your finger, but I can remove the infection so you won't die from blood poisoning."

"Thank you," Curtis squeaked.

Benedict hadn't heard those words in years and the genuine gratitude touched his heart. He missed the kindness and friendship he had known before Stygian had forced him to join the Yfel Brethren. Hunting and murdering magicians—men, women, and children—was a routine occurrence, and the constant moral conflict he faced left him mentally scarred. He was born into a race that had abolished negative emotions and actions, yet the Yfel Brethren broke away from the mainstream and embraced hatred and power. For Benedict to survive his personal torment, he withdrew from reality. A shadow of his former self assisted the Brethren with the carnage. As of yet, he had avoided consuming the power of those that were killed, but it was a matter of time before Everild would initiate him and force him to feed on a victim's energy.

Curtis drifted in and out of sleep while Benedict held his hand and soothed him with a low, humming mantra. Abruptly, Benedict stood up. "Everild has returned from his meeting. I have to go." He carefully draped Curtis' hand on the bed and quickly left the room.

"Aaron is a Cererian slime worm. I don't trust him at all!" Everild shouted after materializing inside the cabin.

"Did the witch meet our demands?" Thane asked.

"Not yet, but she will. Aaron has counseled her, or so he claims, and she has agreed to let him manage everything—from contacting us to arranging the meeting on Denali. He informed me of the plan he concocted. I strongly suspect he will double-cross all of us."

"What makes you think so?" Benedict asked.

"Since we had struck that deal with Aaron to stop poaching from his precious tribe, he's become increasingly demanding and arrogant. He believes he has the upper hand and can order us to do his bidding. But his flaw is his ego. And, even though he arranged one plan with the sorceress, he provided me with a second one, unknown to the witch. That makes me suspicious. He's playing both sides and Aaron only plays for himself." Everild glanced toward the bedroom door and then to Benedict. "How's our piece of meat?"

"The human was consumed with a massive infection because he was too stupid and ran tainted water over his wound. I stopped the infection from invading his blood, but did not heal the finger thus keeping him alive so you can continue to use him." Benedict hoped veiling his response with feigned contempt for the human would convince Everild that aiding the hostage was in his best interest.

"Hmm, an infection?" Everild glared at Benedict as he stepped closer until their faces were inches apart.

"Yes, due to the tainted water from the tap," Benedict repeated. He stiffened, expecting an explosive reaction from his leader, which had been a frequent response.

Tense moments passed.

"Okay. I agree. We need the meat alive because we have a new plan. Gather around," Everild commanded.

Everild sat at the table and beckoned Thane and Benedict to join him as he produced a piece of paper. "This is what Aaron presented to me. We will meet the sorceress at Denali's summit. She believes Aaron is bestowing cloaking magic on her friend so that he can enter the meeting circle to surprise us. In reality, Aaron will feign his cloaking magic, but they won't discover that until it's too late." Thane and Benedict nodded. "But, since Aaron is a known liar and can't be trusted, we will have our own plan. So, when we travel through the portal atop Pilot Mountain to the one atop Denali, we will..." Everild trailed off and glared at the bedroom door. "The human is listening to our plan!"

Everild burst through the door, knocking it off its hinges. Curtis cowered against the headboard, expecting a savage beating. Instead, as Everild strode to the side of the bed, he whipped out a tourné knife. Grabbing Curtis by the hair, he cut off his right ear. Blood spurted and Curtis howled in agony, pressing his hand against the side of his head. "That will teach you to listen to our conversation!"

Benedict suppressed his disgust at Everild's brutal action, and stared at the floor.

"Another present for our witch bitch, Everild!" Thane danced with delight.

Everild held the ear aloft, blood trickling down his arm. "I think Ms. Kemp will finally *listen* to our demands when she receives this. Thane, quickly prepare a transport box." Everild lobbed the bloody ear to Thane.

"What theme should I use?"

"Nothing fancy. I suggest placing it into a new cell phone box. Then you can teleport it directly into Aaron's office. Can you imagine her face when she sees her husband's ear on top of the phone?" Everild roared with pleasure as Thane danced around the room holding the ear, droplets of blood splattering the floor. Curtis held his head and sobbed—the pitiful wail of an animal that knows it doesn't have long to live. Benedict hung his head, powerless to stop the pain and torture.

The Brethren left Curtis alone in his misery.

"My soldiers, in two days, we will stand triumphant, and magicians will lay dead at our feet." A wicked grin spread across Everild's face as he imagined his victory on the summit. "I can smell and taste their powers as every last molecule leaves their body and enters mine." Everild's tongue slithered out of his mouth and flicked over his lips like a serpent.

"What about us? When do we get to share in the spoils?" Thane demanded.

"INSOLENCE!" Everild bellowed as he slapped Thane across the face with such force that he flew into the wall ten feet away. "You will get yours when I say you can! Now, get over here so I can tell you the rest of our plan, and be quick about it."

Thane cupped his cheek, a bruise rapidly spreading across his face. He staggered to his feet and averted his eyes submissively as he joined Benedict at the table. "As I was saying before we were so rudely interrupted, we won't count on Aaron following through on his promise. As a matter of fact, we can assume he will betray us. We will have our own plan, a superior scheme to guarantee our victory. Huddle close, my soldiers, and I'll share the details..."

Everild spoke in a hushed whisper as Thane and Benedict listened attentively. When he finished, he sat back and grinned at his men. Thane spoke first. "Yes. That is far superior to what Aaron wanted to do."

Sickened by the heinous acts described by Everild, Benedict wanted no part in his scheme, but he had to continue hiding his true feelings lest he get punished by his leader. He summoned his courage to lie. "It's an excellent plan, Everild."

Everild sneered and nodded. "Thane, send that package off immediately. Benedict shut that that weak human up. I can't tolerate that sniffling and crying for another minute." Both men scurried away leaving Everild alone at the table. "Soon I will be more powerful than Stygian."

Chapter 16

Betrayal

Reclining back in the chair, Darrius stretched his long legs onto the edge of the bed and watched Hilly sleep. Humans amused him sometimes. Hilly's face stretched down the side of the pillow, her mouth agape, drooling on the sheets. A raspy snore arose from her throat, a sound similar to a saw blade slicing through concrete blocks. Despite the noise, she slept peacefully. The sheets gently rose and fell with each breath.

"Hilly, time to get up." Darrius regretted having to wake her from her restful slumber. She snorted loudly, and turned onto her other side, yanking the comforter over her head. Darrius shook his head. "Hilly, I know you can hear me. Time to get up."

"Go away, Darrius."

"It's seven o'clock, and we need to get to Aaron's office by eight."

Hilly suddenly sat up, and pushed the comforter away from her. Her matted hair clung to one side of her head, a large chunk of sleep sealed one eye shut and fresh saliva glistened on her cheek. "What do you mean *we*? It's your meeting, not mine."

Darrius stifled a laugh as he studied his friend's appearance. "I learned something last night during my walk, and I feel you should attend the meeting with me this morning."

Hilly rubbed a knuckle into the corner of her eye. She yawned wide and long, "You can manage it, I'm sure."

"Please join me," Darrius requested. Without awaiting an answer, he stripped the sheets from the bed, exposing Hilly in her yellow-duck print, flannel pajamas. The sight reminded him of the pink horse jammies Hilly wore as a little girl at The Nine Muses. Some habits never change. "I've ordered breakfast," he bribed.

Hilly perked up. "Did you order coffee?"

"Yes, I remembered how much you love your caffeine, and I'm having an urn brought up, which will be handy when Jake and Chance wake up."

Rubbing her head and yawning again, Hilly mused, "They were a little rowdy last night." She glanced around her bedroom, and then gazed toward the door before looking back at Darrius. "Did you sleep in the other bedroom last night?"

"Jake and Chance never left the living room. They passed out on the couch lying on top of each other."

Hilly giggled. "Are they still like that?" She jumped out of bed and trotted to the bedroom door. Carefully opening it, avoiding making any noises that might wake the sleeping duo. She glanced into the dimly lit room. Chance was on his stomach, taking up the full length of the sofa. Jake was also on his stomach, spooning on top of him, his head tucked behind Chance's ear. They snored in unison. She grabbed her cell to snap photos, and chuckled while maneuvering around the sleeping pair, taking compromising photos from all angles. "They will kill me if they find out I took these." Satisfied that she had taken enough shots, she tickled Chance's nose with her finger. He batted it away, snorted, and returned to a peaceful slumber. She tickled Jake's nose. Raising his hand to swat at the annoyance, he inadvertently slapped Chance across the face, causing him to stir.

"Go away, Janet," Chance mumbled.

"Okay dear," Hilly whispered, suppressing her laugh.

There's a moment when the sleeping brain allows snippets of reality to filter into its cerebral realm and shoo the dream state away. When the door opens between reality and altered consciousness, dreams dance with their reality partners creating confusion in the sleeper.

"What the...?" Chance grumbled. The weight of Jake's body on top of him pressed Chance's face deep into the cushion, allowing only one eye to open. He struggled to focus on the room, his blood shot eye lolling around like a chameleon searching for prey. Hilly leaned into his face and giggled loudly. "Morning, big brother."

Half asleep, Chance mumbled, "Who...what's going on?" The reality floodgates burst wide open, and Chance realized Jake was lying on top of him.

"Get off of me!" He bellowed, throwing an elbow into Jake's side. Jake grumbled and rolled from the force but he continued sleeping. Chance planted his hands firmly on the couch and pushed upward causing Jake to tumble onto the floor. "I said, get off of me!"

"What the fuck?!" Jake uttered as he rolled around the floor trying to connect the images and make sense of what was happening. Hilly roared with delight watching the two men, disoriented from last night's bourbon binge, trying to stand yet bobbing and weaving against each other. "What just happened. Where am I?" Jake grabbed Chance's shoulder to steady himself, and Chance immediately knocked it away, spinning Jake toward the wall. Jake would have collided with a floor lamp had Darrius not caught him in time.

Darrius led Jake to Chance and then placed a hand on each of their heads. He emitted a low buzzing mantra—healing words for the infamous *tipsy* humans are apt to perform on occasion. He had performed the same ritual on Chance and Kai after they had drank too much at The Nine Muses. It was an effective cure for the headache and fogginess that followed drunken binges.

A sharp rap on the door surprised everyone, and Darrius, having completed the hangover healing, left the two men leaning against one another, and opened the door. A young hotel attendant greeted him. "Good morning, sir. Did you order breakfast?"

Darrius invited the bellboy inside and directed him to the table. Passing Jake and Chance, Darrius commented, "Gentleman, if you can manage to stagger into the bathroom and clean yourselves, I'll have breakfast waiting for you. And, yes, there is plenty of coffee for everyone."

While setting the table, the bellhop gawked at the men. Darrius noticed his distraction and placed a fifty-dollar bill into his hand. "That will be all young man. We don't want to be disturbed the rest of the day. Thank you."

The bellboy held the bill up to the light and snapped it for good measure before responding, "Yes, sir. If you need anything, make sure you ask for Stevie." Darrius was already guiding the babbling young man toward the door. Darrius took a long, deep breath and joined Hilly. Together they watched Chance and Jake support each other to the palatial bathroom.

"I suggest you both take a shower. Someone smells like a distillery," Darrius called after them. The men ambled into the bathroom and quietly closed the door. A loud crash suddenly occurred, followed by an angry, "SHIT!"

Hilly glanced at Darrius. "That was Chance."

A noisy thud sounding much like a great beast stomping on the floor, startled them. An irritated voice screamed, "FUCK!"

Hilly sipped her coffee. "That was Jake."

An eerie silence followed, concerning Darrius who stared at the bathroom door, fearing that the previous noises indicated someone was hurt. Soon, the sounds of water splashing accompanied by Chance's singing put him at ease. "I love to go swimming with bare naked women and swim between their legs..."

Hilly groaned and stared into her coffee. "I'm so sorry for my brother's behavior." She rolled her eyes at Darrius. "Some things never change."

He spooned eggs onto his plate and offered some to Hilly before responding, "Hilly, I wouldn't have it any other way. He smiled broadly, a truly affectionate smile.

"So, what's the deal with you wanting me to go to Aaron's with you this morning?" Hilly asked as she poured another cup of coffee.

"I learned some disturbing news last night when I went for my walk, but I want to share it with everyone, so I'll wait for the boys to finish. Also, Aaron contacted me early this morning." Darrius averted his gaze. "He received another package from the Yfel Brethren last night."

Hilly stared at Darrius over the rim of her mug. Her fingers trembled. She fought hard to maintain her composure, but through gritted teeth she hissed, "I thought he was arranging a meeting, not dictating what other part of my husband should be hacked off."

"Hilly, be careful. We don't know anything yet." Darrius lightly touched Hilly's arm, reassuring her that all would be okay. In doing so, Darrius attempted to comfort himself as well. After witnessing Aaron's private meeting with Everild, Darrius found it increasingly difficult to remain positive about his friend.

"I don't trust him, Darrius. My husband is dying one part at a time, and it's apparent Aaron doesn't care."

Darrius looked down and absently forked at his eggs, gathering his thoughts.

Hilly pressed, "Is there something else?"

Darrius took a bite of egg and chewed slowly, taking his time to respond. "Aaron has changed. Something has occurred that altered his behavior. It's made him more volatile, nasty and unpredictable. He's a completely different person."

"So his outburst in the office yesterday was not typical Aaron?" Hilly rolled her eyes. "If you hadn't been there, I'm afraid I might have gone to blows with that arrogant ass." Darrius gazed at his friend, his brow furrowed with concern. "I'm sorry, Darrius, but he was quite rude," Hilly added.

Remembering the terse exchange, Darrius replied, "You were very rude yourself, Hilly. With your newly acquired powers, your emotions have been more explosive than usual."

"Fair enough, Darrius. I did snap at him." Mischief filled her eyes, "It would have been interesting to see what would have happened if he had pushed me too far."

Chance burst into the room, soaking wet with a large, white towel wrapped around the lower half of his body. A trail of puddles followed him, leaving stains on the carpet. "We need more towels. That nimrod, Jake, got them all wet."

"Chance, get out of here. You're soaking everything," Hilly complained, shoving her brother back toward the bathroom.

Jake popped his head out the door, shampoo foaming in his hair. "Did you get more towels, Chance?"

Hilly grabbed Chance's arm and dragged him into the bathroom. Jake stood naked except for a face cloth, which he held over his groin. Hilly averted her eyes as she passed by, surveying the chaotic scene. The shower curtain hung by only two rings, the remainder having been violently yanked from the rod and discarded on the tile. The sink overflowed with soapy water, which flooded the entire floor.

"You guys make me crazy." Turning to Chance, she grabbed him fiercely by the ears and pulled his face close to hers. She managed to find a level voice with just a hint of malice for emphasis, "I'm leaving with Darrius. You and Jake are responsible for cleaning up this mess. It better be done before we get back. Understand?"

Red-faced, Chance whined, "But, we need more towels, Hilly."

"I can't do much with this little old wash rag," Jake added. He waved it in the air, completely exposing himself. Hilly quickly exited the bathroom, completely disgusted with them both.

Darrius met her at the door, holding fresh towels.

"Where did those come from?" She asked.

"I called my new best friend, Stevie. He's very motivated by money." Darrius walked into the bathroom and surveyed the mess. Jake and Chance stood side by side, dripping onto the tile—Chance with his large fluffy towel askew around his hips and Jake holding a face cloth over his privates. "Here, boys, fresh towels. As Hilly said, we expect this bathroom to be in perfect shape by the time we return."

"Yes, Darrius," they replied in unison.

Darrius whirled and exited. "They don't know you can fix that mess with a snap of your fingers," she remarked.

"It's much more fun this way. Come on, let's walk to Aaron's. When we return, I'll bring everyone up to speed on what I heard last night. Right now, it's all about you and Curtis."

There was an eerie calm in Aningan. In the early morning hours, visitors were either sleeping, eating breakfast or recovering from drunken celebrations. Only a few locals prowled the main street, allowing plenty of room for Darrius and Hilly to walk without the usual crush of humanity.

"Darrius, if you can teleport everywhere, why do you choose to walk?"

Darrius gazed around as he answered. "I would miss all of nature's wonder—the people, the buildings, this dirt street, the birds singing, the smell of fresh pine, and the sun's warmth. My mind is stimulated, and my senses are alive when I walk outdoors. You once described your trek in the North Carolina woods as feeling like a voyeur in a fantasy land full of strange sounds, tantalizing smells, and incredible sights. That's how I perceive your world when I choose to stroll. To teleport is efficient and easy, but I would miss all this genuine beauty.

She hadn't considered Aningan as a thing of beauty at all—the constant dusty haze lingering in the air, the vomit in the alleyways, the rude people. "On Ceres, do you walk or teleport everywhere?"

"We teleport everywhere. That's not to say beauty doesn't exist there, but, admittedly, I don't relish walking in it as I do here on Earth. Everything is so different on Ceres. Even after thousands of years here, I still encounter unexpected delights I've not witnessed before." Darrius wrapped his arm around Hilly and pulled her close. "I thoroughly enjoy interacting with humans, despite their eccentricities. Their unique quirks add interesting layers to their personalities." Darrius gazed at Hilly. "It is a rare occurrence, but it's always an extreme pleasure when I find a special human with whom I can share my strolls in nature, and Hilly, you are one of those people. I consider you to be a special friend."

Hilly hugged Darrius back and felt the warmth that came from receiving a sincere compliment—a validation that you are valued and appreciated. Making friends wasn't easy for Hilly and to hear Darrius freely use the word "friend" with her, truly touched her heart and her soul. Arms entwined, they continued on their journey without speaking, just soaking in the surrounding energy.

Turning onto the quiet lane leading to Aaron's office, Hilly stopped and shivered. An overwhelming tide of negative energy washed over her when she realized she'd have to face the inevitable and examine the contents of the package. Darrius held her closer. "Everything is going to be okay. As long as I'm with you, Aaron can't hurt you."

"It's not Aaron I'm afraid of, Darrius. I'm afraid of what will be in the package. I can't bear Curtis being tortured while I'm able to walk about freely."

As they scaled the steps to Aningan Properties, a large raven squawked a welcome. "Your friend is back," Darrius observed.

Hilly gazed at the black bird. "He alerts me to those who are not what they appear to be or those who will do me harm. He's appeared at this office three times. So I'm inclined to believe Aaron will either betray me or harm me. In either case, I'm prepared."

Darrius touched Hilly's shoulder. "Remember my caution about judging too quickly. Use your psychic abilities. Your emotions can sometimes paint the wrong picture."

Hilly drew in a deep breath and slowly exhaled. "I'll try to be calm."

"Are you ready?"

"Not really. But there's never enough time to prepare for evil." Hilly replied, and Darrius pushed the door open. They strode into the dimly lit room. A waft of sandalwood snatched her attention. "I've never smelled that scent in this office before."

Taking Hilly's arm, Darrius led her down the darkened hall. "Perhaps Aaron has rolled out the 'welcome mat' and is demonstrating a softer side by using a scent you enjoy."

Hilly gritted her teeth. The mere mention of Aaron's name made her seethe. And, to think he was changing, being nicer, was a bunch of bullshit. But she wouldn't tell Darrius that. She would keep her word, be patient, and stay in the present.

Darrius rapped on the office door with his knuckle and a melodic voice answered. "Please come in Darrius and Ms. Kemp."

"Remember, Hilly, don't judge." Hilly flashed an exaggerated grin and pushed the door open.

Aaron rose from his desk and gestured toward two chairs. "Ms. Kemp, how nice to see you. And, Darrius, I appreciate your punctuality. Would either of you like some refreshments? Coffee or water?"

"No thanks," Hilly replied, convinced that any beverage would probably contain poison.

"I'm fine, Aaron, but thank you for asking," Darrius politely replied.

Aaron slowly sat down, his eyes steeled on Hilly who returned his gaze with her own glare, her lips drawn thin and draining color. Darrius observed the two adversaries and decided to break the tension. "Aaron, I understand you've heard from the Brethren?"

Keeping his eyes trained on Hilly, he responded, "Yes, the outcome is not what we expected." His mouth turned downward, and his eyes softened as he withdrew a small package from a desk drawer. Hilly watched his emotional display with disdain. He was mocking her and she gripped the arms of her chair to displace the rising anger. Aaron placed the parcel in the middle of the desk, and Hilly studied it, her right leg nervously shaking, anticipating what lay inside.

"I thought you were going to arrange a meeting, Aaron," Hilly uttered. "That was the plan we all discussed. Correction, the plan that *you* and Darrius discussed and agreed upon. So, what happened?" Her right leg bounced as the emotional energy escalated.

Aaron stared at her, taking his time before answering. "Yes, that was the plan. But, as you are aware, the Yfel are unpredictable."

"When did you receive the package?" Darrius interjected. He mentally examined the contents of the box and grimaced at the bloody image flooding his mind.

"I found it on my desk this morning."

"How did the package get into the office? Does someone else have a key?" Hilly pressed, remaining calm except for her right leg which continued bouncing nervously.

"Of course, Sammy has a key," he responded. "And, if the package was delivered to him, he would have run it right over because it's marked urgent." He tapped the box where the word appeared.

"Deliveries are made on Sundays in Aningan?" Hilly's leg pumped furiously, and Darrius reached over, gently placing his hand on her knee, calming the energy. Before you answer that, I don't see the markings of any shipping company. How did the package arrive? By carrier pigeon?"

"Hilly, Sunday deliveries happen all the time. Right, Aaron?" Darrius spoke to thwart Aaron's eminent outburst.

Aaron settled back in his chair and calmly replied, "Yes, Darrius, you are right."

Hilly shot an angry glance at Darrius who winked at her. He continued, "Let's address that which we're reluctant to do. We need to see what's inside."

Aaron moved to unwrap the box. Hilly rose and yanked the package away, snarling, "If you don't mind, this is addressed to me, so I'll be the one to open it." Aaron shrunk back against his chair and folded his hands in his lap. His green eyes danced in anticipation.

Hilly held the box on her lap and carefully peeled off the tape holding the kraft paper in place. She unwound the paper exposing a brightly colored cell phone box. "What?" she uttered as she tilted the box, listening for any sound. Picking the tape off the sides, she held her breath as she carefully withdrew the lid. She gasped.

"Bastards!" Her hands trembled uncontrollably, violently shaking the container. Inside lay a new phone and resting against the screen, in a macabre fashion, was a freshly amputated ear. Decorating the lobe was a single gold stud like the one Curtis wears. Hilly stared at the contents and panted short gasps before looking at Darrius, tears rolling down her cheeks. Darrius plucked the package from her hands. Hilly stared at him, numb and overwhelmed with horror. After studying the contents, Darrius gently replaced the lid and put the parcel on the desk.

Aaron stared at Hilly, a hint of a smile spreading across his lip. It was obvious he enjoyed her misery, and he lapped at her sorrow like an energy thief. Hilly's leg thumped the floor again and her hands opened and closed as if she were dispelling any remnants of the box remaining on her fingers. Darrius addressed Aaron, "Was there a message with this box? The other packages had a message."

Maintaining his stare on Hilly, Aaron calmly replied, "The only message was verbal. The Yfel will meet Hilly at Denali's summit tomorrow morning. Instructions will be sent to your hotel room. They cautioned that she better come alone."

Hilly shook from a violent mix of anger, sadness, and an unexpected pulse of malice rising from the pit of her stomach. The tears that had pooled in her eyes vanished, and a dark shadow passed over her face. An eerie calm descended—the peace one feels when they have finally made a decision and have resigned themselves to the outcome, good or bad. Darrius glanced at Aaron who grinned wide, basking in Hilly's suffering, relishing in her torment as though he sipped on her distress and grew stronger with each mouthful.

A flash of bright light filled the room. Hilly leapt to her feet, her hands outstretched, shooting two parallel rays of white-hot energy directly toward Aaron. The unexpected blast pushed him and the chair back through the wall.

"Hilly, No!" Darrius shouted as he reached to restrain her. But she flew into the air, escaping his grasp, and landed on the desk, propelling the intense heat into Aaron's body as he struggled holding his hands up in defense. Her face twisted with rage as she channeled all her fury into her hands which glowed red from the intense heat. Rotating her hands, she created a small ball of intense energy. The orb throbbed a deep red color, and she threw it at Aaron's head in one final assault. The energy exploded throughout the room. The concussion broke the window and scattered all of the furniture. Suddenly the room grew quiet except for a gentle hiss emanating from Aaron's body. The attack lasted less than three minutes.

Darrius lunged for Hilly and wrapped his arms around her, lifting her from the desk. Darrius held her tight and spoke Cererian words into her ear, attempting to calm her down. "Hilly? Are you with me?" She didn't struggle, but her body remained rigid, her hands still flexed for another assault. She panted furiously and stared at Aaron's corpse like a she-wolf that had just run down and killed her prey.

Darrius glanced over his shoulder at Aaron. The body smoldered and lay in a crumpled heap, the face melted and unrecognizable. The intense energy she threw at Aaron was so direct and focused that only his body bore the marks of an attack, there were no scorch marks on the wall or the furniture.

"Is he dead?" Hilly gasped.

"If he's not, he'll wish he was," Darrius responded Darrius. "Hilly, what did you do?"

"I couldn't take his smugness anymore. Didn't you see how he relished in my misery? He was enjoying it!"

"It wasn't worth killing him. He was our link to the Yfel, our connection to having Curtis returned." He finally released her, and she slowly surveyed the damage. She realized killing him released so much stress and so many emotions. Darrius walked to Aaron, knelt and examined the body, his hands floating back and forth, sensing for any life that may still remain.

"He's dead, right?" Hilly asked Hilly.

Darrius sighed and stood up. He took some time before replying, "Yes, this man is dead, but—"

"Fabulous news!" Hilly cut him off.

Darrius shook his head at her disrespectful display. "Hilly, you didn't let me finish. This version of Aaron is dead. But, after examining the body, I realized that it is a clever doppelganger, and not the real Aaron."

Hilly pounded her fist on the desk. "Are you sure?" She went to the body and kicked at it. It looked like Aaron and still possessed the smirk he was so well known for. "Darrius, are you sure?"

"Yes, and in a few minutes that collection of molecules will soon disappear." They watched as the doppelganger disintegrated and vanished into thin air, not a trace left on the floor, not even the clothes.

"I knew I couldn't trust that fucker." Hilly slammed her fist onto the desk again. "Now what do we do?" She turned to Darrius. The whites of her eyes were blood red and her hands still glowed hot.

"Let's get your hands cooled first." Darrius gently folded her hands into his, cooling them. He was greatly disturbed by her behavior and her disregard for life, even though it had been an imposter. Because of the doppelganger, Darrius believed Aaron might be observing the entire exchange, and mentally messaged Hilly while cloaking his conversation against eavesdropping.

Hilly, listen to me. This whole charade was staged. Aaron knew how you'd react, and he played you like a fool. He used your emotions against you. He understands now what you're capable of and that you want him dead, so I'm sure negotiating for Curtis will be tricky. You may have destroyed our ability to get your husband returned.

Hilly looked away from Darrius, refusing to admit she was wrong. She stared at the ground.

I'm sorry, Darrius. I lost my head. I just couldn't take Aaron's gloating anymore. What should we do?

Darrius gently took Hilly's chin and lifted it until they stared into each other's eyes. *We go back to the hotel room, and we'll take the box with us. I have more to share with all of you, and this little play adds more mystery to what I already know. So, take a deep breath and let's get out of here.*

Darrius collected the parcel and guided Hilly down the hallway to the front room. She yanked the door open and ran outside, into the fresh air and sunshine. Darrius followed her. Nobody noticed the brilliant green eyes studying them from the corner of the front room. In the dim light, the immense, black Persian cat blended into the background, undetected. The cat known as Jeffrey switched its fluffy tail, and slowly, very slowly, he smiled.

Chapter 17

The Family Records

After spending the morning cleaning the bathroom, Jake and Chance sat at the table scarfing down the remains of breakfast and drinking black coffee. They laughed, summarizing the events from the previous night—the bourbon shots, the hand stands that went awry (which explained the broken lamps), and the levitation challenge (resulting in stacked end tables teetering up to the ceiling). They avoided discussing the details of their sleeping arrangement on the couch. Better to erase that memory.

Jake was boasting about a victorious jousting competition at a Renaissance festival when Darrius and Hilly unexpectedly appeared in the middle of the room. Chance spewed coffee in Jake's face.

"What the...," Jake sputtered.

"Sorry for the intrusion," Darrius remarked. The men gawked. Teleporting doesn't create a great flash of light like a portal. Instead, the traveler or travelers simply appear, beginning as blurred images until they completely materialize, all in the blink of an eye.

"Hilly, go take a cool shower," Darrius urged, then added, "I'm sure the bathroom is spotless, right boys?" Jake and Chance nodded their heads numbly. It's not every day that someone materializes right in front of you.

Averting her eyes, Hilly hurried by them and slammed the door. Using her powers to kill the being, who she thought was Aaron, left her drained and sluggish. She stared at herself in the mirror and was horrified—black pupils surrounded by blood-red filled her entire eye, making her appear like a bug-eyed monster. Gently touching her face, the warmth from her energized hands made her sweat, but at least they no longer burned red. She shook her head and sighed, still not comprehending the quickness of her emotions and her fury. *Perhaps I am becoming a monster.*

She peeled off her clothes, dropping them to the floor before turning on the cold water in the shower. She stepped in and placed her head against the wall tile, allowing the cold water to saturate her hair and roll down her back. The water soothed her body, removing the emotional energy that had collected within her pores. Alone with her thoughts, she wept uncontrollably, fearing she was evolving into a beast like Stygian. Streams of water rolled down the side of her face and joined her tears.

"That was quite an entrance, Darrius," Chance said, sincerely impressed. He jerked his thumb at the bathroom. "Is everything okay?"

"Hilly received another package from the Yfel," Darrius replied solemnly.

"Crap. What was inside?" Chance asked.

"I don't suggest you open this until you're done eating." Darrius placed the package on the table.

Jake and Chance eyed the box. "How bad can it be?" Jake asked as he reached for it.

Chance stopped him. "No, don't touch it. I don't want to lose my breakfast. Just wait."

Jake tapped the box. "Just a little peek," he teased.

"Hilly's had a bad morning so far," Darrius advised, gazing toward the bathroom. "When she joins us, we have a lot more to discuss. I have more information about Aaron that will impact all the plans we have made to meet with the Yfel Brethren and get Curtis returned. I need both of you to get yourselves together, and fast!" Darrius stressed. They nodded in unison while shoveling eggs into their mouths.

All was forgotten about the package sitting in the middle of the table. For the time being.

Like an old film projector, images fluttered through Hilly's mind as she replayed the events in Aaron's office. The speed of her anger and the ferociousness of the energy pulses shocked her. It was an ability she hadn't known she possessed. She wondered how the situation escalated. Aaron's smugness and lack of empathy had irritated her, but for her to react in such an extreme manner—it didn't make sense. An ordinary human would have just yelled "shut up", but Hilly's first reaction was to kill, and not just kill, but to incinerate the man. She recalled the rays of light shooting from her hands. Despite her detestable actions, she had enjoyed the power and control. "I wonder if that's how the Yfel feel," she whispered against the cold tile. But no sooner had she uttered the words, that she swore at herself for having such a bizarre thought. Normal people don't think that way. But she wasn't normal anymore. Not exactly sure what she had become, she was definitely not the same Hilly Kemp who fought Stygian three months earlier.

The water was refreshing, and she didn't want to get out. If only life was this easy—jump in the shower and let the water wash all your problems away. But she knew Darrius had more information to share. Sighing deeply, she turned off the water, dried herself, and then looked in the mirror.

Gazing at her nude body, she truly liked the woman that stared back. Her reflection exuded confidence despite the bruises and scars, and she flexed her arm muscles to accentuate her strength. Dipping her hand into the jar of gel, she ran it through her hair, spiking it up at the top, and smoothing the sides. She pursed her lips and kissed the air. "You're okay, Hilly Kemp. Just keep being who you are."

The boys leaned back in their chairs and patted their bulging stomachs. Chance roared a booming belch just as Hilly exited the bathroom. "Nice one, Chance," she noted. "I might have given that one a nine if you had been able to make it last a few more seconds."

Chance almost fell out of his chair by Hilly's comment, and Jake doubled over in laughter. Patting Chance on the top of the head, she tucked a leg under her before sinking into the seat beside him. Darrius poured a cup of black coffee and pushed it in front of her. "Feeling better?" he asked.

"Much better. Thank you, Darrius." She grabbed a piece of toast from a plate that lay beside the parcel, but she didn't even glance at the box. Munching her toast, Hilly casually looked around the room. Jake and Chance stared at her while Darrius sipped his coffee silently. "Whatcha looking at boys?" Hilly challenged.

"Everything okay, sis?" Chance asked, concerned about her well-being.

Jake mentally reached out to her, *Are you okay, Hilly?*

Hilly studied their faces. Her initial reaction was to get mad because she detested scrutiny of her behavior or her wellbeing. *Don't waste your pity on me,* she thought. But, realizing the two men care about her, she reined in her emotions and replied, "I'm okay, despite everything." Forcing a smile, she sipped her coffee and looked away from them.

"We need to talk about the altercation at Aaron's office," Darrius stated bluntly.

Hilly's eyes widened as she stared at Darrius and messaged, *Darrius, no!*

Darrius patted her hand and continued, "Hilly killed Aaron this morning."

"What the fuck!" Chance shouted as he stood up, staring at Hilly.

"Damn, Hilly," Jake exclaimed. "You would need supernatural powers to kill a Cererian like Uncle Aaron." Jake leaned back in his chair and studied Hilly. His jaw muscles bunched as he considered what she had done.

"Please be quiet and let me finish," Darrius stopped them. "Hilly vanquished Aaron, but it was a doppelganger. So, I want to thank Hilly for unearthing that betrayal." Stunned by Darrius' comment, Hilly smiled at him for spinning a more positive view of the events. "The imposter was so well created that if Hilly had not thought to kill it, we may never have known we were being misled."

"In addition to this revelation, during my walk last night, I overheard Aaron talking to Everild—in person. The Yfel leader sat in the office discussing the summit meeting with Aaron who shared our plan. The Yfel are now fully aware of our intentions. So, when Hilly meets them tomorrow, Jake will not have the proper magic to penetrate the meeting circle, which would leave Hilly to fend for herself."

"Shit, Darrius," Jake exclaimed. "Hilly can't face them alone."

"I also have something to share," Chance mentioned as he collected a notepad from his suitcase. "While searching the family records, I found something quite interesting about the Yfel Brethren that will benefit us in hatching a new plan."

"The family records?" Jake asked.

"Chance is Keeper of the Records," Darrius explained. "He possesses an ancient tome containing the historical accounts of all the tribes and families of Earth."

"Ever since I acquired the book I'm addicted and can't stop reading," Chance confirmed. "Every tale and every story is fascinating, almost enchanting. It makes me wonder if these accounts could have been the basis for the fairy tales we know today." Chance closed his eyes. "Sometimes, it calls to me in the middle of the night. I try to resist, but it's very persistent and won't relent until I see what it wants. It always reveals a new page, directing me, pushing me toward the pertinent knowledge for that day. And, it beckoned me two nights ago."

"What was so important that it woke you up?" Hilly pressed.

"Before I knew that anything had befallen Curtis, the records summoned me and led me to a passage written by an ancestor hundreds of years ago. The verses are like deciphering cryptic messages at sometimes, and at other times, it's like reading love letters. I spent an hour contemplating this eye-witness account about an attack from the Yfel Brethren:

Evil befell the family. Though many escaped, we lost some of our lovelies, the youngest, the tenderest to the Yfel. Innocent power is sweetest to the lips, lost on the wicked tongues that lap their essence like cats to milk. Though despicable to watch the carnage, I witnessed one act of compassion, a decision to withdraw from the feast and cloak their fare as a castoff to be thrown into the river. The child was placed on a raft and escaped the murders. The individual's actions never raised suspicions since the others were busy consuming their own victims and relishing in the released power. Today, I bore witness to a crack in the armor of our adversaries. With more force, we may be able to break them apart!

"What does it mean?" Hilly asked.

"Elementary, my dear Watson. The Yfel Brethren are not a cohesive unit. There is one who will break ranks. And, that individual may be instrumental in saving Curtis."

"Do you have a name?" Jake asked, leaning over to gaze at Chance's notes.

"That's the problem. I found this passage, but there is no mention of a name. It doesn't identify any of the Yfel Brethren. Darrius, any ideas on how we can discover more about this person?"

Darrius sat with his hands clasped in front of him, deep in thought. "I've given this a lot of thought. Of the remaining members, only Benedict would be the likely candidate to be our potential ally."

"Can you mentally contact him?" Hilly asked, visibly excited by this positive news.

"Alas, I cannot. They have cloaked their whereabouts from me and choose only to work through Aaron. There is another problem. Since it was Everild's conjuring that bound Benedict to the group, only the death of Everild will release Benedict. He may be limited on what he can do to assist us while he is tethered to the Brethren."

The group sat in silence as everyone considered ideas for how to proceed. Hilly ran her finger around the rim of her cup and stared into the ether. "I have a plan," she proclaimed as she thumped the table with her finger.

"You do realize that we no longer have an advantage?" Jake said as he walked to the front window. "Just what kind of a plan can we create to thwart their efforts when we don't know what they're going to do?" He shook his head.

Hilly rose and joined him at the window. "The best idea is one that nobody would ever consider." Jake looked at her as if she was crazy.

"Hilly, you're talking in riddles."

"But every riddle has an answer. Denali's summit is my home turf, and that gives us home field advantage. The Yfel may have their Cererian powers, but we have the power of Denali, and she will not deny me."

Darrius joined them. "Hilly, there are three of them and one of you. Despite your growing powers, you can't fight them without help."

Her emerald eyes flashed with mischief, and Hilly grinned at everyone. Chance groaned because he knew what that smile meant. It was the same grin he witnessed at The Nine Muses before the battle with the dragon. "Uh, oh, my baby sister has a plan that you'll both love and hate."

Hilly nodded at Chance. "You may question my sanity, but this idea will definitely work." Glancing around the room Hilly considered that Aaron may have spies everywhere. "I'm afraid the walls may have ears, so I'll share my proposal via telepathy." They all joined together in the middle of the room as Hilly mentally messaged her scheme to battle the Brethren and save her husband.

Darrius stood with his hands clasped in front of him. "Hilly, that just might work."

Everild stood in Aaron's office, furious at his host. "The witch is stronger than you led us to believe, Aaron. She displays many of Stygian's skills and there may be more abilities that lie deep, powers yet to be discovered."

"Everild, please calm down," Aaron said attempting to assuage his ally's fears. "There are three of you and only one of her. Her comrade will no longer be able to penetrate the meeting circle. Just remember to play her emotions. She can't control her fury—that's her weakness, and when she's most vulnerable. If you follow our plan, you'll be victorious."

Everild nodded. "When I kill the witch, I'll be able to drink in her extreme power, and I'll surely be the strongest. I will rule this world and everyone will do my bidding!"

Aaron's green eyes flashed and jumped with pleasure. Now that he had manipulated the Yfel and humans into following his devious schemes, he could now focus on his plan to eradicate them all and finally control the Earth.

Chapter 18

The Yfel Brethren

Hilly snuggled deep into the downy comforter pulled over her head, blocking out the chaos of the morning. She lay limp, completely drained, not even enough energy to raise an eyebrow if the Yfel Brethren themselves burst into the hotel room. The moment her head hit the pillow, she drifted off, welcoming the falling sensation that occurs just before the dream's vivid images fluttered through her brain.

The vision landscape was familiar—dark and dreary with lightning and torrential rain. She stood on a mountain with Raven, which channeled the storm's electrical current into a protective halo of energy around her. Searching the heavens, Hilly located her adversary—the black dragon. It flew from the east, screeching its arrival, leathery wings propelling miniature vortices toward her, but the energy bubble surrounding her deflected them away.

Something was amiss. Although the black beast approached, Hilly lowered her sword, unwilling to fight. It was as though she had no control over her movements. Closing her eyes, she mentally scanned her body—there was no fear, no anger, no negative emotions at all. Had the warrior softened and become complacent? She shook her head to clear the cobwebs clinging to her brain, and the vision switched.

Still atop a mountain, holding Raven, Hilly stood naked in a blizzard of snow and ice. The maelstrom swirled around her, yet she was not cold, nor did she feel the sting of the ice crystals. Instead, she felt incredibly warm and alive, more vibrant than she'd felt in months. Big fluffy flakes coated her eyelashes, making it impossible to see, but she sensed that the beast had left, leaving her all alone on the summit. A crack of lightning startled her, and she gazed up into the sky, into the belly of the storm. The face of an old woman smiled back, and she knew immediately Mother Denali was present. A tsunami of peace and calm washed over her. Hilly closed her eyes against the drifting snow which soon encased her body, transforming her into an ice sculpture, a tribute to The Great Mother.

Hilly's eyes fluttered open and she scanned the bedroom, ensuring she was back in the physical world and no longer drifting in a dream. A chilly wave flowed upward from her feet, and she flung the comforter aside, finding goosebumps covering her arms and legs. She bolted into the bathroom and turned on the hot water. Glancing at her image in the mirror, she gasped at the ice crystals clinging to her hair and eyelashes. "Was I on Denali?" she wondered out loud.

A rapping on the door snatched her attention. "Hilly? Is that you?"

Relieved it was Darrius and not the meddlesome duo—Jake and her brother, Chance—she invited him in. "Come in, Darrius. I'm decent."

Darrius slowly opened the door, peering around the corner, before stepping all the way into the room. "You slept a long time. I trust it was restful."

Hilly scooped warm water over her arms, still prickly with goosebumps, and answered, "Yes...and no." Her green eyes twinkled. "Denali visited me in my dream. It helped me realize I have nothing to fear. But it also left me with images that don't make sense."

"Like what?" Darrius was intrigued since Hilly's past visions had always been ominous and foreboding, resulting in injury or death.

"The dragon approached, but it suddenly disappeared, and I was plunged naked into the middle of a snowstorm."

"Very curious. So it started like your old visions but switched to something new? Were you alone?"

"Yes, I was totally alone except for Raven which I held, but not up in battle posture. I held her down and even felt compelled to drop her to the ground because I experienced a complete shift in my emotions—there was no anger or fear, only peace and bliss." A nervous giggle escaped, and Hilly clamped a hand over her mouth. Her eyes widened at the unexpected burst of emotion. "I don't know where that came from," she said almost apologetically.

"Nervous energy," Darrius remarked. "You had accumulated negative emotions over the last few days, and you were able to finally release them in your dream. The giggle was your body's release of physical energy."

Hilly nodded as she dried her arms. "I must admit, I do feel very relaxed."

"Come on, let's join Chance and Jake." Darrius held the door ajar as Hilly passed. She stopped and glanced at him.

"Today is going to be a good day, Darrius," Hilly confidently affirmed, and she marched into the living area.

Something on the table caught Darrius' attention. The box containing Curtis' amputated ear vibrated a subtle low rumble that only Darrius' keen sense of hearing had detected. Dread washed over him as he neared the table and gently removed the box's lid. The cellphone trembled, the display flashing a pulsed light, signaling a call. Curtis' ear jiggled on the screen like a slice of dried meat curiously decorated with a gold stud earring. Darrius knew it was the Yfel. Without touching the phone, Darrius used his psychic powers and answered. "Hello?"

Dead air.

"Hello, is someone there?"

Demented laughter answered him before trailing off to silence.

"Everild?"

"Are you the human's answering service now?" the caller hissed. "Put the witch on, I refuse to talk with you, Darrius."

Hilly started to speak, but Darrius held up his hand to stop her. "She's indisposed right now. Give me the message, Everild."

"NO!" The phone abruptly disconnected.

Hilly cleared her throat. "I'll speak with them, Darrius." She approached the table.

Realizing the lid was still off the box, Darrius abruptly barked, "Stop!" and Hilly halted. Darrius fumbled to replace the lid. "Let me call them back first." Once again, he used his psychic powers to call Everild.

A deep-throated laugh answered and taunted Darrius, "Yes?"

"Everild, what does it matter if Hilly answers the phone as long as she knows the message? Isn't that more important?" Darrius glanced sideways at Hilly who strode toward him with a determined look edged into her face. They locked eyes and continued their conversation in private, through telepathy. *Darrius, let me talk to them.*

"What do you want, Everild?" Hilly demanded.

"Is that Hilly?" Everild purred.

"I'm here." Hilly curtly responded as she joined Darrius by the table.

"Use the actual phone, witch. I won't talk to you psychically." A harsh dial tone indicated Everild had hung up.

Hilly drew in a deep breath as if she needed all the air in the room to move her feet forward. Chance placed a comforting hand on her shoulder. She glanced at him and mouthsed, "Thanks."

The box on the table quivered as the phone vibrated inside. She snatched the package and gently removed the lid. She turned away in disgust, not only from the grizzly contents but also because the ear had putrefied, and liquids oozed from it. She gritted her teeth and picked up the silver phone, tilting it to dislodge the gruesome flesh adhered to the screen, and answered, "Hello?"

A low, growling chuckle responded.

"Answer me now or I'll hang up," Hilly demanded.

"Careful, witch, we still have your husband and can take our time removing more meat."

She chewed her lower lip, willing her anger to disappear. Darrius mentally messaged, *Stay in control, show no emotions. Remember your dream.*

She swiftly nodded and replied, "What do you want?"

"All in good time, my little sorceress," he responded in a drawn-out whisper.

"Goodbye." Hilly abruptly ended the call.

Jake and Chance gasped. Darrius shook his head. "Hilly, that little prank will do more harm than good."

"I'm maintaining control, Darrius. But I'm hoping Everild loses his." Her eyes flashed as the phone vibrated with an incoming call. "Hello?" she answered.

"Don't pull that shit again, witch!" Everild screamed into the phone.

"Then let's talk business, Everild," Hilly replied in a calm, emotionless tone.

Dead air. Hilly knew Everild was playing games with her. Refusing to participate, she remained quiet. A full minute passed.

"Witch?" Everild shouted.

"Here," Hilly responded, feeling her adversary's anger rising.

"Tomorrow morning. Nine o'clock. Denali's summit. Come alone."

"The summit is vast. Where will I find you?"

"You'll find us and we'll find you." The call suddenly ended. Hilly replaced the phone back in the box and stared at Curtis' ear. She lingered for a moment before glancing at the floor and wiping away a tear.

Darrius had listened to the entire call using his psychic abilities and beamed at Hilly. "You exercised extreme patience while chatting with Everild. I know that consumed a lot of your energy, and I'm very proud of you for handling yourself in that manner. I think the call went very well."

"I agree. Now if we can just outsmart them on Denali." She glanced at Chance and Jake. "You can't let me down, guys."

Jake patted Hilly on the back. "Hilly, I reckon tomorrow will prove that either you're a crazy-ass warrior who thrives on recklessness or, you're a very clever firewalker.

"I hope it proves that I'm just Hilly Kemp. I don't need any fancy titles or recognition."

"Fucking bitch!" Everild yelled as he disconnected the call and then slapped Benedict across the face, sending him crashing against the cabin wall. He would have pounded Thane as well if the soldier hadn't quickly ducked. "I can't wait to face her tomorrow. I'll consume her energy and feast on her fear. Is everything ready for the meeting, Thane?"

"Yes, Everild!" Thane responded promptly.

"Good, very good. Soldiers, tomorrow will be the day we finally surpass Stygian in power!" Everild threw his arms wide and closed his eyes, imagining the carnage and the energy feasting.

Benedict sighed. He detested the day before the killings. Pressed into service, he could not deny the orders of his master, but he hated bringing horror to others. He longed to escape from the Yfel but was bound to the group by magic. Benedict gazed at his leader in disgust. He needed to find a way out.

Chapter 19

The Decision

Darrius brooded by the hotel window mindlessly watching people rush along the main road. Some hurried to their jobs while others dawdled, going nowhere in particular, just prowling the streets until something exciting happened. Aningan awoke to a brilliant, blue sky with a hint of wispy clouds hovering on the horizon. It was an ideal day for climbing, and Darrius' thoughts shifted to Hilly, Chance, and Jake. He wondered if they neared the summit meeting at that very moment.

He had bid the warriors farewell at midnight. "May Denali keep you safe," he had called after them as they left the hotel room.

He had stayed awake since their departure and struggled with a decision he knew must be made.

Aaron's betrayal weighed heavy on his mind. He shuddered to think of the consequences if they hadn't discovered Aaron's ruse, or if they had implemented the original plan to use his sham protection magic. After discovering Aaron's deception, Darrius had conjured his own cloaking spell for Jake and Chance, allowing them to enter the meeting circle undetected.

Even though he was able to rectify the one issue for his friends, Darrius realized that as long as Aaron remained in control, people would still suffer from his atrocious acts. Aaron needed to be stopped, permanently. Aaron's transgressions had become too numerous. They had not only been against Darrius' friends, or his own race, but Aaron had a complete and total disregard for humans, especially magicians who had been murdered for thousands of years because of his deeds.

Reporting a Cererian for improper behavior followed stringent protocol. Evidence would need to be provided, and the accuser would be subjected to intense scrutiny themselves.

Darrius had sought counsel from the Senator, a high-ranking Cererian politician responsible for the original expedition to Earth. Not too many individuals were granted an audience with the Senator. It would be fair to say that maybe one in a million were able to spend even a few minutes in his presence. However, the Senator had granted Darrius immediate access. It's not every day that a brave patriot who single-handedly saved his planet from annihilation asks for guidance.

Shortly after midnight, after Jake, Chance, and Hilly left the hotel, Darrius psychically cleansed the hotel room and sat, cross-legged on the floor. He fell into a deep trance, a level of consciousness whose depths spiraled into the solar systems and beyond. It was in this heightened state of awareness that he communicated with the Senator, advising him of Aaron's behavior and known infractions. Having witnessed many of these deeds himself, Darrius mentally uploaded those images and voice memories so that the Senator would have undisputed proof. The entire meeting lasted no more than thirty minutes, and the result did not shock Darrius. Cererian officers would visit Aaron that morning, neutralize his power, and teleport him immediately to Ceres for judgment and, perhaps, rehabilitation.

At eight o'clock that morning, Darrius had received the Senator's confirmation that Aaron arrived on Ceres, and he did not go quietly. When the officers, clad in protective suits, approached, Aaron had bombarded them with a crippling spell that deployed jagged energy crystals into their brains, instantly killing one soldier and severely injuring two others. A cloaked team of shape-shifters, disguised as ravens, had attacked from overhead, dragging an invisible energy net over him, engulfing him, and immediately draining his power. Aaron had clawed at his attackers, attempting to remove the energy web, but it was too late. He ceased fighting and collapsed. His neutralized lifeforce was captured and contained. The remaining officers had surrounded him and watched as his body slowly solidified, a living statue of a once proud Cererian—Aaron's physical tomb for transport to Ceres.

Darrius received the news about Aaron's capture with mixed emotions. Aaron had been his friend. How had he developed into a murderous egomaniac, a tyrant of fury inflicting harm on all who crossed his path? Darrius mused about the Yfel, another group of Cererians who enjoyed torturing and creating pain. Why would a Cererian stray from their natural inclination to be compassionate, supportive, and kind to lusting for blood?

Darrius sighed and turned away from the window.

Chapter 20

Climbing Denali

Jake, Chance, and Hilly departed the hotel at midnight to avoid detection by Aaron's allies. They allowed additional time so they could drive a longer route to Hilly's cabin. Once they arrived, they rested and ate breakfast before hiking the two miles through the wilderness to the sacred granite rock guarding the lupine meadow. It was here, during her vision quest, that Hilly had first felt the earth's energy pulse. It was near this boulder that she realized she could open a portal, a gateway that could shuttle them close to Denali's peak. Since Hilly needed to appear at the summit by herself, the trio planned to arrive just below the mountaintop and join a team of climbers. Incognito, they would avoid detection from the Yfel who would teleport directly to the peak. The Brethren had the advantage of knowing the exact meeting location, a fact Hilly wouldn't discover until she walked into it.

Hilly gently placed her hand on the boulder, and it vibrated eagerly, recognizing the firewalker witch. Spirits of nature always remember magical beings, especially the good ones. "Step aside, gentleman," she directed.

Jake and Chance shuffled out of her way and watched as Hilly raised her hands toward Denali, preparing her magic. Circling her hands in opposite directions, she invoked the spirits of nature, "Denali of the north, sylphs of the east, dragons of the south, and undines of the west join me now to create elemental energy. By the swirl of my hand, may your power open the threshold." Hilly moved her arms in a circle from high in the sky to low near the ground, moving faster and faster until the movement blurred as she cast her spell. "With granite I stand grounded, with air I breathe life, with water I nourish my soul and with fire I open a portal of light." As she uttered the last phrase, she threw her hands toward Denali and a tremendous concussive blast knocked Jake and Chance backward as a large swirling portal opened with Hilly standing in front of its maw.

The suction of the portal pulled at Hilly's hair, whipping it wildly as she turned to face Jake and Chance. "Come on, boys, let's get this done." They joined her and together they walked into the dark mass. As soon as their bodies penetrated the membrane, the gateway closed with a *hiss*.

The portal spat them out by a rocky outcropping six-hundred feet from the summit. A team of climbers had just marched past, their boot prints peppered the snow to a ridge in the distance. The temperature plummeted thirty degrees from the mild climate in the Mat-Su Valley where the portal had opened. They all zipped their parkas, wrapped thermal scarves around their necks, and secured their goggles against the sun's glare.

Hilly glanced at her watch. "Seven, forty-five. We're cutting it close. I need to arrive alone," Hilly reminded. "I'll catch up to this climbing group while you join the next team. Follow the plan," she said before a blast of cold air forced her to shut her mouth against the chill.

Jake and Chance watched Hilly lumber after the climbing party and disappear over a rocky ledge.

"Nervous?" Chance asked, watching his sister disappear over the rise.

"I'm anxious to get going."

Chance grunted in agreement. "This reminds me of when my family prepared to battle Stygian. We had a plan—a risky one—just like today. But we kept our faith in Hilly and it turned out okay—sort of."

"What do you mean sort of?" Jake responded.

"Damn, I always say too much sometimes." Chance groaned. He dropped his gaze and kicked at the snow.

"Tell me," Jake urged. "What happened?"

"Well, the plan worked great. But Hilly had underestimated Stygian's strength, and, well, she died."

Jake whirled Chance around and ripped off his goggles to look into his eyes. "What do you mean, 'she died'? Are we following a ghost to the peak?"

"No, Hilly's not a ghost. Hilly did *die*, but our friend, Prasad, sacrificed his life so she could live and complete her destiny." Chance frowned, because even *he* didn't believe his own words. He stared at Jake's wide eyes and furrowed brow. "You think I'm crazy, don't you?"

"Sounds like a load of North Carolina bullshit to me."

"Look, all I can say is that I would follow my sister to hell and back if she asked me. No one, and I mean no one, has the courage she has. I don't yet understand all her powers, but her magic is second to none, except for maybe Darrius."

Jake studied Chance and mulled over his statement. Yes, he had seen Hilly's abilities. He was aware her skills were more powerful than any other magician he knew. And he strongly suspected she was the lost firewalker, the one that escaped the carnage so long ago, but rising from the dead? This was one detail he couldn't fathom. He'd hide his skepticism for now.

"Okay, brother. I believe you. Look sharp, there's a line of climbers approaching. Let's fall in behind them and get to the top."

Chance repositioned his goggles and nodded to the exhausted climbers as they trudged by. Watching them pass, he and Jake then joined in behind them, pulling themselves forward with their poles, taking each step slowly as they ascended to Denali's summit.

Five hundred feet from the summit, an overwhelming sense of dread washed over Hilly like an avalanche of energy cascading down a mountain slope. Her intuition bucked and bile rose in her throat making her gag. She turned downwind and spat a gob onto the snow. Images flashed in her mind—snapshots of the future flickering through her brain like an old movie.

She grimaced at the horror. Something felt terribly wrong. Her stomach tightened and the hair on her arms stood on end. A creepy sensation slid over her skin as a nagging sense that something shitty was about to happen filled her mind with despair. She couldn't put her finger on it, but something was different—a shift in the force—and the energy had tumbled from an incredible high to a deep, dark low. Death was near and she'd do anything to stop it.

From behind, two climbers hailed, "On your left." Hilly side-stepped a few steps off the path, allowing them ample room to pass. Any movement was laborious, every breath ached. She met their gaze—reflective sunglasses rimmed by fur-lined parkas. The exhausted climbers trudged by. One, whose beard had frozen, sprouted icicles dangling from his face like an icy wind chime. They smiled and nodded as they passed, heads down, poles stabbing the crusted snow as they stepped forward in synch. She sensed their weariness and their determination to reach the summit. She suddenly received Jake's encouragement, *We've got your back, Hilly. See you at the top.*

She mentally replied, *May Denali smile upon all of us today! I love you guys! Go to the summit and wait for me there.* Jake and Chance moved over the rise, and Hilly was alone with her thoughts, and that familiar feeling of dread.

Gazing at the peak, Hilly opened her arms wide. "Mother Denali," she implored, "What do the images mean? Can I change the future or alter the visions you shared with me?" Suddenly she reeled from an explosive pulse of energy. Denali shoved her, testing her strength, measuring her powers. Hilly stood her ground, remembering to remain calm and receptive. Chanting, accompanied by drumbeats, drifted on the wind and filtered through her mind.

Hilly placed a gloved hand over her heart and closed her eyes. The chanting thrummed like a million honey bees in her head and soon fell into rhythm with her heart, creating a warm and welcoming melody. But she noticed another beat, a subtle vibration below the rhythmic hum of the ancients—*thump, thump.*

A slow ripple of energy ebbed and flowed like an ocean caressing the shore, but this vibration emanated from the rocky bones and snowy mantle of the great mountain. Denali's life force rose from the depths of her gigantic granite body and intertwined with Hilly's soul. Two energetic streams spiraled around each other merging their heartbeats.

Thump. Thump. Thump. Thump.

Hilly gasped at the unexpected ecstasy flowing through her body. She closed her eyes and moaned as The Great One spoke to her in whispers delivered on the wind, lightly caressing her with a lacy web of energy from the ley lines crisscrossing the slopes and the surrounding peaks of The Alaska Range.

Denali welcomed her daughter. *You asked about Future, but first, you must understand who she is. She is a devoted sister to Past and to Present. The triplets perform an endless dance through eternity. One does not exist without the others. However, of all the siblings, Future's face can be altered. There is opportunity in the split second before Future becomes anchored to the Present and then slumbers with the Past. Walk cautiously, my child. Past and Present will soon converge on the summit, creating a future that will change humanity.*

Hilly opened her eyes. The chanting drifted away, and Denali returned to her rocky lair. The Great Mother had shared her wisdom—words full of possibility and danger. But as is the tendency of nature's spirits, she revealed only that which was intended for Hilly. Denali knew what would soon transpire on her summit—spirits of nature know everything.

The relentless sense of doom returned with vengeance. Hilly doubled over and violently retched into the snow as a wave of nausea washed over her. Something was definitely wrong. She must keep moving forward, she had to reach the summit and join her comrades to confront her destiny. She adjusted the scabbard slung across her back. Raven hummed in anticipation of the fight that would soon ensue. Hilly planted her poles and pulled herself forward—one slow step at a time—following the line of boot prints stretching upward.

Denali's warning churned in her mind: *Walk cautiously, my child. Past and Present will soon converge on the summit, creating a Future that will change humanity.*

Chapter 21

The Meeting Circle

An anomaly disrupted the atmosphere on Denali's summit. What started as a soft ripple erupted into an electromagnetic wave that burst outward as the immense portal opened near the entrance of a natural cave. Lasting only seconds, the effect shifted the local energy fields, creating dizziness and disorientation among the few climbers lingering in the area. Everild, Thane, Benedict, and their hostage, Curtis, emerged from the gaping maw of the portal.

"I never grow tired of traveling this way," Everild boasted as he surveyed his surroundings. Cererian magic cloaked both the portal and its inhabitants. To the nearby climbers, the landscape hadn't changed, nor could they see the Yfel Brethren and their captive standing twenty feet away. While they had experienced the energetic wave when the energy hub formed, the mountaineers dismissed the effects as altitude issues and continued snapping photos of each other on the peak.

Everild stood in the shadows with his soldiers. "Look at those pathetic humans," he growled. "Lowly Folk, not an ounce of magic between them, believing that scaling a mountain is an extraordinary feat. What do they know of great achievements? I can teleport anywhere in the world. I can vanquish any opponent. I can easily crush their heads with a flick of my hand." Everild extended his arm toward the trio of climbers and mouthed an ancient Cererian incantation. The humans fell to their knees, holding their heads, and screaming in pain.

"My lord, killing these lowly humans is a complete waste of your abilities and valuable time," Benedict interrupted. "Might I suggest reserving your great power for the battle soon to come?" Everild temporarily ceased his magic and glared at Benedict who cast his eyes downward subserviently at his leader. He dared to continue and whispered, "I offer this suggestion with the utmost respect, my lord."

Everild hissed. "You're right. Why nibble on these tasteless appetizers when I have such a scrumptious entrée approaching?" He turned away from the humans who rolled on the ground, groaning from the assault. "I'll leave them. They can skitter back to their filthy, dark holes like the insects they are."

"Thane, prepare the space immediately. The witch will soon arrive. Ensure all is in order." Turning to Benedict, who held Curtis' restraints, he growled, "Secure that piece of meat to the wall." Thane scrambled away while Benedict led the hostage toward a sheltered part of the mountain.

Curtis trembled in the freezing temperatures. "Isn't there anything you do for me?" Benedict gazed into the hapless man's sad eyes and felt his pain, his despair. He wanted to help him and would have magically whisked him away if he wasn't hampered by Everild's cursed spell, preventing him from performing high magic.

"I'm sorry. There's nothing I can do for you." Benedict noticed Everild observing them, and fastened Curtis to the rock before running to his leader's side. "What else can I do for you, my lord?"

"Wait with me, Benedict. I have a treat for you. Today, you will feast on one of the magicians. I know you've been waiting for this moment for years." Everild howled a deep guttural laugh into the icy wind that made Benedict shiver in fear and disgust. Everild loved tormenting his reluctant soldier. He was aware that Benedict detested the idea of feasting on magicians. Forcing him to participate would bring Everild extreme pleasure.

He clamped a clawed hand on Benedict's shoulder. He winced and bent under the pain. "You know I only do this because I like you, right?" Everild cackled and violently shoved Benedict to the ground.

Jake and Chance were approaching the final feet to the mountain peak when they were surprised by three climbers scurrying over the rocky ledge and running haphazardly as though a wild beast was in pursuit. Chance held up his hands to stop the first man who flung his cap and goggles into the air, and screamed, "There's a ghost...a ghost on the summit! We were attacked by a ghost!"

"Hold up, brother. What's going on?"

The man collapsed to the ground, panting.

He stared up and gasped, "Help us...we were attacked by an invisible being."

Jake ensnared the second man who scrambled wildly around his fallen comrade. "Hey, buddy, what's going on? What's the hurry?"

The climber slumped to the ground and rolled onto his back. "Oh, my god...oh, my god..."

Chance and Jake turned to the third man who trembled violently and stared vacantly into space. Jake grabbed him, forcing him to stare into his eyes. "Hey, are you okay?" The man's mouth opened and closed, but no words tumbled out.

Finally, the first man, cowering at Chance's boots, stuttered, "The...summit...is...haunted!"

"Yeah!" the second man agreed. "There are spirits up there, and they attacked all of us."

Jake turned to Chance and mentally messaged, *I think the Yfel Brethren have made an appearance at the top. We need to be very wary from this point forward.* Chance nodded in agreement as he assisted the first climber to his feet.

"I have no idea what happened. One moment, we were taking photos, and the next we were on the ground in pain. It was the worst headache I've had like someone was squeezing my brain."

"Are you okay to descend by yourselves?" Chance asked as Jake helped the other man to his feet.

The two climbers looked at their other companion who remained in a rigid catatonic state. "It may be slow going, but I think we'll be fine. Are you guys still thinking about heading up?"

Jake patted the climber's shoulder. "It sounds crazy, especially after what you just experienced, but my friend and I have been looking forward to reaching the summit all day. If we don't go now, we'll regret it."

"Be careful. I'd heard Denali can be spooky at times, and our encounter was bizarre."

"Definitely," Chance responded as he helped maneuver their startled friend to them. "We'll keep an eye out for trouble or anything supernatural."

The three climbers collected themselves and slowly made their way down the slope, toward base camp, leaving Jake and Chance watching them descend beyond the ridge.

"Well, that was an interesting encounter. Let's see what awaits us at the summit. I'm sure we'll see more than spirits." Chance checked his equipment to make sure he hadn't dropped anything during the scuffle with the climbers.

Jake chuckled. "Luckily for us, Darrius took the time to cast his Cererian magic, so we'd be invisible to Cererians, but not to humans. Can you imagine that trio running helter-skelter down the slope and slamming right into us? We could have all tumbled into a crevasse. Come on, we better get going. We need to prepare for Hilly's arrival."

Everild stood with Benedict in the middle of the meeting circle while Thane completed his conjuring around the outer ring. Walking clockwise, Thane uttered ancient Cererian words as he built the energetic dome over the meeting circle. To seal the bubble, he blew a magical breath along the seam from the ground to the sky, and the transparent bubble closed as if a zipper had pulled it together. He then returned to his leader and announced, "The meeting circle is complete, my lord."

"Excellent. Now, all we need is our sorceress," Everild said as he licked his lips, imagining Hilly in his grasp. "This is going to be an extraordinary day."

Hilly reached the summit and stopped. The azure sky was a stark contrast to the dark entity meeting her in this beautiful place. A hunk of granite rolled along the ground and stopped at her boot. She gazed down at the rock. Looking back at her was a smiley face drawn with a black marker. She grinned at the thoughtful method Jake and Chance used to notify her that they had arrived safely and awaited her signal. Adhering to their plan, she made no attempt to psychically reach out to them lest the Yfel Brethren should hear their conversation.

Removing the scabbard from her back, she gently unsheathed Raven which hummed a welcome to her mistress. Hilly leaned against a nearby boulder and listened. The mountain remained quiet, except for a stiff breeze that tugged at her hair. She surveyed the area, using her heightened senses to find the meeting circle.

It wasn't long before she felt displaced energy to her right. She slowly extended her hand, pushing it forward until it met resistance from an invisible barrier. She continued pushing her hand until it penetrated a gelatinous membrane, disappearing from view. She withdrew it and stared at the space that had consumed it—a wall of magic, reflecting Denali's landscape of rocks, snow, and ice, but providing no details of what awaited her on the other side.

The Cererian conjuring used in creating the meeting space blocked her psychic powers from penetrating the energy bubble, leaving her to wonder if the Yfel observed her antics and if they intended to formally invite her inside. Of course, she also considered grabbing Raven, bursting through the energy membrane, and battling all who confronted her. She thought better of it. *Stick to the plan, Hilly.*

Her plan accommodated anything the Yfel might throw at her. Hopefully, she had anticipated all situations and left nothing out. She walked away from the energy barrier and located a quiet space where she could safely meditate and summon Denali. However, the sacred space was very close to the energy dome, making the proximity tricky since she knew the Yfel could probably observe her every move. Turning her back on the bubble, she silently called for The Great Mother: *Mother Denali, hear my plea. Soon, I will enter the battle arena you foretold to me. I have but one request. Please open a gateway so my companions can accompany me and help me fight the evil which awaits us.* Hilly gazed at the peaks of the Alaska Range as she continued, *Please give me a sign Great One that you will grant me this request.*

The summit was silent. A breeze swirled through the boulders, but the familiar vibration signaling the arrival of The Great Mother never occurred. Hilly turned to leave, to return to the meeting dome when a *screech* caught her attention. An enormous raven, the size of a great bear, flew toward her. Each gigantic wing spanned six feet and the bird's large bill was almost two feet long. Without altering its speed, it soared overhead, scraping Hilly's hair, before settling on a nearby rocky crag. The immense corvid cocked its head and stared at Hilly. Its black eyes gleamed. Denali had delivered her reply via her magical messenger—the raven. The black bird and Hilly gazed at each other, exchanging silent words. Finally, Hilly nodded and bowed toward it. The Great Mother had granted her daughter's request—she would provide a means for Jake and Chance to access the meeting circle.

Relieved, Hilly took a long deep breath and mouthed "thank you." She grabbed her broadsword and strode toward the energy dome. Aware that Jake and Chance silently observed her actions, Hilly swept her brow with an open hand, her thumb jerked skyward—her signal that Denali would grant them access.

As she marched to the energy bubble, a deep rumble stopped her in her tracks. The ominous sound was heard and felt from deep in the earth below her feet. Seconds later, an earthquake shuddered the entire mountain range. Hilly lurched forward and backward, trying to maintain her footing as boulders rocketed past her. She held her sword above her head as a shower of gravel rained down on her from the rocky ledge where the massive raven had once perched. From the corner of her eye she witnessed an opening appear in the rocky crag as the granite split and separated until a small entranceway formed.

Silence.

The quaking lasted less than a minute. Hilly surveyed the landscape. Rocks bunched against the invisible energy bubble. The stack of boulders appeared to seemingly teeter in midair, defying gravity, as the wall of the energy dome held them aloft. Something moved above her. Discreetly she turned her back to the meeting dome while scanning the rocky crag. In that split second, she saw Chance and Jake scurry through the opening in the rock. She exhaled and watched the steam from her breath drift away from her.

Hilly gritted her teeth and whirled. She clenched Raven in her fist and advanced toward the energy bubble, gazing upward and sideways, looking for a doorway, or even a hint that the Yfel were aware of her presence. Her body tensed, prepared for any surprises, but her breathing was slow and steady. Finally, a seam materialized in the dome wall which split open allowing Hilly and Everild to glare at each other.

"Please join us, sorceress, we've been expecting you," Everild hissed, extending his hand in a mock gesture to help her across the threshold.

"Stand aside Everild and I will enter," Hilly ordered. "I want you and all your soldiers to stand back, or I will not join the meeting circle."

He narrowed his gaze on the witch while the corners of his mouth twitched. Finally, he acquiesced to her demands. "Step back soldiers. Allow the sorceress to join our little party." The soldiers stepped back, their bodies on alert, prepared to deliver lethal blows of energy upon their leader's command.

Hilly pushed through the flexible membrane. As soon as she was completely through the barrier the dome sealed shut.

"Please come in," Everild invited as he walked into the middle of the dome, purposely turning his back on her. He whirled around and faced Hilly while Thane and Benedict stood behind him, all three staring at her, expectedly.

She switched her broadsword to her right hand, ready for battle. Raven vibrated as she connected with her mistress' adrenaline surge. "Where's Curtis?" Hilly asked, gazing around the interior of the energy ball.

"The meat you call 'Curtis' is chained to the wall over there," Everild replied, pointing at the granite. He then added, "Just what does a magician see in a Folk person? He's not on your level at all."

Hilly saw Curtis huddled by the granite with his hands tightly manacled to the rock. He couldn't or wouldn't look at Hilly. It broke her heart to see her husband so broken. Tears welled in her eyes and she bit her lip to stop the flood of sadness. The determined warrior suddenly returned. "How do I know he's alive?"

"Poke him, Benedict. Make the monkey dance," Everild demanded.

Benedict walked over to Curtis and gently advised, "You need to move so Hilly can see you're alive." Curtis grabbed his chains in both hands, with his face turned toward the wall, and hefted himself up. Weak from starvation and blood loss, he violently shivered against the granite, his back toward everyone.

Hilly averted her eyes. The Yfel had reduced her husband to a trembling, beaten man afraid to look at his wife. Shocking as it was to see Curtis in this condition, Hilly forced herself to control her emotions. If she was going to win his freedom, she needed to remain strong, stay calm, and fight these bastards for his release.

"Oh, the human is shy," Everild mocked, maintaining his gaze with Hilly so he could witness her reaction to his words.

"Let's get on with it, Everild," Hilly responded bluntly. "What do you want for the release of my husband? Releasing Stygian is *not* an option."

Everild grinned wide. Then he frowned, his face becoming serious and more monstrous as he spoke in a sickly, sweet tone, "My dear, I thought my desires were apparent. I want *you*. I want to consume every molecule of your being and suck in your extraordinary magic. I want your life in exchange for your husband's miserable existence."

Chapter 22

The Battle

The intense hatred Hilly harbored for Everild surged throughout her body. Her muscles tensed, she tightened her grip on Raven, and narrowed her eyes on the Yfel leader. In that moment, Thane and Benedict blurred from her vision as she focused directly on Everild. She sneered as various battle scenes flickered through her brain, images depicting perfect methods for killing all of them. Adrenaline coursed through her veins quickening her heart rate and increasing her breathing. Hilly licked her lips, yielding to the primal urge to annihilate them all.

Thane and Benedict shifted their positions and cast worried glances toward their leader who growled, “Speak, witch!”

Maintaining her stare, Hilly ambled sideways to her right, one leg across the other, slow and purposeful while she swirled her broadsword, not to provoke a fight, but to intimidate and move her opponents away from her. It was critical to move the Yfel away from the center of the dome and the cave, so Jake and Chance would have surprise on their side when they emerged.

“Be ready, my soldiers,” Everild ordered, “The sorceress is crafting a spell.” Everild then hissed at her, “There is no escape, witch. You may have outsmarted Stygian, but you cannot fight three Cererian soldiers at once. Your arrogance makes me laugh. You’re a pathetic excuse for a magician.” He spit streams of green goo at her, attempting to unnerve her.

Hilly maneuvered to the other side of the energy dome, just feet from the cave and her husband restrained against the granite wall. "It's not arrogance you see, Everild. What you're witnessing are the final frames of your life before I kill you." Hilly's bravado shocked her. She'd always been fearless, even as a little girl, but her boldness had exploded since her Revelation at The Nine Muses. Restoring her memories and discovering her true family and powers had unlocked hidden areas in her body and mind allowing an incredible transformation to occur. Truth sprouted the seed within her that had been buried in darkness for decades, giving power to her body and her voice.

Hilly snuck a quick peek toward the cave opening, anticipating Jake and Chance's arrival. Seeing no one, she poked at Everild, hoping to give her friends more time to navigate the rocky passage Denali had created for them. "You know, Everild...Stygian was much more powerful and clever than you. You saw how I handled him." Thane gulped and stared at his leader.

"Choose your words wisely, witch, or I'll kill you and your husband."

Hilly glanced at the entryway again. This time, her action caught Everild's eye. "Nervous, sorceress? Are you realizing just how futile your efforts are?"

Hilly detected gravel skittering off the walls deep within the cave. Hushed footsteps assured her Jake and Chance were close. Moving her left hand behind her back, Hilly held up three fingers visible only to the cave opening—their prearranged signal meaning Jake and Chance would count to three before emerging with their weapons at the ready. She smiled at Everild. "Nervous? No. Grateful? Yes"

"Grateful?" Everild hissed.

Jake and Chance sprang from the cave, their weapons drawn and ready for battle as they assumed their positions on either side of Hilly.

"You humans are detestable!" Everild screamed. "There may be more of you, but that just means there are more magicians for me to feast upon."

He howled into the air, releasing his fury into the energy dome. The echo reverberated around the walls, producing a series of powerful shockwaves that blasted Hilly and her companions to the ground. They struggled to stand as the assault continued. Everild cried out again raising his arms and releasing his magic, a spell that beckoned snow, ice, and wind to join him. Soon a monstrous snowstorm churned up the slopes of Denali, first engulfing and then penetrating the energy bubble.

The Yfel stood shoulder to shoulder opposite the magicians who supported each other in the gales as the tempest spewed snow and ice. A clash of thunder rocked the summit as lightning licked the granite, drawn to the magnetic energy streaming from Everild's fingers.

"Leave her for me!" Everild ordered his soldiers. "You can have the male magicians." Everild sneered. "What's wrong, witch, afraid to start the fight?"

Hilly swirled Raven in her hand. "I'm not afraid of anything, Everild. I'm assessing my opponents. Frankly, I don't see much talent before me." Jake and Chance shot puzzled glances toward Hilly.

"Perhaps you haven't been properly motivated, witch." Everild pushed one hand toward Curtis who clung to his chains on the granite wall. With a flick of his wrist, Everild sent a bolt of energy flowing into Curtis blowing him completely off the rock face and pulverizing his body. Pieces of flesh showered Jake, Chance, and Hilly. Everild howled with delight, his energy release intensifying the blizzard.

Hilly screamed.

Staring in horror at the remains of her husband littering the ground, she welcomed the swell of fury that rose from the depths of her soul. The will to control her emotions died with Curtis. Rage flooded into her brain. Now, she only thirsted for revenge by killing Everild. She steeled her gaze on the Yfel leader and emitted a low growl. Jake and Chance stared at Hilly, alarmed and a little fearful of the primal sounds issuing from her.

"Hilly, control your emotions," Jake shouted at her, hoping to halt the madness. "Don't let Everild provoke you into a blind rage. That's what he's hoping for. Hilly, are you listening?"

Another low growl—a rumble that began in the pit of her stomach and rolled across the back of her throat—burst from her mouth in a savage snarl as she bared her teeth. She glared at the Yfel leader through oily black eyes. Everild chuckled.

"Look, soldiers. Even after her husband has been annihilated, the witch doesn't make a move. She has no courage, and her magician friends lack bravery as well. What an easy fight this will be." He roared into the atmosphere, bombarding the blizzard with electrified particles that bounced around the interior of the dome. The snowstorm swirled viciously, propelling ice crystals which embedded in the membrane, their jagged points jutting dangerously downward.

Hilly snarled again and clenched Raven.

Jake shouted another warning, "Hilly, don't react to him. Look at him, he can't wait to see you explode."

Hilly looked at Jake with dark black eyes and seethed, "I will make him pay for what he's done."

She blinked once and then soared toward Everild. The Yfel leader anticipated her move and launched upward into the dome. Hilly changed course and pursued him, clashing with the Yfel leader near the jagged ice crystals jutting from the ceiling. Extending his hands, Everild fired energy pulses at Hilly who wielded Raven in front of her, deflecting the blasts until she was able to catapult off his chest and slice into his arm. They momentarily hung in the air, studying each other. Everild casually inspected the eight-inch wound on his arm. He ran his finger along the cut, healing it with Cererian magic.

"What a stupid sorceress, if that's all you've got then I will vanquish you in a matter of minutes." Everild discharged a laser beam of white-hot energy toward Hilly who repositioned Raven's blade, allowing it to absorb the energy, storing the charge within the Cererian crystals that comprised the blade. Everild threw himself at Hilly, grabbing her with his claws, and pulling her close. The intertwined duo swirled in the tempest's gales.

As Hilly battled Everild, Jake pounced on Thane with his battle daggers, surprising the soldier, and Chance rushed Benedict who immediately fell upon his knees, hands up and palms forward.

"I will not fight you, human. You may kill me, but I will not raise my hand to you." Chance stared at the man, wondering what to do. Adrenaline pumped through Chance's veins and now this man had thrown the off switch. The Brethren gazed up at his opponent. "The choice is yours to make."

Jake witnessed the odd exchange and hailed Chance, "Leave him. Help me with this one." His friend's words jolted Chance back into action, and he joined in the fight against Thane, using his broadsword to deflect the soldier's energy pulses. Jake managed two well placed stabs into Thane's shoulders, severing tendons and muscles, which weakened him. Using his tremendous strength, Chance battled Thane to the ground, sat on him, and pinned his arms, preventing him from lobbing energy bombs. Jake knelt at Thane's head and grabbed a fistful of hair, yanking his head back to expose his white neck. The soldier frantically babbled Cererian magic, his eyes wide with fright as Jake ran Cadmar across his throat, decapitating the soldier. Translucent wisps escaped from the body and frantically churned in the snowstorm, seeking refuge.

"Look, Chance, we are witnessing the release of magicians who lost their lives to this piece of shit." Spirits burst forth from Thane's ragged neck, and the transparent balls of energy swirled along the inside of the energetic bubble seeking their escape, longing to return to the natural world. The spell on Thane's energy dome broke upon his death, and the transparent membrane dissipated allowing the freed souls to fly away.

Jake and Chance looked skyward at Hilly battling Everild. Unable to fly like his sister and friend, Chance was grounded. "Get up there and help Hilly," he pleaded.

"Already on my way, brother."

Everild and Hilly wrestled against each other, both uttering spells, creating a dense air of chaos around them. Jake approached and was rebuffed by a wall of energy thrown by Everild's conjuring. Catching his breath, Jake soared toward them again, using the energy in the blades of Cadmar and Cathal to guide his way.

The Yfel leader hugged Hilly tighter, probably hoping Jake wouldn't risk hurting his friend. "Get off of me, you son of a bitch," Hilly screamed.

Everild cackled as he pinned her arms in a tight embrace, restricting her access to Raven which dangled in her hand. "Don't you like your new boyfriend, Hilly? Come on, kiss me."

Eye to eye, nose to nose, Everild and Hilly spiraled in a death embrace as Jake encircled them watching for his opportunity. He swiftly jabbed his battle daggers into Everild before soaring away. But his attack was useless. The Yfel leader healed his wounds quicker than Jake could inflict harm.

Suddenly a message broke into Jake's brain. *Use your daggers wisely. Remember the dragon in my vision quest.* Jake gazed at Hilly, her brilliant green eyes had returned. His friend had regained control—at least for the moment. Everild and Hilly twirled faster and faster, spinning in the snowstorm, blurring in the air.

Hilly cast a final spell against Everild, an ancient incantation that would also put her life at risk. Hilly's fire magic bound the two of them together as one, but, in so doing, neither of them could use their powers.

"What are you doing?" Everild howled as he began to realize he no longer controlled the situation and had lost his ability to conjure.

Hilly grinned at him. "Don't you want to dance with me, Everild?" Tentacles of ice and stone wound around their bodies, starting at their feet and rising upward until only their heads were free. Abruptly, Hilly ended the spell, and their twirling bodies slowly stopped. Hilly and Everild were sealed together in a cocoon formed of ice crystals and rocks. Try as he might, Everild could not free himself and struggled against the frozen bonds.

Jake flew above the duo, preparing to kill the beast just as he had done in Hilly's vision quest. Hilly watched Jake maneuver into position behind Everild and slowly closed her eyes. Everild struggled but was permanently sealed against Hilly in their icy tomb. He opened his mouth and howled his frustration into the air as Jake raised Cathal and Cadmar, and drove the twin Cererian blades deep into Everild's brain.

Everild perished and the thousands of souls he had consumed over the millennium raced upward from the depths of his body, seeking their escape, longing for freedom from their prison. With his mouth agape, Everild slumped against Hilly. She was not aware of what was racing toward her until it was too late. With no other direction to turn, the magician's spirits soared out of Everild's mouth, eyes, and nose and raced directly into Hilly. The punch of tortured energy jolted her as a thousand souls entered her body, filling her up with their torment as well as their magical power.

"Jake, help me!" Hilly screamed. But it was too late, the transfer took a matter of seconds, and Jake couldn't break Hilly free of the rocky snare she had wound around herself and Everild. Popping and snapping sounds filled the air. Cracks fractured down the cocoon on both sides. Hilly's conjuring allowed for a ten-minute delay before the vessel disintegrated and plummeted to the center of the meeting place and shattered to pieces on the ground.

Jake and Chance raced to Hilly's side. She panted and struggled to breathe. "What just happened? I feel so odd," she said, holding her head, attempting to make sense of what just occurred.

"Are you hurt?" Chance asked as he gripped her elbow and helped her stand.

"No. I'm not physically hurt, but something's amiss," she responded. She lurched to the side but Jake stopped her from falling.

Benedict silently stepped beside them. He stroked Hilly's hair and softly spoke, "You consumed the souls of the thousands of magicians Everild had killed over the millennium. You absorbed his spirit as well."

"No, I couldn't have. I didn't want that. How?" Hilly cried.

"The proximity of your bodies provided for an easy transfer," Benedict continued. "The souls don't wish to inhabit a body, but in their desperation to escape Everild, you were in the way. No doubt you have a lot of ringing in your ears right now. That's the sorrowful song of the magicians realizing their mistake."

"But I don't want this. I want them to be free." Hilly searched everyone's faces, but the sorrowful looks conveyed the hopelessness of any reversal. "There must be something we can do." She screamed in frustration into the wind.

Benedict shook his head. "The only method I know of is for the host's body to die, which automatically releases the prisoners into the ether."

"I can't bear this. First, I lost Curtis, and now I've brought torment upon myself and thousands of other magicians." Hilly sobbed into her hands, completely overwhelmed.

"Curtis isn't dead," Benedict stated bluntly.

"What?" Jake asked. "We saw him obliterated by Everild."

Benedict led them to the granite wall. "Where are the pieces scattered all over the ground?" Jake and Chance scoured the area looking for the remnants but could find nothing. Only the manacles remained, still hanging from the wall.

Remembering the encounter in Aaron's office, Hilly turned to Benedict. "A doppelganger? Everild brought a doppelganger to the meeting?"

"Yes," Benedict replied. "The doppelganger acted and appeared as the real Curtis would have. The remnants of the body double were absorbed into the wind moments after his death."

"Why bring a doppelganger?" Jake pressed.

"Control," Benedict replied. "Everild always expected ultimate control. If he had brought the human Curtis, who was weak from his injuries, he may have died unexpectedly and ruined Everild's plan. A doppelganger wouldn't die unless it was done on purpose."

"Curtis is still alive?" Hilly asked in a quavering voice.

"Yes," Benedict replied. "He is alive but weak. He remains in his prison on Pilot Mountain."

"Pilot Mountain, North Carolina?" Hilly and Chance both chorused.

Benedict continued, "Yes, we had your husband hiding in plain sight not too far from where you live. We used the same energy membrane around the cabin so nobody would discover his whereabouts."

Hilly collapsed, but Jake caught her before she hit the ground. "Are you okay?" he asked.

"I feel so disoriented like my molecules are rearranging and shifting. I don't feel like myself at all," Hilly answered.

"It's the transformation," Benedict remarked. "The process could take a matter of days. Might I suggest we return to Pilot Mountain so Hilly can regain her strength, and I can begin healing Curtis' body?"

"I don't have the strength to open the portal," Hilly replied, leaning against Jake's shoulder.

Benedict smiled. "Then allow me to assist you. Since Pilot Mountain is a natural energy hub, I'll open the gateway here on Denali, and we can all transport together."

Hilly bobbed her head before she fainted in Jake's arms. He intended to scoop her up but Chance intervened. "Thanks, Jake, but I've got this. She's my sister and besides, I'm much stronger than you." Chance bent down, gathering Hilly into his arms, her head leaning on his shoulder.

"Okay, gather around," Benedict requested. He pressed his hands together at his heart center, demonstrating reverence for Mother Denali, before raising them toward the cave. Silently uttering a Cererian incantation he opened the portal—a dark swirl of energy. Chance exchanged glances with Jake before striding into the maw, Hilly unconscious in his arms. Jake and Benedict followed. The portal closed with a slight hiss. Thousands of miles away, the foursome arrived on Pilot Mountain. Now that Everild had perished, the monstrous blizzard on Denali calmed down. Only a light snow continued to fall on the battlefield, covering the bodies of Everild and Thane in shrouds of ice crystals.

Pyewacket remained hidden behind the boulder, observing the warriors entering the portal and departing Denali. Now that the area was clear, he emerged and surveyed the summit. He sniffed at the bodies of his Cererian brothers, Thane and Everild, before raising his paw above each one and transporting them carefully to the front of the cave. Then, he opened the portal and transported the soldiers back to Ceres. Returning to the center of the summit, he gazed up into the sky and yowled. Soon, the enormous raven joined him, perching on a large boulder.

The words of the prophecy ring true, the cat messaged.

Future's face was altered today. In so doing, the course of humanity has also changed, the raven replied.

Yes, for a millennium, we have waited for this moment, for the arrival of a champion who can restore balance to the world.

The spirits of nature have given her the gifts. Now, we wait to see how she uses them.

Abruptly the raven flew off and Pyewacket watched the corvid soar into the distance. Then with a flick of his tail, the black cat also disappeared.

Chapter 23

Pilot Mountain

THE PORTAL SPAT OUT the weary warriors on a rocky ledge not too far from a family of hikers. Fortunately, Benedict had cloaked their return from the individuals who were enjoying the scenic view. They only felt the displaced energy created by the energy hub like a gentle breeze blowing across the mountaintop.

Summer sun and high humidity bathed The Knob on Pilot Mountain. Having jumped from a freezing blizzard to extreme heat, Jake removed his parka and thermal scarf. Chance laid Hilly on the ground and removed his winter gear and then hers before discarding all of their clothes in a thicket of nearby bushes. "I can just imagine the face of the person who discovers these treasures," Chance said.

Hilly stirred on the ground. She mumbled unintelligible words and whimpered. "Hilly," Chance whispered as he shook her shoulder. "Time to wake up." Still weary from the assault on Denali, Hilly blinked slowly and stretched. She pouted and tried to make sense of what was happening.

"Where are we?" she croaked in a raspy voice. She cleared her throat and coughed as she propped herself up and glanced around the area. Chance pulled her to her feet but she fell limp against his side.

"Still woozy?" He asked as he guided her to a nearby boulder so she could sit.

"I don't feel very well," she admitted. She stretched her arms toward Chance. "Will you carry me, big brother?"

"How long are you going to milk this, Hilly?" he teased as he easily lifted her. Between the heat and her exhaustion, she soon fell asleep, her head against his chest. "Benedict, we're ready to go. Which way?"

The Cererian pointed toward a winding dirt trail and strode off in the lead, followed by Chance and then Jake. The cabin lay just a mile away, but the hiking route was extremely difficult. Chance and Jake took turns holding Hilly as they scrambled over boulders and slid down steep, gravelly slopes. An hour later, Benedict led them up a dirt road into the middle of a forest.

"Now what?" Chance asked, scanning the endless rows of trees.

Benedict grinned. It was the first time any of them had witnessed any other emotion in the man other than obedience and sadness. "We are home," he announced. Raising his hands, Benedict reversed the veiling spell surrounding the log cabin. Like a mirage fluttering in the heat of a desert, the home shimmered into view.

Hilly stirred in Chance's arms. "Where are we?"

"You're home, Hilly. Your husband is inside," Benedict announced.

"I'll carry you over the threshold," Chance said, carrying inside and placing her on the couch.

With drowsy eyes, Hilly whispered, "I need to see Curtis..." Her voice trailed off as she fell asleep, curled up amid the cushions.

"Follow me," Benedict requested, guiding Jake and Chance to the bedroom, Curtis' prison cell. "Your sister will be fine where she is." The men entered the dimly lit room, which reeked of stale urine and feces. Shackled to the headboard, Curtis lay on his side, eyes closed, his breathing labored. Chance cringed upon seeing the raw, infected flesh on the side of his head, a gaping hole where his ear should have been.

Chance was first to reach the poor, wretched man and placed a gentle hand on his shoulder. "Hey buddy, it's Chance. I'm Hilly's brother."

Curtis stirred and mumbled but didn't open his eyes. "Curtis, wake up. I'm going to take you home."

Slowly, his eyes fluttered open. He blinked several times. "Chance? Hilly?" He squinted at Chance and shook his head "Who are you?"

"I'm Chance. I'm Hilly's brother."

"Hilly? Is Hilly here?" Curtis asked in weak whisper.

"She's here." Chance confirmed. Turning to Benedict, he asked, "Do you think you can remove his manacles?"

Benedict stepped forward, and Curtis screamed in terror. "No! They're back to hurt me!" He thrashed as Chance held his arms, trying to calm him.

"Buddy, this is Benedict. He's the good one."

"Curtis, do you remember me?" Benedict spoke softly. "I removed your infection and reduced your fever." Benedict waved his hands over the shackles, which automatically unlocked, releasing Curtis' hands. The metal restraints had rubbed bloody grooves into his wrist and removed a patch of skin from both hands.

Curtis ceased struggling and stared at Benedict and then at Chance. "What's going on?"

"How do I explain?" Chance responded.

"Perhaps I should heal your friend first," Benedict interrupted. "Then his body and mind will be strong enough to accept what you have to say."

Chance turned to Curtis. "Is that okay with you? Benedict wants to heal you. He wants to regenerate your finger and ear."

Curtis shook his head. "I don't want him touching me. Can we just go home?"

"The entire process is rather fast," Benedict explained. "Your ear and finger will look and function just like the ones you lost. And I don't need to touch you. If you like, your friend can stay with you."

Chance smiled at Curtis, "Whatcha think, buddy? I'll be here with you."

Reluctantly, Curtis nodded his approval. "As long as he doesn't touch me," Curtis said, jerking his head toward Benedict.

"I'll prepare my healing potions. You can stay right there." Benedict opened a cabinet and withdrew several amber-colored bottles filled with various fluids. "After I'm done, you can take a shower and change into fresh clothes."

Jake quietly left the bedroom and rejoined Hilly who was sound asleep, a soft snore escaping her mouth. He gazed at her. Even after battling Everild in a blizzard, she looked amazingly beautiful—her mussed hair, her soft lips and—he stopped himself. Just hours earlier, on Denali, she hadn't been his gorgeous friend when he stared into her oil-black eyes, and she growled at him like a wild creature. He scoffed at the memories. What's happening to Hilly? Even before the souls of a thousand magicians mistakenly entered her body, she was transforming.

Hilly grunted as she rolled onto her back. Looking at her now, Jake only saw a peaceful angel, a beautiful woman who possessed incredible power. Hilly murmured again as she stretched long and then settled back into a deep slumber.

Several hours later, Benedict and Chance emerged from the bedroom, leaving Curtis to shower and change into clean clothes. Hilly sat cross-legged on the couch with Jake beside her. "Jake told me you were healing Curtis. How did it go?"

"I'm confident in the physical healing, the ear and finger appear just like the original ones he possessed. However, I'm skeptical that the emotional scars will ever heal." Benedict walked over to Hilly and leaned down to look into her eyes. “How are you feeling? Do you still have the ringing in your ears?”

“The ringing is fading, and I feel my strength returning. When can I see Curtis?” Hilly asked anxiously asked.

“I suggest you give him a little more time. He’s still adjusting to the situation,” Benedict advised.

“Nonsense.” Hilly proclaimed as she stood. “My husband needs me.”

“Hilly, why don’t you give Curtis just a little more time?” Chance urged. “He’ll come out when he’s ready.”

“Get out of my way, Chance. My husband needs me.” Her lips stretched thin as she clenched her jaw. She lowered he head like a bull preparing to charge, and glared at her brother.

Chance stood aside, allowing Hilly to walk to the bedroom door. She knocked and then entered. Curtis sat on the edge of the bed, buttoning his shirt. He didn’t bother looking up when Hilly entered.

“Hi, babe,” Hilly whispered as she approached him. “How are you feeling?”

“Like crap!” Curtis snapped. He glanced at her and then stared at the floor. His hands gripped the edge of the bed, balling the sheet into his fists.

Hilly winced from her husband’s anger. “I’m so sorry.”

A tense silence swirled in the room.

Curtis rose and walked to the far wall, his back toward Hilly. “Why didn’t you tell me about Stygian and the Yfel? Why didn’t you tell me about all these weird magical friends of yours?” He whirled and glared at Hilly. “Don’t you trust me?”

Hilly twisted her fingers together and chewed on her lower lip. “I meant to tell you, Curtis. The timing never seemed right. How do you bring the topic up out of the blue? ‘Hi honey, by the way, I have all this cool magic now, and there’s this really evil alien that I locked up in an interdimensional cell. Oh, and, I’m related to him.’”

“You’re related to Stygian?!” He shook his head in disgust. “What else are you hiding from me?”

“Oh, honey.” Hilly cocked her head and gazed at her husband. “I never intended to hurt you.” She walked within two feet of him and could feel the rage emanating from his body like a sudden blast of heat. She lifted her hand and touched his shoulder, but he dodged it and walked away from her.

“Leave, Hilly,” Curtis whispered. “I need some time. I need time to heal my body—and my heart.” Hilly stared at his back. His shoulders slumped forward, and he suddenly seemed smaller than she remembered. He sucked in a deep breath. “Could you please send in Chance?”

Hilly reached for him, but Curtis flinched under her touch and refused to look at her. “Sure, I’ll get Chance.” She could sense his anger and disappointment. The negativity eked from his pores and filled the room with an oppressive cloud. She finally decided to give him some space and a little more time. “Babe, I still love you.” She lingered in the doorway, waiting for a response, but Curtis said nothing. Hilly slowly left the room. All eyes were on her as she entered the living room. Tears welling, she looked at Chance. “Curtis wants to talk to you.”

Chance knocked on the bedroom door and Curtis replied, “Come in, if you’re Chance.” Chance flinched at the obvious slight to Hilly and entered the room.

“Hilly said you wanted to see me.” Curtis sat on the edge of the bed, and Chance sat beside him. They stared at the floor in silence for several minutes. Chance knew better than to say anything else. Curtis needed his time to process.

"Do you think it would be okay..." Curtis stopped, unsure about finishing his request.

"What?" Chance urged.

Curtis turned to look at Chance. "Would it be okay if I stayed with you for a while? Until I get my bearings again. I'm afraid to stay in our house because that's where they first assaulted me. Plus, I don't want to be around Hilly right now. I need to sort some things out." He paused and sucked in a deep breath. "I know it's a lot to ask since we just met today, but I don't know where else to turn."

Chance studied Curtis. Sorrowful eyes in a gaunt face stared back at him. He wore the look of a desperate man with no other friend in his life. "Sure, buddy, anything you need. If you need a change of scenery, we can help you with that."

"Thanks," Curtis replied, happy to move on from the horrible memories. "This feels like the right thing to do."

"Does Hilly know your plan?" Chance risked asking the question, but he wanted everything out on the table.

"Not yet. I'll tell her." Curtis looked at his brother-in-law again. "Chance, I don't think I can even look at her anymore. I feel disgusted when I see her."

"Give yourself some time. Both of you need a break." Chance gently placed a hand on Curtis' shoulder.

"Thanks for being my friend, Chance. I really appreciate it. I guess I should tell her. Would you please ask her to come in?"

"Sure, buddy." Chance arose and left the room.

Hilly stood up, anticipating good news but when she saw Chance's face, she knew only bad news followed him. "Curtis wants to talk with you, Hilly."

She glanced toward the bedroom door and squared her shoulders. Her hands balled into fists and then relaxed. She looked at Chance with unsure eyes before walking to the door.

Chance watched Hilly knock at the bedroom door before she entered and quietly closed the door behind her. Looking at Jake he declared, "Man, I could use a drink right now."

"What's going on?" Jake asked, nodding toward the bedroom.

"Nothing good," Chance replied. "Curtis needs a break from Hilly—to heal."

"Oh?" Jake's response seemed too hopeful and he quickly followed it with, "That's rough shit."

Hilly burst through the bedroom door and pushed by Jake and Chance as she ran outside. The sudden flood of emotions seemed to have formed a tidal wave of energy within her body, which was still recovering from the assault of thousands of souls shifting within her cells. She raged against the forest, flinging fallen limbs and kicking tree stumps. Anger and sadness took control as she cried uncontrollably and swore obscenities into the sky. Jake and Benedict followed her outside while Chance joined Curtis in the bedroom.

"It's the effect of the spirit transfer," Benedict remarked. "Cererians can easily manage the flood of energy gathering in their bodies. But humans...well, your species is rather fragile, I'm afraid."

"What can we do to help her manage all this power?" Jake asked.

"Return her to her roots. I know she's grounded with Denali. Perhaps her earth mother can intervene on her behalf."

That's exactly what he had wanted to hear—taking Hilly back to Alaska and away from this North Carolina shithole. Hilly belongs with her own kind and not with a whiny Folk husband who doesn't appreciate the magic she possesses. "That's a great idea."

Finally finished with her outburst, Hilly joined Benedict and Jake. "I'm sorry for my reaction. Just this morning, I was fighting for my husband's life and, now he doesn't even want to see me." She glared at Jake, "How would you feel if someone said that to you?"

"I understand, Hilly. You have a right to your emotions." Jake replied. Benedict glanced at Jake, his eyebrows raised skeptically.

"Damn straight!" she agreed, punching her palm with her fist. Not realizing her increased strength, she waved her hand. "Ow, that hurt."

"You have endured much, Hilly," Benedict emphasized. "It will take more time for your energy and mind to balance."

"Benedict suggested that Mother Denali may be able to help you with this new energy you have rattling around inside of you," Jake offered.

"Is that true, Benedict? Do you think Denali can help me?" Hilly asked, hopeful for any good news.

"Yes, you are a sorceress schooled in the ways of nature's spirits. I believe if you return to Alaska, you will also find a way to manage the unexpected load you now carry."

Hilly nodded. "Then let's make that happen. I don't have anything here anymore." She looked toward the cabin, tears welling in her eyes. "But I have a chance in Alaska. I know there's more for me to learn there, so I want to head back as soon as possible."

Chance emerged from the cabin and heard Hilly's last few words. "Going back, are you sis?"

She ran to him and grabbed him in a huge hug. Burying her face in his shoulder she whispered, "Curtis and I need our space." She glanced into Chance's eyes, "I'll be back. Curtis is my soulmate. I will be back." Then she grabbed Chance's head and pulled it down so she could kiss his forehead. "I love you, big brother." She suddenly bounded away to Jake and Benedict. "I'm ready to go. Let's fire up the portal and head back to Denali."

Almost three thousand miles away, on the other side of the country, the slopes of Mount Shasta rumbled. In the magical realm behind the veil, which separated the world of man from Shasta's domain, the elemental entities and nature's spirits wailed in anguish. The great raven—Denali's messenger—had delivered the news that the sorceress had vanquished the Yfel as it was preordained in The Cererian Prophecy. The witch and other magicians would soon travel to Shasta's protected slopes and penetrate their sacred world.

In unison, the supernatural entities voiced their displeasure creating a noisy buzzing which penetrated the forests like swarms of bees.

The great earth spirit, Shasta, shook her rocky crags demanding to be heard, insisting on silence. When the entities quieted she spoke gently to her magical populations: *Be still, my children. The Prophecy will unfold as it has been preordained. The witch is the earth child of Denali. She and her friends will not harm you. My lost son, my champion, travels with her. This magician known as Kai is one of four souls destined to restore peace to our world. But it is your duty to test his mettle, measure his strength, and evaluate his worthiness to join you as a spiritual entity on these slopes.*

If he passes your tests, he will take his rightful place by my side. If he fails, then the world will never know peace again, and the murders of magical people will continue.

Thank You

Thank you for taking the time to read **Denali Rising**, book 2 of Chronicle of Ceres.

Please take a moment to write a review. Your words will help other readers choose their next book.

It's so important for a book to have social proof, and I'd love your help sharing this series with others who embrace their magic.

Leave a review or star rating at your favorite book retailer

For new releases, giveaways, and fun info, subscribe to my newsletter by visiting www.cllavigne.com

Acknowledgements

My readers and my fans who challenge me in my writing and keep the spirits of the Kemps and Cererians alive.

My husband, Chris, who weathers my emotional storms, calms me, and urges me to finish my fantastical tales.

John, Judy and Steve—how could the Kemps come alive without having you in my life?

Super Jimmy who lives on in my fictional Flanagan's Irish Pub.

Brittany and your amazing editing. Imagine my stories without your intervention.

About Author

Born in Alaska and raised in England, CL is an Elemental Specialist who writes magical realism novels that have witch fantasy overtones. Her stories feature real people and natural magic, all controlled by the Spirits of Nature and otherworldly beings.

Residing in the Sunshine State with her husband, four cats and four goldfish, CL incorporates elements of magic, mysticism and mythology into her writings. It's not unusual to encounter dragons, elemental spirits, Leotes (glowing orbs) and even Big Foot as you follow her characters on their adventures.

Find the magic and stay informed about special deals, giveaways, new releases and other great updates by subscribing to her **NEWSLETTER**.

Discover CL's magic:

www.cllavigne.com

www.facebook.com/CLLaVigneAuthor

www.instagram.com/cllavigneauthor/

Also By

Chronicle of Ceres Magical Realism Series

Beginning of Tomorrows, book 1

Denali Rising, book 2

Bluestone Shadows, book 4

Tales From the Crows

Horror short story collection (2 volumes)

www.ingramcontent.com/pod-product-compliance
Lightning Source LLC
LaVergne TN
LVHW010611100826
845148LV00014B/2917
* 9 7 8 1 7 3 2 2 9 3 3 7 3 *